ROGUE WITCH

Illumina Academy Reverse Harem Book Two

TARAH SCOTT

Scarsdale Publishing

Trademark Acknowledgements

Winchester Magnum
Paco Rabanne
Brunello Cucinelli
Porsche
Jewel of Russia Ultra Limited Edition Vodka
Jurassic Park
Uber
Netflix
Twilight Zone
Hyundai

ONE

Leilah

SUNLIGHT BLINDS ME. I THROW UP A HAND AGAINST the glare. Where the hell am I? Seconds ago, I had crashed to the floor while chasing Shadows in a dimly lit kitchen. I slap a hand over the shoulder I fell on, but there's no pain. I turn in a circle, heart pounding. Gone is the mob boss's kitchen in the virtual War Games. Gone is the dragon I conjured to battle the Shadow chasing Chelsea. Gone are Chelsea and Raith. Now, sunlight, silence and cold surround me.

"Leilah."

I whirl at the sound of my name, but I'm alone. My imagination? Or an echo from the world from which I was just ripped? I'm standing on an icy road in a rural countryside that looks like...God, this could be upper Westchester County, New York where Grams used to live before Shadows consumed her mind and spirit.

"Damn you!" I shout to the wind. "Send me back."

I close my eyes then snap them open again, but nothing changes. Is this a part of the War Games we weren't told about? Would The Academy do that to us? Would the Grand Witch do that to us? Raith sure as hell would. That fucking vampire threatened to expel me from Illumina Academy. He would love to see me fail and get kicked out. If he's playing some trick to get me expelled—

My thoughts screech to a halt. If he's playing some trick to get me expelled, why should I fight him? I would love nothing better than to be allowed to leave The Academy. Then I could return home—my new home, Grams' house.

So, how do I oblige?

I look down at my clothes. I'm still wearing the skin-tight, dark brown pants, leather bustier, and calf length, quilted, dark brown waistcoat I wore in the War Games. Even the burn mark from Chelsea's lightning bolt still mars my right sleeve. I clap a hand over the Celtic short sword strapped to my belt on the left and the other hand over two Japanese curved blades on the right. Still there.

I scan my surroundings. Across the street, a large stone house stands twenty feet off the road. To my left, beyond the open field, sits a two-story stone home that's at least forty-five hundred square feet. The road winds around a curve and disappears into trees. All as perfectly normal as any rural street in upper Westchester County. Wherever *here* is, appears just as real as the virtual Shadow world where the war games were taking place. Only that world took place at night, near a large city on the grounds of a crime lord's estate.

Are any of the other students here? Is Chelsea here? When last I saw the teenager, she was fleeing from the house of the crime lord we were sent to capture, a Shadow hard on her tail. I'd conjured a dragon in an effort to get the Shadow to chase me instead. But the Shadow was hungry for fear and Chelsea had plenty of that. Then Raith arrived an instant before all went white. Now, I'm here in—whatever this is.

Instructors aren't supposed to interfere with the games. But then, Commander Raith Vanderkoff, Mr. Vampire Asshole, does exactly as he pleases. *Wait.* Are the teachers still observing us? God, that's perverse and—

Fear whips through me when I remember.

Stony.

I stuff a hand into the inside pocket of my jacket where Stony, in mouse form, had been hiding a moment ago. My fingers encounter the lining. I search left, then right. Nothing.

No. No. No.

I choke back a sob. I just got my familiar back two days ago. To have her ripped from me again so soon is…cruel. I slap my thigh and force back the tears that threaten to spill from my eyes. Stony knows to meet me at Grams' if we get separated.

"Figure out what's going on and we'll be reunited," I tell myself.

Think. I release a slow breath. If the War Games' virtual world has gone wonky, maybe we were transported to somewhere near The Academy in Westchester? But it was just night, now it's day. I look up at the sky at the sun, which is—

No way. *No-fucking-way.*

I stare at a light blue sun.

I shake my head almost violently. This isn't my reality. Where am I? What—

Did the Shadow I was chasing infect me? The Shadows feed on our fears. Some people simply can't find their way out of the darkness The Shadows create, and psychosis consumes them. If we're lucky—if being driven insane with fear can be called luck—the infected only take themselves down. If we're unlucky, we start killing each other like we did in the recent Shadow War where millions died.

If the Shadow did infect me, it would have occurred seconds ago in the War Games. Was the magic I'd used to stop the Shadow enough to open the door to infection? I'd always believed the Illumina was overreacting when they preached that even the slightest use of magic in the presence of a Shadow can allow them entrance into your psyche.

I've practiced magic my whole life and never seen a Shadow until the War Games. The game hadn't been real, though. The Shadows were part of the virtual world—virtualverse, the students called it—created by the Grand Witch of the North—key word being *virtual*.

Fear twists through me. "Stony!" I cry. "Where are you?"

Where am I?

My thoughts abruptly jumble with a horrifying thought. On God, is it possible…is this a…Reaping? I resist the urge to look around for the floating obsidian ribbons that are Shadows. Are they close? Will they attack if I use magic in an effort to figure out where I am? Is Illumina telling the truth? Does our magic feed The Shadows? Damn the Illumina. They make us fear our natural state.

The possibility this is a Reaping is too fantastical. What are the chances that Illumina Academy students could be swept into a Reaping—a magical reality that tests our skills against our mortal enemies, The Shadows—while in a magical virtual reality designed to test our skills against The Shadows? The last Reaping took place five years ago. They never reappear for at least twenty-five years. This has got to be the virtualverse gone wrong.

A bitter wind whips my hair. I shiver. Clouds scuttle across the weird blue sun and the wind turns colder. I smell oncoming snow in the too-crisp air. I glance left then right down the road. Does this reality come complete with cars whizzing by too fast on these narrow roads? In the real upper Westchester County, it's dangerous to walk on the roads, which doesn't stop fools from doing so. There are no sidewalks, and the densely wooded terrain leaves no place to walk except on the shoulder of the road. I take a deep breath and, like just another fool, start walking.

Minutes later, I round a curve in the road. A large red barn borders the road up ahead to my left. The purr of a car engine draws my attention to the road behind me. I step off the road and face the oncoming car, as a blue sedan appears around the curve. I stick out my thumb as the vehicle approaches. An elderly woman is driving. She keeps going. I turn and watch the car disappear down the road, and belatedly remember the sword and knives strapped to my belt. Hell, I wouldn't have stopped for me, either. I'm dressed like a medieval warrior. I have my fellow Illumina Academy student, Fran Shelton, to thank for the funky outfit. I hope she's safe at The Academy.

I start walking, again. Through the trees, I glimpse a massive house about eighty feet behind the barn. Up ahead on the right is a two-story home painted mustard yellow with a stone wall in front.

I shiver with cold and stuff my hands in my jacket pockets. In memory, I smell the cinnamon rolls Grams baked on similar cold winter days. My mouth salivates in longing for the hot chocolate she served with the rolls. No one makes hot chocolate like Grams. I release a fog-filled breath and the sense of well-being increases. I haven't felt this good since…since the last time Grams made cinnamon rolls and hot chocolate.

I'm startled to realize that the last time Grams served cinnamon rolls and hot chocolate was the day before she kicked me out of the house. I was fifteen. An unexpected sob escapes me. My God, I had forgotten that. All these years, I'd focused on the day she kicked me out. Why am I remembering this now? My breath comes out as steam in the cold air. The sense of well-being vanishes and the sweet memory of Grams' cinnamon rolls and hot chocolate collides with the memory of her shoving me out the door.

My attention snaps to rapid movement in the trees ahead. I halt. A figure is racing deeper into the trees. I break into a run across the road, past the stone house to my left, and enter the trees beyond the house. Underbrush and low-hanging limbs force me to slow.

"Hey," I shout. I've lost sight of the person, but they can't be far ahead. "Hey!"

I advance at a fast walk and scan my surroundings but spot no sign of human life. I turn and catch sight of a fist hurtling toward my face an instant before pain splinters through my cheek. All goes black.

TWO

Ethan

I slam my thumbs down on the tablet's controls. "Where the hell is Leilah?"

Streetlight glints off the screen. I blink, certain her sudden disappearance from the feed is a trick of the light. I swipe the screen to the monitor room which displays life signs for all the students, but Leilah—and too many others—are gone.

Raith's roar transmitted over the tablet strikes terror in my mind. I swipe the screen back to the feed in the mob boss's kitchen as Raith slings aside the dragon he's just torn apart with his teeth. He wildly scans the room, the blood of the dragon dripping from his mouth. The Fae, Blade Tyrion, appears frozen five feet from him, staring at the spot near the kitchen island from which Leilah Crowe disappeared seconds ago.

"No," he whispers.

She's gone.

We lost her forty years ago when she died in Caleb's arms. She's only just come back into our lives. We can't lose her so soon.

"*No!*" I roar.

Fire leaps from my palms, incinerating the tablet before I can halt the reaction.

"Ethan!"

I yank up my hands, palms face out, ready to blast my fire.

"Ethan!"

My vision snaps the street into focus. Two students stand five feet away, Juan Hernandez and Kiersten Simms. I blink, then glance wildly about for the other twelve students who I'd been leading in the War Games.

They're gone. Twelve students taken from my team.

A Reaping.

I stagger back two paces.

"Ethan." Juan starts toward me.

"Stop," I say in a hoarse voice, my palms still aflame.

He halts.

My gut knots. My youngest student, one of the students taken, is a girl of fourteen, a sweet mage who belongs in a laboratory, not on a battlefield—and sure as hell not in a Reaping— is gone. Never in our history has a Reaping happened in anything less than twenty-five year intervals. The last was a little less than five years ago. Why now? Why, when Leilah just came back into our lives?

Leilah.

My heart thunders. I close my eyes against the pain. Chelsea Nightlow was also taken, the girl who's tried to kill Leilah *twice.*

I snap open my eyes. Seconds before the Reaping took them, I watched Chelsea throw a lightning bolt at Leilah. How was Chelsea able to harm Leilah? No one was supposed to be able to be harmed in the virtual magical world.

"Ethan," Kiersten says.

Juan Hernandez and Kiersten Simms stare, eyes wide with fear. I blink. I have to get them to safety. We're supposed to maintain radio silence for the first third part of the games, so the volume on the second, emergencies-only radio, which connects Raith, Blade, and I, is set on the lowest volume possible.

I pull the radio from its belt holster, depress the send button, and whisper, "Blade, do you copy? Over."

No reply.

I depress the button, again. "Blade, come in. Over."

Static hisses through the speaker. I try Raith with no better luck. I slam the radio back into its holster and pull the other radio from its holster. I call for Raith and Blade, but still no answer. With a curse, I shove the second radio back into its holster. I was a fool to destroy the tablet. At least, if I'd kept it, I could have seen what they were doing. I've got to get these kids out of the virtual world. No one is supposed to be able to die in a virtual world, but we never considered that a Reaping could take place simultaneously. The virtual criminals will continue to be criminals until we complete our mission, which means we're in danger.

"We're going to return to the real world," I whisper.

The kids glance at each other.

"Were they taken in a Reaping?" Kiersten asks.

"Yes," I say. "But your friends will be all right."

"There are only two of us." She glances around. "What if—"

"There are three of us," I cut in. "I'm here. Remember?"

Their attention darts past me the instant before three shadows fall across the asphalt on each side of me. I spin. Two large men stand on a street corner twenty feet away.

Demons.

I call my fire an instant before the demon on the left throws a ball of churning darkness I recognize all too well.

Shadow fire.

I throw up a wall of dark blue flames that radiates heat. Both students are high potential with immense magical powers, but neither is prepared to face demons—even virtual demons. Kiersten stands frozen, eyes wide.

Juan shouts, "Look out!" and shifts into gargoyle form, tall with pointed ears and a round demonic-like face fearsome enough to strike fear into the hearts of even demons.

He throws his massive bat-like wings around us and shudders when the ball of energy hits him at what I know is a fraction of the ball's energy, before the energy dissipates. I push past the safety of his wings in time to see a second melon-sized ball of dark energy hurtling toward us.

I thrust my palm outward and shoot a stream of white-hot flame as the taller of the demons lunges toward us. My fire collides with the shadow fire and explodes. Kiersten throws a protective shield around us.

To my surprise, she pulls a small round, opaque blue spirit bottle from her pocket. She yanks the cork off and shouts, "Souls of darkness, hearken my command, within this bottle, your spirit must land."

Pride surges. The spell is rudimentary—that's the goal—but effective. The demon who threw the dark energy lets go a wail that sends a chill down my spine, then he evaporates into a long wisp of black smoke that makes a beeline for Kiersten's bottle. When the last of that demon disappears into the bottle, she slams on the cork.

The other demon hisses, then disappears. Kiersten's right hand drops away from the bottle and I see the cork top is even with the bottle top, just as it's supposed to be. No chance of that cork shaking loose. Kiersten stares at the bottle as if uncertain the glass will hold the demon. I press her shoulder. Her head snaps up. Eyes wide with fear meet mine.

"Come on," I say. "We need to get out of here."

We have a twelve-minute jog to the portal.

"Everyone up for a jog?" I ask.

They nod.

"I'll take the lead," I say. "Juan, you have the rear. We encounter any demons or Shadows, we stop, and *I* deal with them."

I start forward and they fall in behind me. Juan remains in his gargoyle form. The kid will make a fine warrior.

"What about humans in need?" Kiersten asks.

"The games are over." I scan our surroundings and pick up the pace. "The humans here aren't real. What matters is us getting back to The Academy."

"Are we in real danger?" Kiersten asks.

Truth is, I don't know. A Reaping taking place in a virtual magical world? To my knowledge, that's never happened. Chelsea was able to harm Leilah. Who knows what else can happen?

"No," I reply. "But we can't complete our mission with most teammates gone."

"You mean we're not experienced enough to take on Shadows and criminals," Juan says. In gargoyle form, Juan is as strong as I am, but that doesn't mean he's ready to meet demons.

"I wouldn't want these odds," I say. I don't say that I have faced these odds.

We get four blocks when two men and a woman—two mortals and a witch dressed in long leather coats—emerge from a side street and step into our path.

"Well, well," the man in the middle says. "Strangers passing through our territory without permission. A gargoyle—and a witch with spirit bottles." His eyes fix on Kiersten's belt. "Just how many demons have you do-gooders imprisoned?"

"That's none of your business," Kiersten shoots back.

I glimpse the man's slight smile and a glint of streetlight off metal inside his coat in the instant before he yanks out a sword. How had I missed that? Because I'm not taking this world seriously.

I lunge and call forth my fire.

"Lookout, Daniel," the man to the left shouts.

I aim my fire at the sword.

The woman throws up both hands and shouts, "*Deflecto.*"

I throw another fire ball as the first shoots back toward us. Behind me, comes the loud flap of wings.

The second man circles to my right. "I hate fucking gargoyles," he hisses as the first dives to the left.

My fireball grazes his arm. He rolls, then jumps to his feet and throws the sword javelin style. My answering stream of fire melts the metal, which hits the pavement with a loud splat.

The witch shouts, "*Corvus.*"

A massive crow appears. Juan screams the chilling scream unique to gargoyles. I shoot a blast of dragon heat at the second man. He blows backwards into the street. The leader yanks a .45 Winchester Magnum from his waistband. I draw a sharp breath. The crow's caw makes my ears ring. Juan's wings are spread full length in readiness to attack.

"Attack!" the witch yells.

We don't have time for these damn games. I throw my hands up, palms face out. Flames blast from my hands as the gun roars. The witch screams, the two men shout. My heat blasts across them and illuminates the silhouette of their bodies. Their skeletons are framed in ash before the bones blow away as dust.

"Ethan."

I whirl at the stark fear in Juan's voice. He catches Kiersten as I spot the blood that darkens the front of her shirt. The crow screams again. I incinerate the creature with a flash of fire. Then scoop up Kiersten, take three running steps and unfurl my wings as I take flight, Juan at my side.

THREE

Leilah

I SWIM UPWARD THROUGH MURK TOWARD consciousness. Cold seeps through my bones. A throbbing in my head thrums in rhythm with the beat of my heart. Dim light filters into my brain and I blink my surroundings into focus. I'm lying, face up, on the forest floor. Light snow flutters down through the bare tree branches. My hands are tied behind my back. Grit scratches my eyes. I blink and try to brush my eyes against my shoulder but can't reach with my hands tied behind my back.

I force my shoulders to relax and close my eyes to allow the scant snow to land on my face. After several heartbeats, the small flakes melt, and I blink repeatedly until the grit clears. I struggle upright and eventually manage a sitting position, then scan my surroundings. I'm alone and—my heart takes a dive— someone has taken my weapons and coat.

I turn my attention to my ankle bindings, which—well fuck a duck—are shoelaces. Oh, this piece of bullshit is going to cost whoever tied me up. Determination to find my attacker bolsters me. Everyone needs goals.

I maneuver my arms down past my butt and shimmy them

along my legs. My belly is flat, but I still have to hold my breath in order to stretch my arms far enough to get my hands past my feet. The asshole who tied me up tied my wrists so tight as to make escape hugely uncomfortable. Plus, my fingers are numb.

I finally work the knot loose from the shoestring around my ankles. I push up onto my feet and stumble. My left leg is partially asleep. I can't catch myself and hit the snow-covered ground. Goddammit, why did this alternative reality have to take place in winter?

I massage my sleeping leg until the pins and needles disappear, then stand. Now, I have to find a way to get the shoestring off my wrists. I examine the knot. It's just as big as the one that bound my ankles. Maybe I should have started with my wrists. But I have to admit, I'm glad to be standing instead of lying on the cold ground.

I consider biting my way through the shoestring, but I'll likely end up with bloodied and chaffed wrists and an even tighter knot. Whoever tied me up knew what they were doing. The knot is near my pinkies, which is much harder to reach than a knot near my thumbs. I remember as a kid, when my shoestrings knotted up, sometimes Grams had to cut the laces because the knot was too unmanageable. I scan the area, but an inch of snow blankets the ground, and I find no rocks that might act as a knife.

"Fuckers," I mutter. They could have left me at least one knife.

Awareness causes the hairs on the back of my neck to stand on end. I freeze. I'm not alone. I whirl, then gasp. A wolf as high as my hip crouches fifteen feet away. My heart thumps like a jackhammer. I've never seen a shifter this large, but this brute has to be one. He stares through eyes the color of tanzanite crystal. So beautiful. Beautiful or not, if he attacks, I can't climb a tree or effectively defend myself. I center my magic in readiness to defend myself.

The wolf growls.

"Easy," I murmur.

The wolf steps forward.

I retreat a pace.

He halts.

"Why don't you just move on?" I ask.

He shakes his head.

I blink. Is he saying no?

A shiver races down my arms. We aren't alone. Who else is here? Another student? Gooseflesh rises on my arms. No Academy student elicits this reaction. Beyond the wolf, I catch sight of a single rippling ribbon of black angled on a slow course toward me. Fear, very different than that I feel toward the wolf, grips my heart with a hand as cold as iron.

Shadow.

FOUR

Blade

FOR THE DOZENTH TIME IN THE LAST TWO HOURS, I force back fear. We must make certain the students still remaining at The Academy are well before Ethan, Raith and I can deal with Leilah being taken in the Reaping. I open the door for the professors filing out from Raith's office—one from each of the clans, Silwood, Longthorpe, Middlewich, and Penncarrow. The job of these powerful teachers is to reinforce The Academy with wards that will ensure the spell that activated the Reaping didn't create gaping holes in the protection around the school. The last professor, Penelope Fairbrandt, is on her way to becoming a powerful witch to rival Olympia. She gives me a tiny nod, then passes out of view into the hallway.

I return to my place near the hearth. Raith and I were more fortunate than Ethan. After the Reaping, we led our students out of the virtual world without incident. But I sensed danger too bloody close for my liking. I prop an elbow on the mantle and shift my attention to Raith, who sits beside the Grand Witch on a sofa that faces another sofa in front of the hearth. Raith is listening to something she whispers to him. We have removed our body armor, but he still wears the same blood-stained t-shirt. At least, he had the good sense to wipe the dragon blood from his mouth. Raith is subdued, but his eyes reveal a struggle raging inside him.

Seton and Carter sit on the couch opposite Raith and Olympia. I'm astonished the Grand Witch allowed them to stay. I had counted on her ordering them out with the clan professors. I even hoped she would give Headmaster Domini some task that would take him away. No such luck.

A Watchman appears in the open doorway. He knocks and steps just inside the doorway.

"Any signs of Shadows?" Raith demands.

"No, sir," Ciaan replies.

"I want double watches all night," Raith orders. "The slightest problem, call me immediately."

"Yes, sir." He leaves as Olympia's assistant, Franklin, enters.

Franklin ignores us and says, "Mistress Olympia," then crosses to her, and extends a palm sized tablet.

He bends and whispers something in her ear. Olympia stands and they walk to Raith's desk, away from us, and continue their whispered conversation. Raith meets my gaze, and I know he's listening with his heightened vampiric hearing. The slight thinning of his mouth tells me he isn't pleased with what he's hearing.

Another light knock sounds on the open door and Professor David Cromwell enters. He stops, then looks at Olympia, whose attention is now on the tablet Franklin has handed her. Cromwell glances from Headmaster Domini to Raith. A sheen of sweat glistens on the portly man's bald head.

"What is it, David?" Raith asks.

Cromwell takes three more steps into the room—in an effort to put distance between him and the Grand Witch, I suspect—and says, "The list of students taken in the Reaping has been uploaded into the system. You may access the data any time. We escorted the remaining students to their rooms and ordered them to stay there for the night, as well as informed them there is a general curfew of six p.m., until further notice. Professors and teachers are patrolling the halls to enforce the curfew."

"Make sure the students know we're available, if they need us," Raith says.

Cromwell nods. "Already done. Several students had mates taken. Two had siblings taken. We have teachers with them now. Faculty members are calling parents and loved ones of the missing to explain the situation."

My chest tightens. Those parents and loved ones won't sleep for the next week.

"What of Kiersten Simms?" Olympia asks.

A smidgen of relief appears on Cromwell's face. "She's doing well. Her father died when she was young, but her mother lives in New Jersey. We've sent a car to bring her here. Juan Hernandez refuses to leave her side."

"From what Ethan said, the young man deserves a medal," Olympia says.

As if called by the Grand Witch, Ethan steps into view in the hallway behind Cromwell and hurries past him into the room. "I've ordered Watchmen to patrol the site of the virtual games where the students were taken," Ethan says.

Cromwell frowns. "The students can't possibly return before next week."

"Thank you, Cromwell," Domini says.

Cromwell hesitates and looks at Raith, who gives a slight nod. Cromwell angles his head toward Olympia and says, "Grand Witch."

She looks up from the tables and nods acknowledgement, then returns her attention to the tablet.

He sweeps his gaze across the room, says "Gentlemen," then leaves.

Ethan closes the door behind him, and Olympia returns to her seat beside Raith, as her assistant quietly leaves.

When the door clicks shut, Seton narrows his eyes on Olympia. "You said no one could get hurt in your virtual world. How could you have been so wrong?"

His anger is palpable. Seven years ago, Seton and Leilah were close. Her sudden loss clearly has him reeling.

The fire cracks and a wave of heat ruffles the sleeve of Olympia's robe. Her cool eyes lock onto the man. "Perhaps the arrival of the Reaping disrupted the laws of our virtual world."

Seton throws his hands into the air. "The Grand Witch of the North has no answer."

Headmaster Domini opens his mouth, but Olympia's reply could freeze rain on an August day, "Careful, Child. I understand your worry, but I do not tolerate disrespect."

"I assume no one considered the possibility that a Reaping might take place while we were in the virtual world—magical world," Carter says.

Olympia lifts a brow. "Even I cannot predict a Reaping." She looks to Raith. "I want to be kept apprised of the investigation into how our magic failed in the virtual world."

"You do realize that Leilah Crowe was taken in the Reaping, along with her would-be killer?" Seton says.

"Chelsea Nightlow," the Grand Witch says.

Seton leaps to his feet. "You know Chelsea tried to kill Leilah with that lightning bolt?"

"I just watched the video feed leading up to the students' disappearance," Olympia replies.

I keep my expression neutral. If she watched the video feed, that means she saw Raith tear apart the dragon that Leilah conjured. What will Olympia make of that?

"We can do nothing," Olympia says. "Ms. Crowe is a powerful witch. She can take care of herself."

"We didn't ask for the War Games to take place in a virtual magical world," Seton mutters.

"Enough," Raith snaps. "Grand Witch, I suggest you notify the Council of Kispu to investigate what went wrong in the virtual world. This is your creation. The workings of a magical world are beyond our abilities to decipher."

"That is a drastic measure," Domini says.

Raith pointedly ignores the Headmaster. "No one can match the Kispu witches' understanding of magic."

Except Leilah, I think, and I know Ethan and Raith are thinking the same thing. Many incarnations of practicing magic has made her—our Ciarah—a natural. Right now, her biggest hindrance is being twenty-two years old and not remembering past lives.

"Calling in the Kispu Order may not be a bad idea, Grand Witch," I say. Olympia once warned me not to think that my ability to charm her would always work in my favor. Let's hope this isn't that moment.

The chill in her voice returns when she says, "I will give it consideration."

Raith's eyes turn to slits and I start when I'm certain I glimpse his front lip protrude slightly as it does when his fangs elongate. Only two things cause an ancient vampire like Raith to show his fangs: hunger and extreme anger. Raith fed on Ciarah less than two weeks ago, which means he's not hungry. Olympia will not take kindly to the vampire unleashing his anger in her presence, or worse, on her.

"If you like, Grand Witch," I attempt a casual tone, "I will be happy to handle the matter."

Her mouth thins, and I know she isn't pleased with the idea of the Kispu Order being called in, for that implies she might have made a mistake, and the Grand Witch doesn't make mistakes.

"I will, of course, work closely with them to ensure you are kept up to date with their findings," I say.

"You always keep me up on the findings of your investigations, don't you, Blade?" she replies.

She is referring to my inability to penetrate the Zidruhin, the priests who worship our enemy, the demigod and Shadow mage Damien. My temper flares, but I maintain a cool smile. "As you know, not everyone shares information as readily as the Kispu Order."

She gives a mirthless laugh. "I never considered you naïve, Blade. The Kispu don't share information they can later use to their advantage."

"They are not the Gestapo, Olympia."

Her eyes flash with indignation, but the merest hint of a flush appears in her cheeks.

"I believe I can persuade them to be forthcoming," I say. "And lest you forget, they will likely find that the Reaping is the cause of the glitches in the virtual world."

Her gaze sharpens. "There can be no other answer."

FIVE

Leilah

REAPING, MY MIND SHOUTS. THIS IS—*MUST BE*—A Reaping.

The Shadow gliding closer is nothing like the one in the War Games. The Shadow in the virtualverse was two dimensional compared to this elegant, thick black ribbon that floats in the air like a fish in water. This Shadow makes me want to reach out and touch it.

A dizzying sense of déjà vu assails me. Blurred images of a *place* fill my psychic vision. I strain so hard in an effort to grab the memory that my head throbs. Recall rubs against the edges of my brain and makes me want to scream in frustration. A growl vibrates in my chest. I jar and the wolf snaps into focus. He is staring at the Shadow, his lips pull back in a snarl.

White light, my inner voice whispers. *Now! White light.*

I jam my eyes shut and try to envision white light. Darkness surrounds me. I snap my eyes open. The Shadow is closer. The wolf widens its stance and continues to growl.

"God, I can't see the white light."

"*Sure you can, sweet pea,*" Grams' voice assures me in memory. "*Can you see a streetlamp?*"

Yes, that I can see.

"Look at that light. That is the essence of protection. Spread the light out from the streetlamp. Let that light surround then fill you."

I ignore the discomfort of the shoelaces that bind my wrists and open my eyes. I envision the bright white light spreading from the streetlamp to surround me. The wolf growls, low and rumbling. Even if the Shadow leaves, that damn wolf can still kill me. The wolf looks over his shoulder at me, eyes intense. He's standing between me and the Shadow. He's protecting me.

What did Professor Cromwell say? Fear and doubt are the enemy. We must trust. Trust a big ass wolf? He returns his attention to the Shadow, lifts his head high, and howls. I tremble. White light floods me just as the wolf stops howling and snaps his powerful jaw at the Shadow.

The Shadow intends to infect the shifter. Then it will eat away at the wolf's soul until he either kills himself or commits a heinous act that damns his soul to Shadow Hell. I command more white light to surround us. Blinding white light pierces my eyes. I jam my eyes shut. Dammit. I guess I *haven't* forgotten how to call white light.

Above the thudding of my heart, the wolf's snarls fill the air. I reach out with my third eye and locate the animal, teeth bared in a ferocious snarl. The Shadow glides around the wolf. The wolf's fear and anger will ultimately open a door for the Shadow to enter and infect him.

I push the white light around and inside the wolf. His head whips around and he stares at me. I flush, oddly embarrassed. The white light falters and I imagine the Shadow's satisfaction. I clear my mind. No, not my mind, I realize with a touch of panic. *My heart.* Serenity comes from the soul. I can't allow the shifter to sacrifice himself for me. Rarely, are people truly selfless. Stony is selfless. My heart swells with love. She is a true friend.

"Give into the light," I telepath the wolf.

His mouth relaxes and the snarl disappears as he returns his attention to the Shadow. Sadness tinges my peace. How can something so magnificent be evil? The white light dims. What the hell? I jerk my attention onto the ribbon of obsidian. It hovers five feet from the wolf.

Waiting.

That's how the thing is working me. Sidetracking me with sadness over the waste of such beauty.

Sneaky mother fucker.

I dim the white light until instinct tells me the light won't blind me, then open my eyes. The white light remains visible to my third eye, but I'm also seeing the rippling ribbon of black against natural sunlight—if natural can apply to a blue sun. The shifter twists his head and looks at me. I swear, he's frowning.

"What?" I say.

Thankfully, he doesn't answer. I would have serious doubts about my sanity if he did. Even here in this weird place.

"Why don't you shift into human form?" I demand.

I watch the Shadow from the corner of my eye and refocus on relaxing. Peace and harmony are my swords. The wolf stares at me, but I sense he's watching the Shadow from his peripheral vision, as well. I long for my sword or even a knife.

Shit, weapons don't help against Shadows.

"Why don't we get out of here?" I ask the wolf.

He continues to stare.

"It'll go away if we ignore it," I say. God, I hope I'm right.

The wolf doesn't move.

I sigh. "Okay, then. You stay. I'm leaving."

I start to turn. He gives a low bark.

I halt. "What? You think I'm going to face off with that thing?" I shake my head. "This might be your home, but it's not mine. I've got to find my friends—not friends, so much." I roll my eyes. I'm an idiot.

He looks at the Shadow, then lowers onto his belly and

drops his snout onto his front paw. I blink. Nap time? I realize the white light has dimmed. I concentrate my third eye on the white light. The Shadow slows its ripple. Is the white light having an effect? I increase the brightness, but the Shadow doesn't change.

The wolf heaves a deep sigh and I wonder if he *is* taking a nap. The Shadow grows fainter. What's happening? I take two steps left so I can see the wolf's face. His eyes aren't closed, but he appears as docile as a kitten. I experience the strange desire to drop to my knees and run my fingers through his thick fur.

Dare I?

I study the Shadow. It's still hovering. Is its color a little fainter? The teacher didn't cover any of this in class. I look back at the wolf. His eyes are almost closed. I wonder if my touch will startle him, then realize that's stupid. It's almost impossible to sneak up on a wolf. But will he allow me to stroke him—and do I want to get closer to that fucking Shadow? I take a step toward the wolf.

His head jerks up and he looks at me. My heart jumps into overdrive. Okay, so he doesn't want me near him. The Shadow grows darker. What the hell? Did the slight tension I just felt feed the Shadow? Not just me, the shifter clearly experienced some stress when I stepped closer. Excitement whips through me. Hell, that's why the wolf laid down. He was relaxing, putting himself at rest…at peace.

The need to free my wrists nags at the back of my mind. My fingers are numb and will hurt like hell when I get loose. I look at the shoestring. "How the fu-heck"—I flick a glance at the Shadow, which doesn't so much as flicker—"am I going to get untied?"

The wolf cocks his head.

"Any ideas?" I return my attention to the shoestrings. I guess I'll have to gnaw them off.

The wolf pushes to his feet. I retreat, step on something

uneven beneath the covering of snow and slip a few inches before catching myself. He stares at me.

Warmth begins a slow creep up my cheeks. "All right, fella. Let's keep our distance."

He takes another step closer. Fear tightens my stomach. The Shadow's ripple grows more pronounced. My heart picks up speed. The wolf sighs—I think that's a sigh—and lowers his backside to the ground, then lifts a paw in the air as if waving. Or inviting me to come closer.

No way. He can't be—

He nods.

Nods? Fuck, I really have fallen down the rabbit hole.

"Sorry, big fella," I maintain a casual tone. "I'm not getting closer."

He drops onto his belly and I swear he's inviting me to stroke his back.

"Maybe we can play after I get these shoestrings off," I say.

How the hell am I going to get the damn things off? A sudden wave of homesickness makes me wish I was back home at Grams' house. Blade once told me that The Academy was my home. My heart lurches when I remember him saying, *"I call being surrounded by people who love you 'home.'"*

I long for Stony. I hope she's enjoying Chinese food at *our house.*

The wolf whines.

I sigh. "I know, it's been a shitty day."

I shiver and realize the temperature has dropped—and the Shadow is gone. I blink. Is that how we get rid of them? Don't get angry and they leave? If the answer is that easy, how did they wipe out millions of Margiddians? Sadness grips my heart and a sense of hopelessness overwhelms me. The Shadows wiped out millions because we are a species that thrives on anger and sadness. I start at a bump against my leg and realize the wolf is leaning against me.

I freeze. If he decides to eat me, I'll be in serious trouble. His head reaches my waist. He looks up to me and I swear I see nothing but warmth. Wolves aren't renown for their friendliness. In fact, they can be downright anti-social, and aggressive if you invade their space. This is one strange place.

He startles me by licking my hands. I can only stare. I have never been particularly fond of wolves. I consider them on the arrogant side. But this beast is as sweet as brown sugar. His teeth brush my wrists and I gasp. He stills and his eyes lift to my face. My heart is pounding. His eyes remain on me as his teeth brush the sensitive flesh of my wrist.

"What are you doing there, big boy?" I ask.

If I leap away, he will be on me before I flinch. Panic is causing my insides to shake and the trees spin around me. I try to focus on some kind of spell that will get me out of here. I can't use magic. Magic will call The Shadows. I can't—

Is the wolf—? I squint at my wrists. He's gnawing the shoelaces. The laces abruptly loosen. I yank my hands up and work the laces off. Immediately, a thousand pins and needles prick my hands from the inside. I groan and shake my hands as blood rushes back into numb fingers. I try to bend my fingers. My left pinkie doesn't move. Panic tightens my chest. The wolf woofs. I jerk my gaze onto him. Damn, if he doesn't seem to be telling me to stay calm. My pinkie moves and I release a breath. My fingers still hurt like hell, but that'll pass. Then I'll be able to—

A shout causes me to look up. I scan the forest as I turn. "Where did that shout come from, boy?"

The wolf doesn't move. Another shout. I'm sure it came from somewhere to my right. I take off running. The wolf catches up with me in three seconds and barks. He bumps my leg.

I stumble, then catch myself. "Hey!"

He looks up at me.

"Do that again and I'll kick you," I growl, but I wonder if I have the courage to carry out my threat. He could catch my leg in his powerful jaws and snap the bone without missing stride.

I dodge a large elm and leap a fallen branch. Seconds later, we break from the trees, leap the ditch, and stumble to a halt on the road. I stop, breathing heavily, and scan my surroundings. Nothing. Then another scream. I glimpse someone in the trees across the street and take off after them.

The wolf growls. I leap the small ditch on the far side of the road, land on soft ground and skid a foot before propelling myself forward. A small figure darts behind a large tree. I dodge limbs and attempt to pick up speed but can only go so fast through the damned trees and snow. I catch sight of another wolf. Although tall and wiry, the animal looks anorexic compared to the one at my side. Another scream. The kid shoots lunges from the tree and my heart jumps into my throat.

Jonas.

The last time I saw the kid, he'd broken past the imprisoning spell Blade had cast around my dorm room. Jonas races across a clearing. I duck a low branch and leafless branches slap my shoulder. The kid looks over his shoulder at the wolf, which is closing in. I swallow a scream. Three Shadows trail the wolf. Adrenaline pumps my heart faster. One of the Shadows slows. Damn, has it sensed my presence?

"Jonas!" I shout.

His head whips in our direction. His eyes lock onto *my* wolf and widen. The Shadows pick up speed, headed directly for him. He's got to do something to stop the Shadows' advance. But he can't, I realize. Fear has an iron grip on him.

Hell, I don't blame him.

SIX

Ethan

BLADE RARELY GETS ANGRY, BUT THE DARKENING OF his blue eyes tells me he's losing patience. None of us know what went wrong in the War Games—least of all, Olympia. Worse, Raith, Blade and I don't know if Ciarah is safe. Safe? She isn't safe. The possibility of another Reaping occurring so soon and Ciarah being taken hadn't factored into our plans. Anger ignites my fire and warms my palms. There must be a way to help her. There must be.

Normally, when a Reaping occurs, we do our best to go about our business until our loved ones return—or not. The Reaping lasts a week, at most. Seven days of hell. For Raith, Blade, and I, beings who have lived millennia, it's an eternity.

My thoughts screech to attention. Forty years have passed since I last sensed the subtle shift in air that signals the arrival of a god, but there is no mistaking the feeling. A hiss from Blade tells me he, too, senses the god's arrival. Olympia freezes and I almost swear that Domini flinches right before the goddess Eldione appears.

Whereas Aphrodite, the Greek goddess of love, possesses a beauty that warms the heart, Eldione, an Atlantean goddess, has stark beauty cold as ice. A blaze of copper locks frame alabaster skin and emerald eyes not of this world. To touch her is to freeze one's heart. She wears the ancient, flowing white gown that reminds us that she and the other gods existed before our ancestors lived.

"Eldione," Olympia says in a cool voice. "To what do we owe the honor of your presence?"

"*You* do not have the honor of anything, witch," Eldione replies, and Blade visibly winces. "You have nothing to do with the matter." Eldione faces Raith. "I am here—" Her head snaps in Seton's direction and her eyes narrow. "Since when does the Illumina associate with *skyloi*?"

Dogs? The Atlantean gods refer to the gods of the Greek pantheon as *skyloi*: dogs.

Raith's eyes jerk to mine.

"Skyloi?" Olympia whispers. "A Greek god?"

"No god," she sneers. *Demigod*, I think, as Eldione adds, "Demigod."

Seton's brows raise. "You don't mean me?"

"Tychon," she half growls.

Tychon? "Son of Alastor?" I blurt, and Blade finishes, "God of family feuds and avengers of evil deeds."

Blade takes two quick steps toward me as Raith leaps to his feet and I command fire into my palms.

Eldione's eyes meet mine and she gives a low laugh. "Will you uphold your alliance with the Pantheon and protect me from him? Or will you make the same mistake Zeus did?"

The Atlanteans have never forgiven Zeus for not taking their side when Damien's Atlantean sorceress, Elexea, sank Atlantis. Their ancient rivalry evolved into a bitter feud that left a bounty on the sorceress's head.

"What is your intention, Eldione?" I demand.

"So, *you* have made your choice," she hisses, then swings

her gaze onto Olympia "The Grand Witch of the North has allied herself with the ancient deceivers."

"Ancient deceivers is correct," Olympia says in a voice so cold, chills prickle my arms. "We know him as Seton Alexander, a graduate of The Academy."

I can't believe it. Seton Alexander, graduate of The Academy —childhood friend to Ciarah—and a Greek demigod No. Tychon is centuries old. He is no youth. He took the form of a young man to— To what? Befriend Ciarah? My thoughts race and I snap my gaze onto Blade. He's staring at Seton with eyes that have turned golden. Fae eyes. My heart jumps into overdrive.

"Raith," I begin, but he has already started toward Blade.

"He has betrayed us," the Fae's voice breaks the silence. "Betrayed *her*."

Raith reaches Blade as a gale force wind whips through the room. A floor lamp crashes to the carpet. I'm not sure if Blade has called the wind, or if one of the gods are responsible. Maybe even Olympia, who has thrown her hands into the air and is chanting. I turn my shoulder into the wind and start for Blade as Raith seizes his shoulders and shakes him. One of the things that make the Fae so powerful is their connection with nature. Like dragons with fire, they need only think *wind* and the elements obey their command almost without exception.

A snarl mingles with the roar of wind and magic courses through the room. I look over my shoulder. Eldione stands with one hand stretched toward Seton. Not a hair on her head so much as rustles with the wind. Seton has turned his head aside as if to protect himself from the wind. I stumble back two paces before bracing my legs to keep from being forced against the wall. Carter leaps and tackles Seton. Seton's feral growl is nearly as loud as the wind, then he vanishes. Carter's arms close around air.

Eldione whirls to face Olympia, and demands, "What is the

meaning of this?" The wind ceases and her last word comes out a shout in the now quiet room.

"You gods claim to be all powerful, then blame us for being fooled by your kind?" the Grand Witch snaps.

Her voice is hard as granite, but I see fear in her eyes. I'm afraid, too, but I bet for a very different reason. Why did Seton take human form and befriend Leilah? Does he know about our relationship with her? I shudder to think the lengths to which Olympia will go to find the answer to that question. If our relationship with Leilah is exposed—

"Tychon is a *demigod*," Eldione snaps. "He is not all powerful."

"He is powerful enough to take human form and fool us all," Domini cuts in.

I glance at Raith, who has a hand on Blade's shoulder. They're both staring at Domini.

"Why would a demigod befriend a young girl?" Carter asks.

Damn Carter.

Eldione rakes her gaze down Carter's length. "Another vampire." She swings her eyes onto Olympia. "But he does raise a good point."

Olympia pins Raith with a stare, and I swallow.

SEVEN

Leilah

THERE'S ONLY ONE WAY TO GET THAT WEIRD WOLF off the kid's tail. I reach deep inside my core and draw up a hairline of silver light. When in doubt, go back to the basics, Grams used to say. Silver is a natural repellent. I don't allow myself to glance at the wolf loping at my side. I can't chance even a whisp of silver finding its way to him.

Jonas disappears among the trees. Dammit, I need to see my intended victim to be sure the silver hits the animal's heart. If the wolf leaves my sight, he'll get the kid before I can take him down.

I spin the silver upward like a missile and out through my eyes. A blinding instant of pain rips through my eyeballs, then the silver races toward the wolf. The wolf beside me barks so loudly, I wince. I leap a fallen tree branch. One of the Shadows turns and veers toward me. I have to get the silver to the wolf before I lose sight of him—and before that fucking Shadow reaches me.

The wolf—my wolf—growls. He shoots past me, on a collision course with the approaching Shadow. I want to cry but force back the compulsion. The silver is almost upon the wolf chasing Jonas. The animal reaches the trees. I squint to keep him in sight and barely miss a rock the size of a cantaloupe that protrudes from the ground.

The wolf is a blur. My silver spear disappears into the trees and I concentrate to keep my connection to the thing. The silver is close. Yes, another few feet. I push out a harsh breath on a warrior's scream, as if throwing the spear with all my might—then steel myself against the pain as the spear pierces the animal's ribs. His warm, pounding heart beats in rhythm with my own for three heartbeats. Then he squeals and collapses.

Now, I have to catch the kid before the Shadows get him. I shoot into the trees and slow. Where is he? I scan the trees. Movement to my left yanks my attention in that direction. Jonas stumbles and falls ten feet from three Shadows. He rolls onto his back and crabwalks backward—not from the Shadows—from the wolf. My wolf.

My wolf peels his lips back and growls. My heart leaps into my throat. He's going to attack the kid. *God, please, no.* Sorrow, soul deep, causes tears to prick. I have to kill the wolf. I halt and cup my palms in front of me.

"Forest spirits, I call upon you to gather wind."

An eddy of wind coalesces in my hands. I push my palms together and form a ball. With a deep breath, I draw back my right hand to throw the ball of energy. I step forward with my right leg and—

The three Shadows veer toward the wolf. The wolf spins to face them and growls. He's drawing their attention away from the kid! I throw the energy ball, spinning slightly to the left in the last second. The ball of energy whizzes past the wolf, ruffling the animal's fur. The Shadows race toward him. Fury oozes from the shifter. The Shadows will eat him alive.

A noise beyond the wolf and kid startles me, then I recognize the crunch of snow and leaves beneath pounding feet—

many feet, I realize. I freeze, pulse racing. An instant later, the Shadows veer toward the noise and I discern half a dozen people running toward us. The wolf whirls toward the newcomers. He's no longer growling, but his teeth are bared. Jonas remains frozen, his wide eyes on the approaching newcomers.

"He's here!" a guy in the lead shouts.

I don't know his name, but I recognize the guy from campus. He grips a branch about the size of a bat on one end like he's ready to swing. But the small ribbon of obsidian that slithers around his neck is what has my heart pounding like a locomotive.

"I knew it," a girl says.

I know that voice. *Ariel*.

They stop ten feet from Jonas and the wolf and the leader looks my way as Ariel steps around him. I take a step back. A Shadow slithers around her face, twisting and turning as if its growing excited.

"Well, well, well," she says. "I told you this would work out." She starts toward me and the wolf growls. Ariel halts, eyes narrowed on the shifter. "Leave it to a *witch* to have a familiar with her."

"Ariel, do you realize you've been infected by a Shadow?" I whisper.

The Shadow slithers down her cheek. Eyes locked with mine, she opens her mouth and it disappears inside. My stomach lurches.

"We're in a Reaping," I say. "It's not your fault."

"Another Reaping isn't due for about twenty more years." She returns her attention to the wolf.

He barks.

Her mouth twists upward in a malicious mile. "You think you can take on all of us?"

"Don't be a fool," I say.

The floating Shadows turn in my direction.

"We need to put a lid on this," I say.

Ariel and the guy laugh.

"Really?" the guy says.

I glance from him to Ariel. "You're infected by Shadows." I look at the other students. They're younger, probably fourteen to seventeen. No Shadows slither across their bodies, but their eyes are wide with fear and some cast terrified glances at the nearby Shadows.

I focus on the oldest boy. "Tell them," I say.

His eyes widen.

The leader glances his way and gives him a mean grin. "Yeah, Bobby, tell me."

Bobby shakes his head.

"Jonas," I say. "Come here."

He doesn't move.

"Come on." I give him a reassuring smile. "It's okay." I look at the other kids. "You all, too. Come with us."

The leader slaps the branch against his palm.

"Come on, everyone," I say. "I can protect you."

"I would think twice about that." The leader sweeps his gaze across his small band.

"Don't listen to him," I say. "Come on. Jonas, come on."

"Anthony won't hurt Jonas," Ariel says. "He just—"

"Is this what you all want?" I stare at Bobby.

The kids glance at each other.

"Clear your minds and think positive thoughts," I tell the students.

Ariel snorts. "You think you can control Shadows with positive thoughts?"

"Do as I say," I urge the other students.

Bobby says, "We can't."

"Why?" I ask.

"Because these two will get us long before the Shadows do."

Anthony starts toward Bobby.

Fuck it.

"Rock," I murmur. A rock the size of a baseball appears in my hand. "Hey, asshole," I call, and throw the rock at Anthony.

"*Deflecto,*" Ariel counters, and the rock veers left.

I shove my fisted hands forward, then open them palms outward, directing power that splits the rock into a thousand pieces aimed at Anthony. Ariel screams and ducks—the stupid bitch thinks I have no aim. Anthony spins toward me. His eyes widen and he dives for the ground.

"Run!" I shout.

The students freeze.

"Run!" I shout, again. "*Now.*"

They break from their stupor, spin away from Anthony, and run. Except Jonas. I start toward him, then halt when the Shadows head in my direction. Oh, God. My use of magic is calling them to me.

EIGHT

Blade

Tychon is gone, but the hate that still radiates off Eldione feeds my barely controlled fury. I start to step forward with the intention of leaving, but Raith's hand on my shoulder keeps me where I stand.

"Tychon disguising himself as a human and befriending Leilah Crowe must have something to do with Miriam Crowe," Olympia says.

I fist my hands at my sides. I will find Tychon and tear him limb from limb.

"The witch who died while practicing Shadow magic?" Eldione frowns. "What has she to do with Tychon?"

"Leilah Crowe is Miriam's granddaughter," Olympia replies.

Eldione stares. "The woman Tychon befriended?"

"Yes." Raith removes his hand from my shoulder. "Seton's friendship with Ms. Crowe must have something to do with her grandmother."

"A rogue witch and an Atlantean demigod." Eldione blows out a breath. "At least we need not worry about the witch."

Olympia draws a sharp breath.

Eldione pins her with a hard look. "Don't act as if *I* am the one with no compassion. A high witch who practices Shadow magic is ruthless. Normally, I would not bother to interfere—"

"Indeed?" Olympia cuts in. "Then why are you here?"

The goddess's eyes blaze. "We saw the Reaping take place."

"It came early," Raith says. "*Very* early."

"Your Reaping pales in comparison to finding allies harboring a mortal enemy," Eldione sneers.

"We had no idea of Seton's true identity," Domini interjects.

I snap my gaze onto him. Domini, I realize, has been too quiet. I expect a man of his supposed power to take action. Instead, Carter took Seton—Tychon—down.

"If we had known his true identity, we would have contacted you," Domini continues.

Eldione frowns. "Who are you?"

"Mage Edd Domini, at your service." He executes a slight bow.

Eldione studies him, then returns her attention to Olympia. "The great Grand Witch of the North cannot recognize a demigod?"

"You can't have it both ways, Eldione," Olympia replies. "Either you gods are powerful enough to fool us or you aren't."

"I have never heard the Grand Witch admit that anyone could fool her," Eldione says.

Olympia offers a cool smile. "No one is invincible."

Eldione's eyes snap with power.

"Eldione," Raith says. "What do you want?"

The goddess' mouth thins. She dislikes Olympia. But Olympia is a diplomat. She may allow her frustration to show, but she will never gainsay the goddess. Caleb, on the other hand, cares nothing for politics and wouldn't tolerate her bloody bullshit. The last time the goddess appeared was just before Ciarah, called Nova in that lifetime, died. Caleb, in wolf form, had bared his teeth and growled at Eldione. I suddenly long for the wolf's company. He would hunt down Tychon with me. The wolf howl in the virtual war games unexpectedly rises in memory. I haven't heard a wolf howl since Caleb disappeared.

NINE

Leilah

A WOLF HOWLS IN THE DISTANCE. I JERK MY GAZE from the approaching Shadows and scan the area, but glimpse only the retreating backs of the fleeing students.

Jonas sidles closer. "Is the howling getting closer?" he whispers, one eye on the Shadows, which hover five feet away,

Yeah, I think, but say, "I don't know."

How many wolves roam these woods? We weren't trained to battle Shadows while fighting for our lives. Hell, I have no real training in fighting Shadows. I look at my wolf. His ears are pricked and he's staring in the direction of the howl. He looks at me and barks.

I blow out a breath. "If you're saying we should run, I agree."

He whips around and bounds away from the howling pack.

"Come on, kid. We're getting out of here," I say.

Jonas runs after the wolf. I back up several paces, squinting into the tress in an effort to discern movement. I see nothing, glance at the Shadows, which haven't moved, then spin and hurry after Jonas and wolf. We can't go on like this. We've got to find a place to get out of the cold, find food and water, and plan.

I get no more than a dozen steps when magical energy abruptly pushes at my psychic space. I slow and look around but see only the kid and the wolf up ahead. I twist and look over my shoulder. The Shadows are gone. I face forward and jog to catch up with Jonas and the wolf. Is Ariel using magic to try and find us, or maybe someone is in trouble and is trying to save themselves?

This is probably how The Shadows ensnared so many people in the Shadow War. We use magic in order to save yourself—or help others. Then, boom! They've got you.

Another wolf howl jerks me from my thoughts. Magic presses harder against me and I stumble. Maybe someone really is in trouble. But as the thought forms, a sense of familiarity washes over me. I have encountered this magic before. The Academy? A chill slides down my back. No, the War Games. The lightning bolt that nearly sizzled me in the war lord's house.

Chelsea.

I had forgotten about her. I figured she had conjured that lightning bolt because something spooked her. Just like something must have spooked her now. I want to throw out my senses in an effort to find her, but that's sure to draw attention to me—to us. I dodge a low hanging branch. Dammit, Chelsea can't be more than fifteen. Exhaustion rolls over me. We've been here less than a day and I'm so tired. How can I possibly help the kid, Chelsea, the wolf...or anyone else? Fuck, I can barely help myself.

Longing for Stony rolls over me with such force that I want to cry. I push back the question of why she didn't transition into the Reaping. Stony is a powerful creature. A fucking Reaping can't do her in. I force back tears. If Jonas sees me crying, it'll freak him out. I half wonder how the wolf would react. Hell, I wish that damn creature would shift into his human form. I want—need—to talk to another adult, an adult who can help me plan. Another wolf howls. I whip my head around and peer over my shoulder That one was close. My heart jumps into my throat when I discern several furry blurs.

"Run!" I shout, and run faster.

Jonas has already picked up the pace. The wolf turns and races toward me.

"Keep going." I wave him forward.

He darts past me. "No!" I halt and spin. "We need you."

He looks back at me, and I swear his eyes soften. Then he faces forward again. What will we do if something happens to him? What will we do if those wolves catch us? I whirl toward Jonas. He's thirty feet ahead and hauling ass. I spot movement amongst the trees up ahead to the left.

Shadows.

Oh, God, they're on his tail. I stumble forward.

You can't have him, mother fuckers.

The Shadows veer toward me. Fear causes my stomach to roil and I feel like I might vomit.

Relax, I tell myself, then realize my mistake. I want them to chase me—not Jonas. He hasn't slowed and is much father ahead. A new fear swirls in my stomach. What if Ariel and her band catch him? I run faster. Maybe I can ditch the Shadows somewhere.

The wolves howl a chorus and I look over my shoulder. Are they the same long nosed, weird wolves like the one I killed? I shiver, then face forward. The Shadows are within ten feet of me.

"Get lost," I shout.

They halt, and I stumble to a stop. They ripple in place, like thick, wide ribbons, as if uncertain what to do. I know the feeling. If I move, will I break whatever spell holds them immobile?

"Leilah!" Jonas shouts.

He's stopped and is looking back at me. The Shadows head for him.

"Run!" I shout. "Run!"

He runs and they pick up speed.

Anger bursts from me and I sprint after the Shadows. "You leave him alone."

They reverse course and start toward me again.

"How the hell do I kill you?" I shout.

Another wolf howl echoes through the trees, much closer. I veer to the left, away from the kid. He's out of sight. My heart thunders. I need to ditch the Shadows and find him. I hope like hell I *can* find him. I resist the urge to head in the direction he disappeared. A wolf snarl I recognize emanates from some-where to my right.

My wolf.

I scan wildly for the source of the growl. The damn wolf must be fighting the other wolves. If I can get to him, he can track Jonas. Growls and barks yank my attention to the right. Vicious growls are followed by a wolf's yelp of pain. How many wolves is he fighting? I follow the noise, then stop when it seems the snarls and growls are emanating more to my right.

I throw my hands up in the air and turn in a circle as I shout, "Where the fuck are you?"

The Shadows start away from me. Are they headed toward the wolves? Good. I can follow them. Wait, not good. They might infect my wolf.

TEN

Blade

THE WOLF HOWL BOUNCES OFF THE INSIDE OF MY
skull. I shake my head in an effort to clear the sense of reality
that grips me. The wolf in the virtual world wasn't real. *Not
real*, I mentally repeat.

Understanding brings a clarity that nearly buckles my
knees.

The virtual world wasn't real.

The Reaping, however, is very real.

Leilah.

I cut my gaze to Ethan. He frowns, then his gaze sharpens
in question.

"I assume you have no idea what triggered the early Reaping?" Eldione asks.

I tense. The gods cannot see into our minds but can sometimes sense our thoughts.

"What do you care triggered the Reaping?" Carter demands.

The goddess bares her teeth at him.

"One might get the idea you don't like vampires," Raith
says.

"You are the exception, my sweet." Eldione locks gazes with

him, and I release a slow breath as I ease thoughts of Leilah into the recesses of my mind.

"We must talk privately," Eldione says.

Raith looks at Carter and jerks his head toward the door. Carter glances around, then stalks from the room.

Eldione nods toward Domini. "That one, as well."

"He is our Headmaster," Olympia objects.

"I understand completely." Domini cuts in. He angles his head Eldione's way, then says, "Good night, all," and leaves.

When the door clicks shut behind him, the goddess says, "The nightmares have returned."

"A Reaping, and nightmares amongst the gods," Raith murmurs.

A chill winds through me. That's not all. Just over two weeks ago, Olympia confided that the fallen angel Samayaza—one of the direct Sons of God—visited her after a five- hundred-year absence to warn her that he believed Damien had located his demon bride and is no longer hiding. Damien, ruler of the infernal regions, the upper levels of hell, Shadow mage, and... demigod of Nightmares.

"Samayaza was right," Olympia says.

"Samayaza?" Eldione repeats.

Even the gods understand the gravity of the situation when an angel of the Most High speaks—even one that has been MIA for centuries.

"What did he say?" Eldione asks.

"That Damien has crawled out from whatever rock he's been hiding under," Raith mutters.

I had hoped against hope that Samayaza was wrong. When the war began nearly forty years ago, we suspected Damien had returned, but had no proof. He is The Shadow Mage. When the Atlantean king sent his most powerful assassin to kill Elexea, he had no idea he would be loosing The Shadows into the world—or that when Damien's sorceress fought the powerful assassin that she would sink Atlantis.

"When did the nightmares begin?" Olympia asks.

"Three weeks ago," Eldione answers.

Olympia stares. "Three weeks and you are only just now telling us?"

The goddess tosses her head. "We are not obligated to tell humans *anything*."

"We are not humans," Olympia says. "And before you come back with a cheeky retort, remember, Damien's nightmares have the ability to destroy you."

"Destroy?" the goddess sneers.

"I suggest you set aside your pride," Olympia snaps. "Either that, or we leave you gods to your own devices until the nightmares drive you insane and you destroy one another."

"We will destroy the world in the process," Eldione hisses.

"But you will still be dead," Olympia says.

"Might Miriam have caused some sort of disturbance when she practiced Shadow magic?" Raith asks.

"There can be no doubt that she is the catalyst of these calamities," the Grand Witch says.

I comprehend how a high witch practicing Shadow magic can have far reaching ramifications—this is the reason we forbid the use of magic without training—but a Reaping? That is beyond our all powers.

"A Reaping and the return of the nightmares are strange coincidences," Ethan says, and I'm struck by the realization that Ciarah returned about three weeks ago. Surely, her connection to her grandmother didn't ignite some sort of disturbance? No. The Grand Witch is right. These events are connected to Miriam alone.

"You must send one of your Council of Kispu back with me to Olympus to cast a spell to rid us of the nightmares," Eldione says.

Olympia nods even as muscles in her jaw tighten. She wants to keep secret that the Reaping occurred within her virtual war games, but too many people were involved. The Council of Kispu will find out and demand an investigation.

"Return in two days," Olympia says. "We will have someone ready."

Eldione nods. "Until then, try to clean up your mess."

Olympia opens her mouth to reply, but Eldione vanishes.

Olympia whirls on Raith. "I watched the video of the last moments of the War Games. There is no doubt Chelsea Nightlow tried to kill Leilah Crowe. Why would she do that?"

We three freeze for several heartbeats before Raith says, "We don't know."

"Is Chelsea responsible for the attempt on Leilah's life in Ethan's class?"

"That's my guess," Raith replies. "I find it unlikely a second person tried to kill Ms. Crowe."

Olympia's lips thin. "I agree. When the Nightlow girl returns—if she returns—she is to be confined to her room. I will deal with her. A Reaping and the gods' nightmares are strange enough. The attempt on Leilah's life is...." She shakes her head. "I don't like it."

I am in complete agreement.

"I am going to the Crowe Potionary," she continues. "Miriam is the key to all this."

Raith angels his head in assent, but I recognize the barely disguised impatience in his eyes.

Olympia's gaze sharpens. "The Wall didn't name Seton as a High Potential. Didn't Miriam nominate Seton as a student for The Academy?"

"Bloody hell," I murmur. "Miriam did nominate him."

Olympia's eyes glaze. "I have no one but myself to blame. I should have kept a closer eye on Miriam. If Blade is right, and she isn't dead—"

"Miriam not dead?" Raith blurts.

Olympia's brows shoot up. "Blade didn't tell you? I thought you three shared everything."

If Olympia had any idea how right she is….

"Apparently not." Raith's mouth thins. "What is this about Miriam not being dead?"

"Just a theory," I say. "The night before the War Games, Zedkeil visited me here at The Academy."

Raith barks a laugh. "A high angel of the Most High deigned to set foot on Academy grounds?" His amusement dies. "He came to tell you that Miriam is alive?"

"He informed me that we must prevent her from finding a way into Hell."

"What?" Ethan blurts.

"Shocking idea, don't you agree?" I say. "By the end of our conversation I deduced two things. One, the angel wasn't being completely honest when he said we have to prevent Miriam from finding a way into Hell—because he fears she's already there."

Raith scowls. "That's ridiculous."

"You haven't heard the best part," I say. "This second point I know is truth, though Zedkeil denied it—far too vehemently. Their god Elohim is locked in Hell."

Ethan and Raith exchange a glance that says they question my sanity.

"You can't be serious," Raith says.

"He's quite serious," Olympia says.

"That explains the god's silence all these centuries." Raith laughs with dark amusement. "Another good reason to make sure the Hell Gates stay locked."

"Maybe," Olympia says. "If Blade is right and Miriam was looking for a way into Hell—"

"Forgive me, Grand Witch," I interrupt. "But I never said I believe she was trying to get into Hell."

Olympia waves me off. "None of us know for certain, but that would explain much. If she succeeded, that means there's a breach in the spell binding the Hell Gates. That could explain the early Reaping, the gods' nightmares, and Tychon's interest in Miriam."

She's reaching. There's nothing to indicate the Reaping has anything to do with the Hell Gates being locked or breached. More and more, I'm convinced the Reaping was triggered by the War Games taking place in Olympia's virtual world, but I remain silent. She will look long and hard to find a way to redirect blame away from herself. Still, the possibility that the War Games trigged a Reaping is troubling.

The first Reaping took place after the great Shadow War in the fifth century. The spell is as powerful as that used by Senorn and Eledin to lock the Hell Gates, and so complex that even the Council of Kispu have been unable to break the spell. In a way, Olympia's virtual Shadow world is not unlike the Reaping. I don't like any of this. The accusation that Miriam might have been trying to open the Hell Gates is enough to bring Leilah deeper under Olympia's scrutiny.

"If Leilah Crowe returns from the Reaping, you are to continue to watch her," Olympia says.

I silently curse. I hate being right.

"As you wish, Grand Witch," Raith says.

She nods curtly, then faces me. "Blade, walk with me."

"Of course, Grand Witch."

She stands and waits while I fetch her long coat from the couch where I'd draped it when she arrived. I hold the coat while she slips her arms into the sleeves, then wait for her to precede me out the door. With a glance at Raith and Ethan that says I will return soon, I follow.

Olympia remains silent until we step from the building into the cold predawn, then says, "You must learn what the Zidruhin know of Damien."

"Grand Witch, we—"

"No excuses," she snaps. "The situation has become critical. There can be no doubt Damien has come out of hiding. Whether or not Miriam found a way into Hell, if Zedkeil believes it's possible, that means Damien will have heard."

"The angels managed to keep secret for centuries the fact that their god is trapped in Hell," I say. "They could keep this secret, as well."

"You never cease to amaze me, Blade. How can a being as old as you be so naïve? The fact that Zedkeil came to see you demonstrates their desperation. Do you think you are the only person Zedkeil talked to about Miriam? Everyone knows she *died* while practicing Shadow magic. I have every confidence that Margiddians know she blew a hole in her basement in the process. You cannot be the only one able to put two and two together."

We turn the corner of the building and continue along the shoveled walkway.

"All that need happen is for Damien to believe Miriam found a way into Hell. That would embolden him," she says.

She has me there.

"His priests must surely know what he plans," she continues. "Powerful as he is, he can't accomplish his goals on his own." She gives me a sideways look. "Can you imagine his and his bride's Shadow power should they unite?"

Power that sank Atlantis. I shake my head. I do not want to imagine their power. She faces forward again as we take the walkway around the building, headed toward her private apartments.

She pulls her coat closer about her. "The next *conflict* won't be a war, but a slaughter. That cannot be allowed."

"The gods will intervene," I say.

She laughs without mirth. "They are slippery as eels and as

tricky as jinns. The only help we will give is if they face annihilation and they need us."

"They need us to stop the nightmares," I say, but know I'm being foolish.

"Are you suggesting I withhold help in ending their nightmares in trade for their help?" She snorts. "They have time before the nightmares become dangerous, which means they will find our weaknesses and exploit them to their advantage. We don't need them poking into our business."

The way Tychon was poking around in our business? In Leilah's business? Fury bubbles to the surface, but I force back the emotion. I will deal with that specific demigod myself.

We reach her building. I open the front door and let her pass before entering.

In the hallway, she stops and faces me, "I will go to Miriam's home. You find a way to penetrate the Zidruhin." Without another word, she turns and starts up the stairs to her apartments.

I whirl and hurry back outside. In the space of hours, the world has gone mad. The only thing worse than Leilah being taken from us is the possibility that Damien has found his Demon Bride. If that happens, nothing will save us, not the bond between myself and the other four men who are bound to Ciarah, and not our love for her. We five have often wondered if anything could kill us. The Shadows can kill us. Worse, if they infected us and we lived indefinitely.... Might another Shadow war might be triggered?

Leilah's words the night we brought her back from her grandmother's house rise in memory, "You defeated The Shadows in the final battle."

"You were there, too," she'd said to Ethan, then to Raith, *"The two of you together."* Then, her attention turned on me, *"You, too, Blade. Miss Mack called you Commander, but I didn't know you were there. Why?"*

"Because my part was more…covert," I'd said.

"What did you do?"

"It's best you don't know."

Memory catapults back twenty years. Unnatural silence reigns in the midnight forest that surrounds the field where Raith and Ethan sit face to face in the middle of two intersecting circles of light, light created by the twenty witches who make up the two circles. The Grand Witch of the North sits at the head of the first chain behind Raith, and High Witch Miriam Crowe sits behind Ethan, each occupying space where the two circles intersect. White light ripples off the witches across the field and is blocked by the trees that encircle the field. The sense of peace that reaches me makes me want to weep. If we could teach every Margiddian to conjure such pure, sweet, white light, fear would disappear, and The Shadows would be rendered powerless.

A full moon hangs overhead, but it's the light the witches create that makes Raith and Ethan's faces glow. Even concealed within the trees, I discern their relaxed expressions. How I wish I knew whether or not the battle had begun.

Attack within an altered plane has never been tried. We have no idea if we can defeat The Shadows in an alternate plane —or if Raith and Ethan can die there. They would never admit to it, but I suspect they believe they can die. I fear they are all too right.

"Damn you, Raith," I murmur.

I should be sitting in that circle. Another Fae could have taken my place to guard the clearing's fourth quadrant. I release a frustrated breath. Raith convinced the Grand Witch I should stand guard, so here I am. In truth, it's Matthias's fault I'm here. As a gargoyle, Matthias is the paradigm of a guardian. If he stood here, instead of me, nature, the angels, and probably even some demons, would heed his beck and call. That's the nature of gargoyles. But Matthias went in search of Caleb and hasn't been heard from in decades.

Noiselessly, I slip from a pine to an elm. My earpiece crackles. I wince. The witches' psychic light is an energy magnet. Even though I require connection to the other watchers, I've twice turned down the device's volume, but to no avail. Wind ruffles my unbound hair. The nature spirits are quiet, but restless.

I scan the woods for Shadows. Those inhuman ribbons of obsidian glide silently. Even with a full moon, I will have difficulty discerning them in the natural shadows of the forest. Still, I sense no unnatural presence, and the other Fae have sounded no alarm.

A Fae's connection to nature isn't magic, but natural talent, which is why we chose this place. Despite my fast-beating heart, I whisper to the nature spirits. An instant later, from the corner of my eye, a tiny light appears amongst the trees. Then another and another. Water sprites. They leave a small trail of light behind them, like a shooting star. My heart warms. I had forgotten the simple beauty of these elemental spirits.

I stiffen at the awareness of a presence.

Shadows.

As quickly as the thought forms, I register the whistle of wind and the flit of a dozen sprites through the trees. The interlopers aren't Shadows, but our own—*Margiddians.* Two... three. No. More. A dozen...two dozen? One is a powerful witch.

Carefully, I press the button of my earpiece and whisper, "We have visitors. At least two dozen Margiddians. Anyone see anything?"

"Nothing here," Josh replies.

I wait for the other two Fae to respond, but nothing.

"Melinda," I say.

Nothing.

"Harrison."

Nothing.

I press the button. "Josh, Anything from Melinda or Harrison?"

I get an earful of static. Bloody hell. We should have known we would have trouble with headsets.

"Josh, if you can hear me, we have company. Stay alert."

The sprites flit from tree to tree in a nervous rhythm. Forest spirits are not part of Margidda, despite being kin to the Fae. They have nothing to fear from The Shadows, as their magic is nature born, and shadows abound within their realm. But they fear the darkness that could choke them.

I slip behind a two-hundred-year-old oak, press my back to the massive trunk, and connect with a solid strength that grounds me to the earth. With a whispered thanks, I scan the forest and send out a plea, asking the forest to guide my search for the interlopers.

A prickle slides down my spine. Something familiar resides in the energy that presses against me. A rustle of leaves to my left snaps my attention in that direction. I freeze. Is that…yes, Jessica Bailey. My heart twists. Jessica is a beautiful young witch who threw away a promising future when she teamed up with vampire crime boss Elijah Walker. I'd begged her to leave Elijah even after he gave himself over to the Shadow infection that enhanced his power and made him the most powerful crime boss on the Eastern Seaboard. But she loved the power. No doubt, Elijah is here with her.

My anger wells hot and fast before I can prevent the rush of emotion. Elijah's profits come from the sacrifice of his fellow Margiddians. I release a slow breath and center my being in line with the white light emitted by the witches. I can't risk drawing Shadows with my anger.

How did Elijah and Jessica learn we were here? Only the witches, Raith, Ethan, myself and the three other Fae guards knew of our plan to battle The Shadows. That means there is a traitor in our midst. Is the traitor one of the witches? No. If that were so, the chain would already have broken. That leaves the three Fae—but nots Josh. I've known him since his childhood.

As long as the chain of light remains unbroken, Jessica and Elijah can't step into the circles of white light. I must deal with Elijah in a calm manner that doesn't open the door to the anger he's so skilled at inciting. Jessica, well…that witch is another story.

She's powerful enough to have joined the witches who form the circles around Raith and Ethan and she will not hesitate to use her magic to stop us—even if that means killing us. Like Elijah, her powers are enhanced by her Shadow infection—and she knows I can't risk using magic.

I'm a fool. I hadn't considered that we might fight anything other than Shadows. Then again, I hadn't considered the possibility of a traitor in our midst. All the lifetimes I've lived, I can still be naïve.

As long as I remain hidden, Jessica can't use her magic directly on me, which requires line of sight. The whisper of leaves crunching beneath a light tread alerts me to their location in the instant before I discern a shape amid the trees. A slight form comes into view amongst the murk of the forest closer to the clearing.

Jessica.

Behind her, a larger, bulkier form follows.

Elijah.

"Show yourself, Blade," Elijah calls.

I mentally laugh. *Not bloody likely, you bastard.*

As if having read my thoughts, he laughs, low, and with an amusement that comes with immense confidence. I should have killed him two years ago when I had the chance.

"Boss," my earpiece crackles with Josh's voice.

"I know," I reply. "Remain calm."

I fear saying more. I have no idea who betrayed us—or how many others are hidden among the trees.

Spirit of wind, I telepath, *show me who hides amongst the trees.*

A breeze rustles the canopy, creating a murmur of voices that says, *"One for one they match the twenty who protect the two—with four to spare."*

Twenty-four witches? My heart pounds.

"Not of your world, their lives are charmed."

Charmed?

I stiffen. Elijah hasn't brought witches or even Shadow-infected Margiddians. He's brought humans he's fed on. Humans he controls, but who have no power over Margiddians. Why do that? Then I know.

I press the button on the headset and say in a bare whisper that I pray Elijah can't hear, "Josh, there are humans in the trees. They intend to attack the circles. Radio the others and find them—stop them. Anything. *Now.*"

The radio's high-pitched squeal is my answer. I scan the trees. Where are the humans? They must be on the other side of the field Melinda and Harrison patrol, or I would have seen them.

I need to locate the humans. Jessica and Elijah can't enter the white light, but if the witches' chain breaks, the white light will extinguish and the witches will be vulnerable. Double fool that I am, I thought four Fae would be enough to guard the witches. I should have brought a battalion.

To my right—in the direction Jessica and Elijah have melted back into the trees—the sprites flit and surge like a flock of birds evading a predator.

"Sprites, I command you to protect the witches."

Wind whips my hair. The sprites fan out, leaving an intricate webbing of light in their wake that blocks Jessica and

Elijah from the witches—for at least a few precious moments—should the circle falter.

I throw my fists heavenward and shout, "Spirit of lightning!"

A roiling black mass blocks out the moon and stars and a deafening thunderclap shakes the ground. The circles of light flicker. I lunge toward the field. With a banshee cry, humans break from the trees on the far side of the field.

Their screams tell me they have been worked into a frenzy that can only be sated with blood. Lightning strikes the ground in front of the attackers. Leaves and brush burst into flame. The humans race through the flames despite screams of pain.

"We are kin far removed," I speak to the earth as I jump a log. "In kinship's name, I call upon earth, wind, fire and"—I hesitate. Once spoken, the result can't be altered—"*air.*"

A blast of wind throws me to the ground. The white light flickers. Panic twists through me. I shove to my feet, breathing hard. Massive energy emanates from across the field beyond the circle of light. I recognize the energy as originating from nature, but it's massive. I have no idea *what* has responded to my call. Has Jessica found a way to control nature spirits? I start at a run through the forest, then halt as a creature steps from the trees from which the humans emerged. Fear constricts my throat. A naked man—a giant—towers ten feet higher than the trees. Earth hangs from his hair and dirt smudges his perfectly muscled body.

An *eudaimon*, I realize. I stare in shock. I've never seen one of the ancient forest spirits. They are believed to be extinct. He bellows an unearthly animal cry that reverberates inside my skull and leaves my ears ringing. He bends and, with a back-handed blow, sends half the mortal attackers flying through the air like rag dolls, back toward the tree line. The remaining scatter in terror. The creature reaches them in one massive step and backhands left, then right. They hurtle through the air.

Their screams are silenced when they crash into trees and drop, limp, to the ground. The witches' light flickers. Again, I start running toward the clearing. The creature takes ground-shaking steps toward the witches. Legend says the *eudaimon* are guardians of light and goodness. Will the forest spirit harm the witches?

"Boss!" Melinda shouts into my earpiece, as she bursts from the trees on the other side of the field.

Movement to my left yanks my attention onto two figures, one slight, one large, running through the trees toward the clearing.

Elijah and Jessica.

What are they doing? They can't enter the circle of light.

"Earth spirit," I call to the giant, "the two traitors who would destroy your forest intend to attack."

The creature turns away from the witches, headed in Jessica and Elijah's direction. Oh, yes, it knows exactly who I'm refer-ring to. Can the forest spirit can kill them? *Eudaimon* are extremely powerful.

Half a dozen Shadows stream past on my right. Anger whips through me. So, this is Elijah and Jessica's plan. They attracted The Shadows with the intention of infecting us Fae, and, if the chain broke, infecting the witches, Raith and Ethan.

The *eudaimon* steps into the forest ahead and to my right, not harming a single tree. The Shadows veer toward the crea-ture. Surely, Shadows have no sway over such an ancient earth spirit? My stomach clenches. The sprites appear and dance in front of me, their pattern instantly recognizable.

"I know," I half growl, and head toward the field, toward the intense white light that, thankfully, remains strong.

The eudaimon heads deeper into the forest. I discern no sign of Jessica and Elijah, but the Shadows— A force seizes my shoulders and drives me backwards. The backs of my legs strike something and I fall across the trunk of a dead tree. The sprites flit around my head in a disjointed dance. Fingers of iron wrap around my throat.

The *eudaimon* bellows.

Use magic, a voice urges.

I claw at the fingers around my throat, but my fingers pass through them. I have to break Jessica's magic. I center power deep in my belly. Energy swirls inside me even as the fingers tighten. I can't draw breath. Power ripples through my chest, down my arms—

The night goes abruptly dark and the full moon which I hadn't been able to see through the witches' white light fills the night sky. I choke back a sob. The Shadows won. They quenched the light. The witches. Raith...Ethan.

Fury rips through me.

"No!" I shout.

My power rushes outward. *Kill them.* I will kill them.

The bands encircling my throat release. I shove to my feet, choking, but throw out my senses in search of the witch and vampire. I can't swallow past the pain in my throat. My energy hits a brick wall. I focus on a large figure blocking my path.

Rage blinds me. I charge.

"Blade!"

I collide with a hard body and we crash to the ground. The roar of a growl penetrates the thundering rush of blood in my ears. I pummel punches to a belly hard as steel. I'll drill a hole through him straight to hell.

"Blade!"

Iron fingers seize my shoulders and yank me backward. I hit the ground so hard the breath rushes from my lungs.

"I'll kill you, you bloody bastard!" I shout.

A bellow shakes the ground. The *eudaimon*. Then silence.

"How did you manage to call an eudaimon?"

I jump to my feet breathing hard and stare at the man I was pounding. "Raith?" I swing around and face—yes—Ethan. "Jessica Bailey and Elijah Walker showed up," I blurt. "I tried to stop them. But the humans...." I search Ethan's eyes. "I failed."

"Failed?" Raith says.

"We won," Ethan says.

I stare. "What?"

"We won," Raith repeats.

"No more death?" I whisper.

"This is the beginning of the end of the war," Raith says.

"The humans." I stumble back two paces.

Ethan seizes my arm and steadies me. "What humans?"

"Elijah brought twenty-four humans. I called upon the forest spirits to protect you. The *eudaimon* appeared and—" I recall how easily he snuffed out the lives of twenty-four mortals, mortals whose only crime had probably been crossing Elijah Walker's path. "Twenty-four more casualties of this war," I choke out.

Their screams pierce my confusion. A thought, both horrifying and hopeful, strikes. What if they didn't all die? What if some of them are lying on the ground, inching toward death in agonizing pain? I lunge past Ethan and Raith.

"Blade!" Raith shouts.

I ignore him and race through the trees and break into the clearing. The witches cluster at the far side of the meadow, some kneeling beside bodies.

"*Blade*," Ethan shouts behind me.

I race across the meadow to the nearest body.

"What happened here?" Miriam Crowe demands when I reach the body she kneels beside.

There is no recrimination in her question. Or is there?

I drop to my knees beside the fallen man. The side of his head is caved in. Blood has pooled on the ground beside his head and I glimpse—

My stomach heaves. I raise my face to heaven and shout,

"This is wrong—so wrong!" I shove to my feet and stumble backwards. I begin to fall.

Strong hands seize my shoulders. "Blade!" Raith shouts.

"Get away," I shout into his face.

"Blade!"

The meadow disappears and The Academy administration building snaps into focus against twilight. I blink into Raith's face.

"You remembered again, didn't you?" Ethan demands.

I look past Raith at him.

"Come on." Raith shoves me. He and Blade fall into step on either side of me. "We need a very strong drink."

ELEVEN

Leilah

I RACE AFTER THE SHADOWS THAT ARE DRAWN BY MY wolf's fury. Beyond the Shadows, the wolf pack comes into view. My blood goes cold. Six wolves encircle my wolf. His lips are drawn back, hackles raised, legs wide, but even with his size, he can't take on six packmates.

One lunges. Mine catches his attacker's neck and, even at twenty feet, I hear bones crunch before he hurls the limp body toward the circle of wolves. Okay, maybe he can handle the wolves, but those Shadows will do him in.

"You Shadows leave him alone!" my shout is hoarse.

The Shadows halt.

That is just too weird.

The wolves' faces turn in my direction.

Fuck. I run past the Shadows and stop ten feet from the wolves. My wolf's eyes narrow on me.

I meet the gaze of the wolf closest to me. "Take your buddies and get lost," I order.

He bares his teeth.

I bare my teeth.

They all bare their teeth and growl. My wolf lunges at the

wolf nearest him. His powerful jaws close around its neck. My stomach lurches at the crunch of bones. The four remaining wolves stalk toward me.

I throw out my hands, palms outward, and shout, "Deflect!"

The wolves are hurled backwards. My wolf pounces on one and makes short work of her. Three remain. The Shadows start toward me.

"Stop!" I shout.

They don't obey.

"Take them." I jab my finger at the three wolves, who now circle mine, teeth bared.

Their ferocious growls rumble through the air. My heart pounds. They are planning a joint attack. One eye on the Shadows, the other on the wolves, I take a step back.

Don't freak out, I tell myself. The last thing my wolf needs is to have to rescue me.

Movement among the trees draws my attention. Another wolf approaches, this one as big as my wolf, its obsidian eyes glaring. Oh God, he's got to be infected by the Shadows. They're all infected. Not my wolf. The Reaping pulls in High Potentials from all over the world. What if the other wolves were foreign Academy students? My heart lurches at the thought. The Shadows slow their progress toward me.

What the hell? Did they slow because of my compassion for the pack wolves? The new wolf reaches the pack wolves and they part for him. If the wolves are students infected by Reaping Shadows, does that mean they will be infected when they return to the real world?

My wolf has killed three of them. Does that mean he's killed three students? Panic sends my heart into an erratic rhythm. What if that's the case? I can't let him kill students. But I can't let them kill him, either. Indecision knots my stomach. The new wolf bares fangs that makes me think of a science fiction movie gone bad. What do I do?

My mind jumbles with the recollection of the earth magic I used in the virtualverse. Maybe—maybe I can get control. I yank up the trembling index finger of my right hand and twirl it in a circle.

"Please," I beg the nature spirits, "help me."

Nothing.

I watch the Shadows and turn the circle faster. "Anything—*please.*"

Nothing.

The other three wolves growl and lower their heads in an attack stance aimed at my wolf.

"Curse you, nature spirits," I shout, then command, "Raven," and a giant raven appears above them.

The bird swoops and the wolves scatter—all except my wolf. His head snaps in my direction, his eyes on the Shadows, hovering three feet from me. The bird's caws make my ears ring. It swoops again, this time grabbing one of the wolves. The animal twists and snaps at the bird, but the crow deftly navigates through the canopy.

"Don't hurt them," I call after the bird.

The crow caws and drops the wolf. The Shadows reach me. I take a step back and thrust out a hand in a "stop" gesture. I freeze when one of the Shadows wraps itself around my arm. My heart gallops. I tell myself to move, but I can't. Through my shirt sleeve the Shadow feels like cool silk caressing my flesh. I want to command it to leave, but the same sense of familiarity I experienced when I saw the Shadows upon my arrival overwhelms me. Then the thing coils up my arm and slips down my shirt. I seize my collar and yank the shirt back in time to see the Shadow disappear into my chest—right above my heart. I can't breathe. Am I having a heart attack? Is that how infection happens, they got inside of us like some ghostly possession?

Furious barking penetrates the ringing in my ears. The raven dives for my wolf. He's three feet away, snapping at the raven as if he means to eat the bird. Fuck, that's an image I don't need.

"Be gone," I command the crow.

My chest tightens and a tiny pain pricks as the bird gives one last caw then vanishes. I drop to my knees, breathing hard. A Shadow is inside me. It's all my fault. I used magic. But how could I not? I couldn't allow other students to die. Am I sure they were students? Who else is in this hellish place besides students and Shadows?

Something bumps my arm and I start. The wolf is nudging me with his nose. I shake my head. He nudges my arm, the arm the Shadow touched. Well, it didn't really touch my skin, though the soft caress of fabric felt as if it did. I'm being stupid. The Shadows touched my skin, my chest, the valley between my breasts, and is inside me!

A sudden vision assails me of Blade on his knees, head raised skyward while loosing an eerie shout that sends a shiver down my spine. The vision evaporates and my surrounding's spin. I drop onto my ass.

I shake my head. What just happened? The knowledge comes to me almost before the thought completes. The blood pact. What was Blade doing on his knees shouting to the heavens? Can a blood pact connection span the gap between the mundane world and the Reaping? The wolf whines. I realize I'm gripping his fur. When had I grabbed him? I let go. He looks at me and waits.

"If a vampire, Fae, and dragon ever ask you to make a blood pact with them, don't," I say.

The wolf sneezes.

"My sentiments exactly," I mutter.

His head snaps to the right and he stares into the trees.

"What do you see, boy?" I ask.

A wolf's growl is my answer. The massive wolf comes into view five feet away. I jump to my feet. After all this, that thing is back? The desire to blast the mother fucker to kingdom come nearly overwhelms me. I take a step forward, but my wolf leaps forward and clamps his mighty jaw onto its throat.

The wolf twists free and sinks his teeth into my wolf's shoulder. My wolf howls and transforms into a tall, muscular man whose hands grip the wolf's jaw and snout and yanks them apart like a chicken wishbone. Wolf blood spurts onto the man's chest. He drops the limp body and whirls to face me.

TWELVE

Matthias

ON DAYS LIKE THIS, I LONG FOR THE SERENITY OF the monastery. I could escape the quagmire of lies and secrets that define this world. Though a bittersweet homecoming awaits me, for the sooner we lose Ciarah, the sooner I return home.

Two years have passed since I reentered the greater world and small creature comforts like this padded chair in the Grand Witch's apartment are still foreign. Such luxuries, too, will soon end.

The front doorknob turns, and I wait as the door opens and the Grand Witch's light tread approaches, footfalls softened by the carpet in the entryway and adjoining hallway. She steps into the living room, slips off her coat, and throws the garment over the back of a chair as she continues toward me.

"I believe I have asked you not to enter my chambers without an invitation." She halts before me.

"Did you expect me to wait outside in the snow?"

She sits in the chair opposite mine beside the fireplace. "You are a gargoyle who turns into stone. The cold has no effect on you."

"In stone form, that is true," I say. "In human form, I feel cold."

"Perhaps if you were in the arctic," she says. "Why are you here?"

"Sadly, I do not bring good news. News unrelated to the Reaping that plucked students from your virtual war games."

Her mouth thins. "Who leaked the rumor?"

I smile gently. "You are not so naive, Grand Witch. By now, all Margidda knows about the Reaping."

"And clearly, the virtual war games."

I angle my head in acknowledgement.

"That still means someone leaked the story."

I shrug. "Such is the way of the world."

"Please, none of your philosophizing, tonight. I have had a trying day. What is your news?"

"The Zidruhin are sealed tight. I made no progress on that front."

"You could have sent a messenger with that news." She blows out a frustrated breath. "I felt sure Blade was hiding something."

"What is there to hide?" I ask, though that Fae is capable of hiding many things.

"I don't know. Perhaps nothing," she says. "If you are unable to infiltrate their ranks, maybe he's telling the truth."

"Have you reason to distrust him?"

She emits a small laugh. "The Fae are never to be fully trusted."

I imagine she distrusts this particular Fae more than most because of his relationship with an ancient vampire and dragon. She would be wise to keep that association in mind.

"The Fae are most accomplished," I say. "If anyone can find a way inside, he can."

She gives a single slow nod. "Perhaps. Still, I want you to keep trying. Damien is back. I am certain."

"Why are you certain?"

She turns her head to the left and stares at the fireplace before facing me. "Eldione visited us today. The gods are experiencing nightmares."

I make the sign of the cross. "God have mercy."

"That isn't all."

I wait.

At last, she says, "An alumni of The Academy who graduated a few years ago—a Seton Alexander—turns out to be a childhood friend of Leilah Crowe, Miriam Crowe's granddaughter."

"I've heard of her."

"Seton was the Atlantean demigod Tychon in disguise."

"Tychon? What has an Atlantean to do with"—I almost say "Ciarah" but catch myself—"Miriam Crowe's granddaughter?"

Olympia slowly shakes her head. "I don't think Leilah Crowe is who he was interested in, but Miriam."

I have no idea why an Atlantean demigod would be interested in Miriam Crowe. Ciarah, however.... A woman who draws to her five ancient beings throughout centuries of incarnations... well, a demigod might find that interesting. Might he suspect her connection to us? That would not bode well for anyone.

"The Wall didn't name Seton as a High Potential. Miriam nominated him as a student," Olympia says.

"That *is* odd," I say.

"Very odd," she agrees. "Upon reflection, another thing I find odd is that someone tried to kill Leilah Crowe."

I start. "What? Someone tried to kill Leilah Crowe?" I manage to add "Crowe" just in time to avoid sounding like an afterthought.

"Strange, wouldn't you say?" she murmurs.

"The girl is unharmed?" I manage a casual tone, although my heart pounds.

"Yes. We now know who tried to kill her—though we don't know why. I wonder if Tychon is involved."

I force calm and ask, "Who assaulted her?"

"One of our young students, a skilled witch."

"Why?" I ask before remembering that she said they didn't know why. "What makes you think the demigod is involved? Does the girl know him?"

Olympia rubs her temples. "I don't know."

"Perhaps I should—"

She shakes her head. "No. You have more important things to do."

No, I don't. My first order of business is to talk with Raith, Ethan, and Blade. I had assumed Ciarah was safe in their care. Apparently, she isn't.

"I have been to Crowe Potionary," she says. "Though I plan to go again."

I relax a fraction at the memory of finding Leilah there during my visit. I recognized her instantly. Her glory doesn't dim through the passage of centuries. Even young, there is a grounded quality to her that was absent in her last lifetime. As Nova, she was beyond impetuous, and self-absorbed. Her magic is far better developed in this lifetime than it was then. That, I am certain, can be credited to her grandmother.

"Did you find anything new?" I ask.

"More strangeness," she replies. "Miriam was a powerful witch."

"Indeed, she was," I reply carefully. Why is Olympia avoiding the question? "Miriam was one of the witches present when you turned the tide of the Shadow War in our favor," I add.

Olympia's expression grows distant. "I would never have believed that such a powerful white witch could fall so far."

"As I mentioned, I am not certain she did fall."

Olympia taps the arm of her chair. "You detected the blasting spell she used in the potionary."

"That doesn't mean she was trying to open the gates in order to help Damien join forces with The Morning Star and gain control of Margidda," I say.

"Why else would she have used such a powerful blasting spell—and with the power of Shadows?"

"Miriam may have found a way into Hell, but that doesn't mean she had a nefarious reason," I say. "Or that she can get out."

She laughs. "You're right—even if you are gullible. It would serve her right to have found a way in, only to become trapped. In any case, do you recall that her granddaughter's room looked as if Miriam hadn't touched it since the girl left?"

I nod. "It seemed almost to be a shrine."

"I thought the same thing—as did Blade. What Blade failed to tell me, however, is that the school textbook—a chemistry book, if I recall—that sat open on the small desk is gone."

"Gone?" I blurt. I understand what she means, but the possible dozen reasons that rush to the surface boil down to the strongest possibility: Ciarah returned to the potionary since I found her there. "What do you think happened?" I ask.

Olympia locks gazes with me. "I think someone returned to the potionary for whatever the charmed chemistry book hid."

THIRTEEN

Ethan

UNLESS BLADE IS KEEPING SECRETS, WHICH IS QUITE possible, his flashback to the night we turned the Shadow War in our favor is the first in seven years. Fae feel emotions too deeply. He couldn't have known the forest spirits would react to his plea for help by sending the ancient *eudaimon*. Even if he had known, he'd had no other choice.

We reach Raith's private chambers and Blade and I settle on the couch near the hearth where, thankfully, a fire burns. Raith pours three glasses of whiskey then passes Blade and I ours. We down the liquor and Raith refills the glasses, then sits in the armchair across from the couch.

He looks from me to Blade. "How did we miss that Seton was a fucking demigod?"

That had me flummoxed, as well. "Just goes to show that no matter how old we are, we can still be fooled."

"How reassuring." Blade finishes his drink, then sets his glass on the coffee table. "What does he want with Ciarah?"

"I think Olympia is right," Raith says. "Miriam Crowe is at the heart of this trouble."

Blade nods. "No white witch has dabbled in Shadow magic for centuries."

"Maybe Miriam thought herself to be Elexea," Blade says.

I blink. "Damien's Demon Bride?"

He shrugs. "Elexea was a powerful Shadow Mage. Miriam certainly qualifies."

"Elexea hasn't been heard from since she sank Atlantis. Maybe the Anunnaki are right and she's trapped in Hell," Raith says.

I grunt. What do they know? If Blade's right, their god Yahweh is trapped in Hell. That would explain his continued silence. I would love to believe the Demon Bride is trapped with him, but that would be too easy.

"Maybe Ethan's right and Miriam is The Demon Bride," Blade says.

"A high white witch a Shadow Mage?" Raith shakes his head. "We'd have picked up on that long ago."

Blade rises and crosses to the liquor tray where he pours another drink, then he faces us. "You just don't want to entertain the possibility that Leilah is The Demon Bride's granddaughter."

Raith scowls. "You're confusing me with Ethan. He's the one who wears rose colored glasses."

I ignore the jab. "Seton—Tychon—didn't arbitrarily befriend Leilah. If his reason has something to do with Miriam, why didn't he ingratiate himself into her life instead of Leilah's?"

Raith shrugs. "I don't know."

"Miriam did nominate him as a student to The Academy," I say. "*After* she sent Leilah packing," I add,

Raith rubs his temples. "I hate the machinations of the gods."

"Either way, that's not our only problem," I say.

"Ciarah being taken from the Reaping," Blade murmurs.

"All we can do there is hope for the best," I say, despite the fear that tightens my chest.

"Maybe." Blade looks from Raith to me. "I believe I connected with Leilah earlier."

"What?" I blurt in unison with Raith's, "What do you mean?"

"After Eldione appeared, I heard a wolf's howl," he says. Raith and I exchange a confused glance and Blade continues. "I was remembering the wolf howl in the virtual war games. The howl suddenly became as real as if the wolf stood in the room with us. I can't be a hundred percent certain, but my instincts tell me we connected."

"The blood pact," I murmur.

Blade gives a single nod. "Yes. That's not all."

"What?" My heart begins to beat faster.

"Don't you remember?" Blade asks.

"Remember what?" I demand.

Blade looks at Raith and understanding dawns on Raith's face. "Ciarah was taken in the Reaping that took place in the early part of the seventeenth century."

How could I have forgotten that?" I whisper.

"She never forgave herself for getting infected," Raith says as if speaking to himself.

"That doesn't mean she'll be infected this time." I look from Raith to Blade.

"No," Blade says gently. "And let's not forget, Leilah is a different person from Emma."

"Yes," I say. "Leilah's much stronger. I really didn't think anyone could be taken a second time. Yes," I quickly add before they can reply, "I know our philosophers and religious leaders theorize about the possibility of being taken in different lifetimes, but...I guess I thought—or hoped—the universe wasn't that cruel."

"Now we know," Blade says.

"And we can't tell anyone that we know—which would lead to how we know," Raith says.

Blade scowls. "You needn't remind us of the danger."

"I know," he replies with uncharacteristic humility. "But we need to keep in mind that this lifetime with Ciarah is different than other lifetimes."

"For more than one reason," I interject.

"Maybe," he says. "But the danger of our relationship to Ciarah being exposed is greater than ever before."

"You just haven't forgiven her for stabbing you in her last lifetime," I say.

"True," he replies too reasonably. "But this isn't about that. Modern technology alone is enough to get us noticed. Worse, we're closely associated with one of the most powerful witches alive."

I start to reply, but Blade says, "He's right. Olympia is already suspicious."

"Not of us," I quickly put in.

"Of Miriam and Leilah," Blade replies.

"I can't argue with that. "When Leilah returns from the Reaping, we can take her somewhere far away from Olympia."

"Run away with a High Potential who's likely as powerful as Miriam?" Blade says. "And now that we know Miriam isn't dead—"

"We don't know that for sure," I cut in.

"That doesn't make the situation with Leilah any easier," Blade says.

I scowl.

"This lifetime with Ciarah isn't going to be as easy as past lifetimes," Raith says.

"What do you care?" I snap. "You don't want anything to do with her."

He shrugs. "Fine, I'll watch while Olympia begins to

wonder why you're interested in Miriam Crowe's grand-daughter."

This is the old Raith. Though not quite. He's too calm.

"Let's worry about Leilah when she returns," Blade says. "And keep something in mind, Ethan. She's not ready to run off with any of us, much less all of us."

"Raith isn't going," I shoot back, but I know I'm being belligerent.

"She's not ready to run off with any of us," Blade repeats. "We have other problems to solve. *Now.*"

"Yes," I say in frustration. "Damien is on the hunt for his Demon Bride."

Blade flashes a smile. "Right."

Raith, Blade, Caleb, Matthias, and I weren't alive when Atlantis fell. The best we can figure, we came into existence at relatively the same time, sometime during the height of the Mesopotamian empire. In the millennia since, Damien has made only a handful of appearances. The last sighting was over a thousand years ago. None of us have seen him. Few have.

"Is it coincidental that all this trouble comes to a head when Ciarah shows up?" Raith asks.

"She has nothing to do with Miriam or Tychon," I say. "We all know that Olympia's virtual world triggered the Reaping."

"I imagine you blame her for the god of the angels being locked in Hell," Blade says without a hint of amusement.

"Ask yourself why Miriam kicked Leilah out at fifteen," Raith says.

"I would rather ask how she almost died while under your watch," says a familiar male voice with a slight Eastern European accent.

Our attentions snap to the doorway.

Matthias stands there, hand on the doorknob.

"Well, well," Blade murmurs.

Raith jumps to his feet, reaches Matthias before I can blink, then rams a fist into Matthias's jaw.

"Raith," I shout as Matthias stumbles backward into the doorjamb.

Blade and I reach Raith at the same time, but I pass Raith, grasp Matthias's arm, and steady him. "Are you all right?" I ask, but immediately whirl on Raith. "What the hell is wrong with you?"

"That pent up rage had to go somewhere," Blade says grimly.

Attention on Raith, Matthias massages his jaw. "Feel better?"

"Not by half." Raith spins, crosses to the table, and pours another drink. "As for any censure from you about Ciarah, you gave up your right to say a fucking word when you went MIA for thirty years."

"I returned when she returned," Matthias says.

"Did you find Caleb?" I ask.

He shakes his head. "The wolf does not wish to be found."

Or he's dead.

"Don't look so glum, Ethan," Matthias says. "He'll show up. Now, tell me about this attempt on Leilah's life."

"She was in my class," I say. "Someone used magic to hurl an unused spear at her. Raith saved her life."

Matthias lifts a brow. "Shared your blood with her?"

"We had no other choice," I say.

"I understand a young witch is her would-be assassin."

Blade, Raith, and I exchange a surprised glance, then Blade says, "How do you know that?"

"Olympia told me."

"Fuck," Raith mutters.

"You'd better sit down and tell us everything." I gesture to the couches in front of the fireplace.

We resume our seats on the couch and Matthias claims the chair nearest me. We fill him in on the two attempts on

Leilah's life and he admits to working for Olympia the last two years and describes her theory behind Miriam Crowe's disappearance.

"Two years and you didn't deign to contact us?" Raith's quiet question tells me he's still angry.

"To what end?" Matthias asks.

"So that we knew you were well," I say.

He gives me that gentle smile I've seen countless times. "You know I'm fine. Olympia is already suspicious of the relationship you three share. I wanted to remain above suspicion."

Raith barks a laugh. "Hear that? Father Mattias is implying he's part of the Grand Witch's inner circle and we're not."

"That's not what I am implying," Matthias says, as Raith rises and crosses to the sideboard where he keeps the whiskey. "And you may address me as 'Bishop James.'"

Raith's head whips around and we all stare.

Blade whistles. "So that's what you've been doing these last thirty years."

"Just the last twenty," Matthias replies. "The first ten, I searched for Caleb."

Raith faces us, a glass of whiskey in hand, and leans against the edge of the sideboard.

"Did you find any leads on Caleb?" I ask.

"I caught his trail a couple of times. But you know how wolves are." Matthias shrugs, "When they don't want to be caught, they turn into wolves and run."

"At least he was alive, at some point," I say.

"Cheer up," Matthias claps me on the shoulder. "With Ciarah's return, we will, no doubt, see him soon."

Matthias is right. At their very heart, wolves demand freedom, and their instincts make them nearly impossible to capture. But he loves Ciarah as much as we do. He'll show up.

"What did a bishop have to contribute to the latest Shadow war?" Raith asks.

"There are Margiddians in the Church. As you well know, Raith."

Raith lifts his somewhat-full glass in salute. "Oh, yes, I know."

"You three did quite well in defeating The Shadows," Matthias says.

"It was your job to be here," Raith says.

"Should I have abandoned defenseless members of the Church?"

Raith's eyes narrow.

"Do you think Tychon sent the Thol'guk to the potionary to kill Ciarah?" Matthias asks.

"What?" Blade blurts in unison with my "You know?" and Raith's "I should kick your ass."

Amusement ticks at the corner of Matthias' mouth. "You should have seen Ciarah. She was magnificent. And that night howler pig." His eyes gleam. "I have never seen one in its natural form. The creature is formidable."

"You were there when the demon attacked?" Blade demands.

"Don't get your knickers in a bunch." *"Knickers in a bunch"* is said with a good approximation of Blade's British accent. "She was quite safe. She had me and her familiar. The night howler pig gave the demon quite a beating. Ciarah—" He pauses. "She did something I have never seen her do before. She conjured black balls of churning magic."

"What do you mean 'black balls of churning magic'?" Raith returns to his seat on the couch and pins Matthias with a stare.

"Just that. They were balls of wispy black fragments."

"Shadows?" Raith demands.

Matthias's brow furrows. "No. Nothing like Shadows. Shadows are solid black ribbons. These were wispy, translucent, swirling."

"I don't like it," Raith mutters.

"I don't know why not," Matthias says. "She defeated the demon."

Raith grunts. "Demons can be defeated with Shadows."

Matthias snorts. "In what world?"

Raith scowls and takes a gulp of whiskey.

"So, there was an attempt on her life," Matthias says, "and she encountered a Thol'guk at her grandmother's house."

"You think the Thol'guk was sent there to kill her?" Blade asks.

"That is what they do best." Matthias shrugs. "The night howler pig gave the demon no opportunity to talk. Thol'guks are sometimes used to capture someone."

"Bounty hunters," I say. "I suppose we should be glad it wasn't an Il'gis."

Matthias's expression darkened. "One of the unholy creatures attacked and killed a priest a couple of years ago."

I exchange a look with Raith and Blade.

Blade gently asks Matthias, "A priest in your order?"

Matthias audibly sighs. "I believe the creature either mistook Father Lucci for me or was trying to get to me. The demon lived up to its reputation for inflicting pain. I was forced to imprison it in a spirit bottle."

And I'm betting he buried the bottle somewhere so remote and so deep no one will ever find it.

"Miriam's death isn't a secret," Raith says. "Maybe someone thinks she faked her death and is looking for her."

Blade straightens. "Olympia feels Zedkeil isn't the only one who wants to know if Miriam found a way into Hell."

"Who better to find an open door into Hell than a demon?" Matthias asks.

"Leilah just happened to be at the wrong place at the wrong time," I say.

"How did the demon get past the wards around the potionary?" Blade says more to himself than to us.

"Miriam has been gone for three months," Raith says. "There are bound to be weak spots. That the wards still hold at all is a testament to her power."

Matthias's attention focuses on Blade. "Olympia informed me that Zedkeil told you that they believe Miriam was trying to enter Hell—and that God is locked inside."

Blade grunts. "Who would have guessed?"

"That would explain much," Matthias says.

"You're not going to tell us how God has been silent all these years?" Raith sneers.

"One could make a case for that point, but no," Matthias replies. "I was going to say that Miriam might have been trying to free *Him*."

"So, you do believe she was trying to find a way into Hell?" Blade asks. "I was certain that was rubbish."

"Few witches in history surpass Mariam's abilities. I find it unlikely her magic backfired."

Raith says, "Few are strong enough to use Shadow magic."

"True," Matthias says. "I detected a blasting spell in the basement where she disappeared."

"We didn't discover any blasting spell." Blade looks at Raith. "I took Judith Holwen."

"Of the Kispu Order?" Matthias chuckles. "You had to know she wouldn't tell the truth. I'm surprised Olympia allowed anyone from the Order to participate in the investigation."

"Olympia didn't have a choice," Raith says. "The Kispu Order insisted on an investigation."

"Of course," Matthias says. "I imagine they said nothing about the hint of magic—almost an echo—in Leilah's room? It was subtle. So subtle, I couldn't locate the source."

Blade's mouth thins. "I must be losing my touch. I detected nothing."

"Perhaps that was because you didn't know that the room belonged to Ciarah."

Blade blinked and opened his mouth, but I cut in, "You knew? Dammit, Matthias, why didn't you tell us? We were blindsided by learning that the new High Potential, Leilah Crowe, was Ciarah."

"Would you have been any less blindsided had I told you earlier?"

"Hell, yes," Raith snaps. "We would never have allowed her to be recruited."

Matthias laughs. "You couldn't have stopped it. The Wall named her as a High Potential."

"Why didn't you tell us?" Raith repeats.

"Raith," I warn.

"No," he says without taking his eyes off Matthias. "I think he owes us an answer."

"I suppose because I thought she didn't deserve to feel the brunt of your anger any sooner than necessary," he replies without rancor.

"Keeping her away from The Academy would have kept her safe," Raith says. "Then you wouldn't have to worry about my anger."

Matthias shrugs. "I'll keep that in mind next time." Raith's eyes flash, and Matthias adds, "I, on the other hand, have no trouble dealing with your anger."

Raith shoves to his feet. "Are we done here?"

"One more tidbit," Matthias says. "Olympia went to the potionary."

"She told us she was going," Blade replies.

"What she didn't tell you is that the chemistry book on Leilah's desk is gone," Matthias says.

"Gone?" I repeat.

Blade's eyes widen. "Is Olympia certain?"

"The chemistry book had to be charmed," Raith cuts in. "A concealment spell. Goddammit. How did we miss that? Who broke the spell?"

"Has Ciarah been there since the night I found her there?" Matthias asks.

"She must have returned the day she broke out of her room," Raith replies.

Matthias laughs. "Broke out of her room?"

"After the attempt on her life, I locked her in her room," Blade says. "A spell was the only way to keep her safe—or so we thought. One of my students got past my magic and freed her."

"Maybe you *are* losing your touch," Matthias says.

Blade scowls. "I caught her sneaking back into her room. I was so angry, I gave no thought to where she'd gone. Bloody hell, I didn't care. Someone had tried to kill—" he broke off.

He must be envisioning what I was: Ciarah laying on Raith's sofa, blood pouring from the wound in her belly, while I forced Raith to drink her blood.

"That bad?" Matthias asks.

I nod, half numb. "We almost lost her."

Matthias releases a breath. "Well, we didn't, and we should find out what the spell on the book was hiding—and perhaps what she's hiding."

"Do you think Miriam left the enchanted book for Leilah to find?" I ask.

"I don't know," Blade says. "But I suspect Olympia is wondering the same thing."

"I told you, Ciarah is nothing but trouble," Raith growls.

Matthias's brows lift. "Since when did a little trouble frighten you?"

"Ciarah is a tsunami," he shoots back.

"We need to search her room," Blade says.

"Matthias leans forward. "If her grandmother managed to break into Hell, whatever Leilah is hiding, might be the key to, well, opening Pandora's box."

FOURTEEN

Leilah

THE TALL, MUSCULAR, NAKED MAN STARING AT ME IS no Academy student. He shifted from wolf to man too effortlessly. He must be an instructor. The spattered blood on his chest and face makes him look as formidable as he did as a wolf.

"You couldn't stay out of things, could you?" the shifter says in a slow drawl. "Some things never change."

"What?" I frown. "That wolf bit your shoulder. Where's the wound?"

Another wolf's howl reaches us, then another, and another and, quickly, too many to count.

"I'm a quick healer." He glances over his shoulder, then starts toward me. "Let's get out of here."

I start to ask how he plans on going anywhere so gloriously naked when he shifts into wolf form and lands on his forepaws with practiced grace. An instant later, he reaches my side.

I narrow my eyes. "So, you *were* giving me dirty looks earlier."

He whoofs.

I figure that's a strong affirmative. When this is over, Mr.

Wolf and I are going to have a talk. For now, I say, "We've got to find Jonas."

He barks and bounds away from the howling. I hurry after him. I manage a brisk walk for about twenty minutes, until we reach the road. We stop and I scan the area. Light snow is falling. No signs of life, no footprints or tire tracks on the road. How long have I been here? I look up. The sun's blue glow behind the clouds sits at about its zenith. What's that, like twelve or one in the afternoon? The sun was pretty bright when I arrived. Have I really only been here a couple of hours? I would have bet on closer to twenty-four hours.

I catch sight of movement beyond the trees that line the far side of the road. The wolf sprints across the road. Someone screams. The wolf reaches the woods and races into the trees.

"Dammit," I mutter, and run after him.

I break through the trees and slow enough to scan the forest. A blur of fur catches my attention up ahead on the left. Beyond the wolf, in a clearing, two dozen people encircle a large oak. My heart jumps into my throat. Four Shadows hover around the group. There's something odd....

I squint. One rope is slung over a thick branch on the right side of the massive tree. A second rope is slung over another branch on the opposite side of the tree. I once saw an oak this large in Westchester. The tree is between two- and three-hundred years old.

I can't see what the ropes are for. Too many people block my view. I creep forward.

The wolf shoots from the woods to my left, headed for the group. Some people turn toward him. I spot Ariel. Two guys to her right grip one end of the rope thrown over a branch. The other end of the rope encircles another guy's neck.

I gasp. A hanging?

I jerk my gaze to the branch on the left, where a rope is tied around a girl's neck.

Chelsea.

She's gripping the rope around her neck, which is held taut by a girl and a boy who can't be any older than her. The knot used to tie the nooses isn't a slip knot. These are hangman's knots with the full thirteen wraps of rope that make the noose. Where did they get rope tied in a real hangman's noose? There would be no breaking free of those nooses.

"Ariel!" I shout. "For God's sake, stop!"

My heart thunders. I break into a run, leap a fallen log and skid on wet, snowy leaves. I catch myself and dodge a small bush. My wolf growls and more heads turn toward him. Surprisingly, the Shadows pay him no heed. Three guys break from the group, headed toward the wolf. They stumble forward onto all fours.

Shifters.

A chant begins among the students facing the tree. "Now, now, now."

I shoot into the clearing and the deafening roar of a large crowd drowns out the chanters as I skid to a halt. A dizzying force of magic assails me. My vision blurs as surrounding forest is replaced by a Roman coliseum's-tiered seating. The apparition wavers like heat waves off a highway. I blink tiny snowflakes from my eyelashes and turn a full circle. The seating surrounds the clearing. How did I miss all those people when I came upon the clearing?

My wolf dodges the first of his canine attackers and the crowd's roar makes my ears ring. The second wolf jumps in my wolf's path and lunges for his neck. My wolf snarls and whips his head around in time to bite the wolf's snout. Blood spurts from the attacking wolf's jaw. My wolf bites his leg. The shifter drops to his belly, shifts back into human form, and begins dragging himself away from my wolf. My wolf whirls and charges the students. The other two wolves cut left on an intercept course.

"Hang the traitors!" shout the onlookers.

What is this? Who are all these people?

"Back up," Ariel shouts to the students gripping the ropes.

They obey. My blood goes cold. Shadows slither across the arms of the girl and two Shadows spin around the neck of the guy. Chelsea grabs the rope above her neck and yanks. The two pulling her rope yank harder. Chelsea's face contorts.

"No!" I shout, but they take another step backward.

Ariel whirls, hate in her eyes, and she shouts something that's drowned out by the shouting spectators. Three students on the far side of the hanging tree run toward the surrounding forest. I stumble forward, legs heavy, as if I'm slogging through water. My boot catches on something. I jerk my gaze to the ground as I stumble over a damn rock. I whip my attention back onto Chelsea. She and the guy are now balanced on tiptoes, both of them gripping the ropes that encircle their necks.

Panic tightens my chest to near pain. Chelsea isn't using magic. Her ability to use magic has to be suffocated by the magic pressing in around us. My sluggishness goes clear through to my bones. We're supposed to overcome The Shadows with peace, harmony, and love—and trust, mostly trust in one another. How the hell am I supposed to trust Ariel or fucking meditate? By the time I enter an altered state, Chelsea and the guy will be dead.

Red hot fury ignites my chest. "Hey, bitch!" I shout at Ariel.

She snaps her gaze onto the four Shadows and points at me.

A maniacal laugh bursts from me. "Come get me, mother-fuckers!"

The Shadows don't move.

"*Get her*," Ariel shouts.

Two girls break from the crowd, headed my way. Oh, this is just perfect. I'm supposed to fight students? My wolf approaches the students near the tree. Two more scatter, then whirl and run for the trees.

"Hey!" Ariel shouts.

One of the Shadows shoots after the fleeing students. The two shifters reach my wolf. My wolf leaps onto the nearest wolf and tears a chunk of fur from his back. The wolves' snarls are lost amid students' shouts of "Get the bastard!" and "Pull harder!"

I push through the weight of apathy as the two girls are within five feet of me. I narrow my eyes on them. The girl on the right freezes.

"Run," I whisper.

Her eyes widen.

"Fucking run," I hiss.

She whirls and runs. The other girl lunges and spins, leg thrown high for a roundhouse kick. I dive to the ground as her boot grazes my cheek. I roll and come to my feet in a squat. She spins, but I hook her ankle with my foot and yank hard. She lands on her ass. I leap on her and ram my fist into her jaw. She goes limp. I push to my feet, breathing hard, and stumble toward the tree.

Someone shouts, "Look out!"

Half a dozen students spin and surge toward me. Growls and snarls fill the air. The phantom spectators cheer. Magic presses against me so hard I drag in a breath. I can't stop all my attackers by brute force. The Shadows hover, waiting. I hesitate. If I continue to use magic, I *will* be infected like Ariel. If I don't return home, Stony could die. Familiars don't always survive the loss of their witches. I swing my gaze from Chelsea to the guy. Neither can I let them die.

Then I've got to be *very* careful.

I square my feet and center my magic, throw my palms up, and channel power up through my abdomen, chest, and down my arms.

I chant to the tune of Humpty Dumpty,

"Academy students built a magic wall.

"Academy students' magic wall fell.

"All the students and all their Shadows couldn't put the wall together again."

The students headed toward me fly backwards and land on the ground. The Shadows are five feet away. I don't care. I'm out for blood.

"Finish them," Ariel shouts at the students pulling the ropes.

The students gripping the ropes pull hard. Chelsea and the guy swing free of the ground. They're clawing at the ropes around their necks as they spin. The weight of magic increases. I laugh without humor and extend my hands, palms up. The same swirling balls of black fire, smoke, or whatever it is that I conjured against the Thol'guk, form in my palms. I throw one like a baseball, then toss the left-hand one into my right hand and throw it, too.

Students scatter, but those pulling the ropes continue their backwards steps. Chelsea and the guy hang five feet in the air and kick wildly. The phantom crowd leaps to their feet and cheers when my balls of energy strike two students and they fall. A guy conjures a spear and hurls it in my direction. I jump out of the way and throw another energy ball at the section of rope above Chelsea's head. The energy ball slices through the rope and she drops to the ground.

Power surges through me. I conjure another ball and draw back my hand to throw the ball of energy. My wolf charges me, barking madly. Yeah, I know. When this is over, he'll give me hell for interfering. Fuck him, too. As long as the Shadows don't come any closer, I can keep going.

Four students fall upon Ariel and begin beating her with their fists. My heart thunders. About fucking time. I'm tackled from behind and hit the ground face first. I can't catch my breath. I try to push off the ground, but my attacker weighs a ton. A knee presses into my back and spots race across my sight. I conjure the vision of—

The weight leaves my back. A wolf snarls inches away from my head. I roll away. My wolf's mouth is clamped around my attacker's arm and the guy is trying to shake him off. My God, the guy is a mountain of muscle. Where did he come from?

Someone screams behind me and I jump to my feet. The press of magic has vanished. Several students are yanking Chelsea's arms as if she's a rag doll and they intend to tear her arms from her body. Ariel throws her hands up and her attackers fly backwards.

Chelsea's eyes flash. She shouts something I can't discern, and a giant eagle appears above her. The bird dives toward her and her attackers scatter. The people in the stands scream in a frenzy of blood lust. My head throbs. I've had enough of this circus.

"Spirits of the earth," I shout, "I call upon you to remove from our sight those things not rooted to the soil."

The stands and the crowd vanish. The screams of the students fleeing the eagle sound almost quiet compared to the phantom crowd's shouts. The eagle screeches and my head throbs again. That damned thing has to go.

"Be gone!" I command, and the eagle disappears.

"How dare you?" Chelsea yells.

I frown at her, then catch sight of the free end of the rope around the guy, now tied off on a low hanging branch. He's hanging, arms limp, head lolling to one side as his body makes a maddeningly slow turn.

I shake my head. "*No*. I threw the ball of energy at his rope." But I hadn't. The guy tackled me before I could throw it. "No," I whisper. "No, no, no, no." Each word is spoken louder until I'm shouting, "No!"

I drop to my knees. "No." The whispered word is mingled with tears.

The Shadows inch closer. One reaches me and slides over my body, almost a caress, as if to comfort. I jump to my feet.

"This is your fault," I shout.

The Shadow leaps off me. The others withdraw, and I have the impression they're cringing.

"*You* did this."

Without thought, a swirling ball of black energy appears in my palm. I throw one, then another, and another and another at the Shadows. With each strike, they falter. I throw energy balls until I realize the Shadows are absorbing each one and I'm breathing heavily. I stagger forward with the intention of catching the Shadows and strangling them with my bare hands. My wolf in human form blocks my path. I suddenly wish that I was back in Grams' house before she kicked me out, before I realized she didn't love me. Then I pitch forward into his arms.

FIFTEEN

Blade

DAMIEN'S FOLLOWERS NUMBER ABOUT A THOUSAND, with fifty-three known Zidruhin priests and priestesses. What they lack in numbers, they make up for in the blackness of their hearts. We believe their order is one of the most ancient and we fear that they co-mingle with demons to widen the gene pool of their ranks—after all, with Hades as Damien's father and the Morning Star as Hell's ruler, Zidruhin and demons are kissing cousins. The Zidruhin have one potential weakness I hope to exploit tonight. They like to party.

My cab pulls to the curb ahead of half a dozen other cabs parked in front of the Brooklyn warehouse where tonight's illegal rave is taking place. The guest list is exclusive, a scant two hundred of New York City's elite—which always includes the Zidruhin.

The cab driver looks at me in the mirror. He's not seeing the tall, blue-eyed, long-haired blond Fae. He's seeing a tall man with shoulder length brown hair and brown eyes. Every Zidruhin priest will know me on sight. The charm disguising the real me is an herbal potion created by one of our most skilled witches. The hope is that the Zidruhin will have a more difficult time detecting earth magic than they would a spell created from pure magic. The catch? I turn into a pumpkin at sunrise—a mere four hours from now.

The beat of music thumps against the car. I exit the cab and pay the fare with a five-hundred-dollar tip. "Remember," I tell him. "Don't move from here until I come back out and I'll pay you a thousand dollars to take me home. But not a word to the woman that'll be with me." If I'm fortunate enough to connect with one of the Zidruhin.

"Sure thing, sir," the drive replies. "I brought coffee and a book." He glances around and laughs. "Out here, I can take a leak around a corner and no one will be the wiser."

"Good man," I say, then turn and scrutinize the warehouse.

I haven't attended a party like this in years. Normally, I would love a night out on the town, but wager tonight will be a waste of time. Olympia doesn't like truths that conflict with the truth she wants to hear. Thus far, the Zidruhin have proven to be impenetrable. We haven't gotten near them with any kind of shapeshifter. Tonight, I'm trying to get someone drunk enough to invite me back to their place.

The key to my plan is the strong powdered sedative in my jacket pocket. If, by chance, I connect with a Zidruhin, the sedative might be the only chance I have to knock them out long enough to search their home—if I get into their home. My only other weapons are the drop of faery water hidden inside the ring on my right hand—and the switchblade in my right boot. My backup is a bruiser of a wizard Olympia made my partner for the night. Barry Goldstein. His father is a powerful wizard, his mother a rabbi. It takes all kinds.

Two young—very young—women in four-inch heels and dresses so short they flash matching lace panties as they pass me. They both look over their shoulders at me and smile. I sigh. Two sweet things who think they'll meet a prince who will treat them like the princesses their fathers told them they are. I wonder what Susan B. Anthony would say to these young women who think they need a man to take care of them.

I head for the door where a bouncer faces a couple dozen party-goers—almost exclusively women—who hope to be deemed beautiful enough to enter. If all goes as planned, Barry should already be here. Should I spot him, I can't so much as look in his direction. We can't risk someone catching on that we know one another. The music inside the building grows louder as I draw closer. The two young women who passed me turn as I approach and make eye contact in obvious hope that I'll be their ticket inside.

"Hey, Bruce," I say.

"Mr. Blackwell." The bouncer pulls the sliding metal door aside.

The music blares so loudly my chest vibrates. I give an almost imperceptible nod to the big man and continue past him. Late last night, after I left Raith, Ethan, and Matthias, I'd made a point of tracking down the rave and finding out who would be watching the front door, then visited him at the party where he was working as the bouncer. We got acquainted to the tune of a thousand dollar tip.

I step inside and Bruce slides the door closed behind me and at least four hundred people are bouncing and gyrating to the music blasting from the speakers positioned at the corners of the massive space. I guess I'm not the only one who gave Bruce something on the side for the privilege of joining the party.

I push through the crowd to the bar set up along the far left wall where Barry will be keeping a watch for me. At the bar, I notice Barry at the edge of the dancefloor, back against the wall as if he's people watching. I snag the bartender's attention and order a vodka straight up. I down the drink, then order another. Once I have the second drink in hand, I turn and survey the room. Now all I have to do is find the dozen or so Zidruhin who are sure to be here and hope…hope what? That one of them will unburden themselves?

I spot a tall redhead at the far end of the bar wearing a Paco Rabanne silver sequin dress. The dress goes for at least three thousand dollars. The Zidruhin don't believe in denying themselves the better things in life. Especially when they're as beautiful as High Priestess Hazel Surral. I'm not certain whether or not she's worth my time. As high priestess, she'll know a great deal about the Zidruhin's plans. But she will also be far more skilled at keeping her secrets. I had hoped to find one of the younger members, someone under fifty years of age who hadn't yet reached the upper echelon but might be privy to enough information to hint at Damien's plans.

In truth, we don't know how much Damien tells his priests and priestesses. They are fanatical followers, but the same can be said of half a dozen other religions, yet their gods remain silent.

Hazel spots me and brazenly rakes her gaze down my body, then returns her attention to my face. Yes, she likes what she sees. My Brunello Cucinelli leather jacket will make me a top catch of the night. She has to be sure I can entertain her in the style to which she is accustomed. She pushes through the people that separate us and heads my way. I focus on my drink and swirl the liquid in the glass.

Despite the heat in the room, a moment later, I sense her warmth behind me. A sultry, deep voice whispers in my ear, "Would you like to buy me a drink?" She steps up to the bar so that I can see her and locks eyes with me.

I signal the bartender to give us both another drink, then shift so that I face her. Her expression makes me half wonder if she wants me to drag her into the men's restroom and fuck her against a stall door.

The bartender delivers another vodka, and a martini for Hazel. She takes a healthy swig, then sets the drink back on the bar. The music segues from one fast club beat to another and she grabs my coat lapels and backs up while pulling me onto the dancefloor. We nearly fall into the crush of dancers and half dance and are half thrown against each other by the other dancers.

By the time the song blends into the next song, she's pressed against me and bumping and gyrating against my hardened cock —I am a man, after all—and, I imagine, she's halfway to what probably isn't her first orgasm of the night. The high priestess is getting a great deal more out of our dance than I am.

Someone bumps me from behind. Not the typical bumping I've experienced since being dragged onto the dancefloor. This is personal—and very male. Hazel's eyes shift past my shoulder and recognition flashes across her face. Another Zidruhin member?

I twist and look over my shoulder to find a man my height with short, dark, tousled GQ-style hair. He's dressed in skin tight leather pants that leave nothing to the imagination and a white, fish net tank top.

Hazel grasps my face and forces me to look at her. In her four-inch heels, we're eye to eye. She kisses me while the guy gyrates against my arse. I force some interest into the kiss. She throws an arm around my neck and plasters herself against my body as she traces my mouth with her tongue. I thrust my tongue inside her mouth and her moan tells me I made the right move. Hazel reaches between us and cups my erection.

I'll be taking care of that beast tonight when I reach my apartment—alone. But to keep up the charade, I growl into her mouth. She gives a throaty laugh, breaks the kiss, then whirls and shakes her arse against my cock. The dancers close even tighter around us and the man dancing against my back grabs my waist and yanks me against his body.

The song segues into another with almost the same beat

and I pull Hazel's back against my chest and say in a loud voice, "You want to get a drink?"

She faces me, grasps my hand, and tugs. The large hands around my waist reluctantly release me. We reach the bar with a few jabs to the ribs and stomach and a couple arse squeezes. Hazel orders two more drinks, then turns, her back to the counter and pulls me close.

"Want to get these to go?" she asks.

"Sure thing," I say.

She smiles. The woman is beautiful and as dangerous as they come.

Our drinks arrive. She drinks hers in one long, beautiful gulp. I do the same, then she grasps my hand and pushes through the crowd to a chair at the end of the bar where a knee length mink coat hangs over the back. She hands me the coat, then turns.

I help her don the coat and say into her ear, "I see you like to live dangerously."

She faces me, brow lifted.

"Someone could have walked off with your coat," I say in a loud voice I'm not sure she can hear over the music.

A smile touches her full mouth. "People are inherently good."

I wish I could agree—despite knowing she's lying. I laugh, then take her hand and elbow us through the crowd. We reach the door and exit into the cold night air. I clear my lungs of the smoke and sweat.

Hazel slips an arm in the crook of my arm. "How about my place?"

I smile. "I can't think of anything better."

"Did you drive?" she asks.

"In this neighborhood?" I shake my head. "I'll grab a taxi."

"No need," she says.

We walk past people lined up to get inside the club and

continue to where a dozen cabs wait at the curb. My driver is parked one car length ahead of the cab at the head of the line. Arm linked with mine, Hazel hurries across the street to a Porsche 911 Targa 4S. She pulls a key fob from her coat pocket and presses the unlock button. A high pitched chirp sounds and the car's lights flash. I follow Hazel to the driver's side and open the door. She casts me a sultry look from beneath her lashes, then slides into the seat and I close the door. Barry's going to have a fit when he discovers I didn't take the assigned cab.

The car purrs to life. I take my time in walking around the car and cast a final glance at my cab driver, who's looking in my direction. I glance at the building's front entrance, but no sign of Barry. Well, this is a fin cock-up. The cabbie starts rolling down his window. I quickly get into the car and the car jets forward.

To my surprise, instead of heading toward the bridge leading to Manhattan, Hazel exits onto I-278, headed for Staten Island. We cross the Verrazano bridge and, fifteen minutes later turn onto a private drive. She continues through an open gate leading to a stone mansion overlooking the bay. To the right, on a flattened hill, is located a pool, a long table and chairs, a large barbeque pit and a pool house. Even what little I can see, the house must sit on at least three acres with lots of trees and privacy. Perfect for Zidruhin rituals.

We exit the car and we hurry up a dozen steps to the home's large oak door. She unlocks the door and backs me into a spacious foyer. A small smile curves her full lips upward as she slips off her coat and tosses it onto a chair near the door.

She grasps my hand and walks backwards three steps. "Would you like a drink?"

"Of course." I follow her past a circular staircase that winds upward to an open hallway with two visible open doors before the open hallway disappears from view.

I follow her into a parlor and we continue through another short hallway into a room with a bar that stretches across a mirrored wall. At least a hundred different bottles of liquor line three shelves against the mirror. A fire burns in a large stone hearth on the wall to the right of the bar. A chocolate brown leather couch sits in front of the hearth.

"Vodka?" She continues around and behind the bar.

I smile. "You were paying attention.

"To you?" She arches a brow. "I'm sure you're used to attention."

I drop onto one of the stools at the bar. She pulls a bottle from the back row of bottles and shows it to me.

I whistle. "Jewel of Russia Ultra Limited Edition. Very nice."

"I thought you'd like it." She pours two tumblers, neat, and slides one of the glasses toward me.

I pick up my glass. "To…wild nights," I say, and we click glasses.

She locks gazes with me and takes a healthy sip. I do the same while wondering how I can distract her and slip some of the sedative into her drink. I'm betting she's got a hidden room or basement for Zidruhin rituals and spellcasting.

"How about some music?" Hazel reaches beneath the bar and a similar techno beat like the one at the rave blasts—though not as loud.

She finishes the drink in a flourish. I follow suit and reach for the bottle.

"Forget that," she says in a loud voice, and rounds the bar.

When she reaches me, she kicks off her shoes, then throws her arms around my neck and gives me a slow, warm kiss clearly meant to drive me mad with lust.

Hazel breaks the kiss, then grabs me by the lapels and pulls me to my feet. She walks backward, leading me, I realize, to the couch. Bollocks. She intends to have sex here and now. Even if Leilah hadn't returned, I wouldn't follow through with this woman. There's been a great deal of speculation—by me as much as any other Margiddian—on the possible negative effects of mating with someone infected by Shadows. We're not certain the Zidruhin are infected with Shadows. In truth, we can't be certain infected Margiddians don't still walk amongst us. We assume, they do.

The one thing we do know is the negative effect of a child born to an infected parent. There's not a condom in the world secure enough for me to risk fathering a child with this woman. So how will I get out of this—and get a look around?

We round the couch and she twists so that I fall onto the leather cushions with her on top. She straddles my hips and grinds herself against my cock. The woman is a skilled seductress. If anything were to give me away as a spy, it won't be a flaccid cock. I grasp her waist and steady her as she throws her head back and rocks against me in rhythm with the music. She seems to have a penchant for dry humping. Perhaps I'll get away with—

The press of a gun barrel against the top of my head is followed by a second individual stepping into my line of sight at the edge of the couch. The man points a nine millimeter luger at me. So that's why Hazel turned on the music. She wanted to be certain I didn't hear her friends' approach. Clever girl. The second man edges around the bar, reaches down, and the music cuts off.

Hazel halts and snaps open her eyes. She looks at whoever has the gun barrel against my head, then twists and looks over her shoulder at the man still pointing his gun at me as he walks around the counter.

"You could have waited a few more minutes," she said.

"Find someone else to fuck," the man pointing the nine millimeter says.

Hazel looks down at me and tilts her head to one side. "I bet you're fantastic in bed."

"I guess you'll never know," I say.

"If you like an audience...."

I grunt. "Love, I doubt even I could perform with two guns pointed at me."

A slow smile spreads across her face. "Think of the danger. Doesn't that turn you on?"

I lift a brow. "Knowing I will likely be shot when we're finished? Not a big turn on."

"You'll delay being shot," she replies.

"So, we have established I'll be shot." I toss her over my head. She collides with the man behind me and his gun fires. My ears ring. I throw out my right hand toward the hearth and shout, "Fire!"

Flames leap from the hearth and fly across the room. The man at the foot of the couch screams and the nine millimeter roars. I roll from the couch. Pain sears across my left shoulder. I hit the carpet and leap to my feet. The man who I threw Hazel into lays motionless on the carpet. Smoke rises from the other man whose charred body is lying twisted on the floor.

Hazel stands, legs spread, arms spread, and eyes blazing. She chants in a low voice in a foreign language. Ancient Akkadian, I realize, and catch the word *Mushussu*. Marduk's servant dragon, a scaly animal with hind legs like eagle talons, lion-like forelimbs, a horned head, a snake-like tongue, and a long neck and tail. A formidable creature that will eat me alive.

I lunge for her. Mushussu appears in front of me. He rears up on his hind legs and hisses. I twist and dive left. A talon seizes my leg and yanks me high into the air, head down.

"Earth—"

My call to the earth is cut off when his tail whips around me, clamping my arms to my sides and cutting off my magic. I release a slow breath.

Hazel steps close. "You probably killed Thomas." She

glances at the burned man, then looks back at me. "But I can forgive you if you tell me who you are."

"*Ngish dug*," I curse.

She bends and whispers in my ear, "Sorry, darling, but you lost your chance to fuck me." Hazel grasps my hair and yanks my head back so that I'm forced to meet her gaze. "Tell me who you are, and I'll make your death quick."

"Your negotiating skills leave something to be desired," I say.

She releases me and the dragon shakes me so hard my teeth rattle.

"Mushussu is hungry," she says.

The room is still spinning when his tongue snakes out and licks my face. I will my pounding heart to slow. I needn't worry about Shadow infection, just the dragon's venom should he get testy.

"I can be merciful and kill you before he starts taking bites out of you," Hazel says. "All I want is to know who you really are."

My head begins to throb. "John Bartholomew," I reply.

She cants her head and studies me. "I think not."

"Killing is against the law, you know," I say.

Her gaze sharpens. "Who will punish me?"

Here is where she believes I will give her a clue as to who sent me.

"The authorities."

"Someone like Cane Darkmour?"

"If I were friends with the Head of the Assembly, do you think I'd be here?"

"Why *are* you here?" she asks.

"I thought, for a good time," I reply.

"Then why use magic to disguise your identity?" She leans close and sniffs my face, then draws in a deep breath. "You reek of earth magic. Juniper berries, chicory....

Foolish boy. Mushussu will peel your skin layer by layer until we reach the real you, then he'll eat your warm organs basted in that ridiculous herbal magic while you're still breathing."

That's one way to see past a charmed disguise. That and wait until sunrise. I'm estimating I have an hour and a half. I doubt Hazel will wait that long to feed me to Mushussu.

If I use my full power to try and break Mushussu's spell, she will too-easily guess that I'm not an average Margiddian. Thus far, we have—I believe—been able to avoid detection while trying to infiltrate the Zidruhin. Or have we?

"Why are you doing this?" I demand.

She studies me. "Are you going to pretend you're an average Margiddian?"

I frown. "I don't have to pretend."

"Average Margiddians don't command fire with such ease. I'm guessing you're a dragon...or perhaps Fae."

"Just an average Margiddian who likes to play with fire."

Mushussu's gives me another shake. My brains are bouncing off the inside of my skull.

"An average Margiddian who can curse in ancient Sumerian. *Ngish dug,*" Hazel adds the last in a whisper.

I curse inwardly. I rarely lose my temper. "Why did you bring me here?" I demand.

"To find out why you came in disguise," she responds.

"That's no reason to threaten to kill me. For all you know, I don't want my mate to know I'm stepping out on her."

"Then I suppose this is the last time you'll step out on her." She turns and walks around behind the bar.

Talking is a waste of time. I thumb the top off my ring and ram the ring into Mushussu's ribs with all my might. The spot where the faery water makes contact with his scaly hide sizzles and steam rises like a small tornado from the wound. The crea-ture shrieks and his tail loosens around me. The press of magic wavers. I yank my right leg up and seize the switchblade from my boot.

"No!" Hazel shouts.

I flip open the blade, cut Mushussu's tail, and drop to the carpet as Hazel reaches us, a bottle of liquor in hand.

"*Enlil,*" I shout. "Come. *Now.*"

The Mesopotamian god of the atmosphere and ruler of the skies and earth appears in a roar of wind and stinging rain, spear in hand. The beard that reaches to his bare chest whips in the wind and the hem of the loincloth wrapped tight around his hips snaps against his knees.

Mushussu bellows. I jump to my feet as Enlil thrusts his spear through Mushussu's belly. The dragon crashes to the carpet. The wind and rain cease, and I rake back the soaked hair plastered against my face. The unconscious man stirs.

Hazel backs away from the god, the bottle she grips held out before her. "I've changed my mind"—her eyes cut to me —"I prefer you live—as my slave." She yanks the top off the bottle and a Shadow emerges.

My heart picks up speed. The thing glides toward me. Enlil is immune to Shadows. I am not. No more magic for me.

I will my pounding heart to slow and, with one eye on the Shadow that hovers five feet from me, I command the god in a calm voice, "Kill her."

Enlil looks from her to me, then says in Sumerian, "I am no killer of women."

Bollocks.

Satisfaction floods Hazel's expression and her eyes narrow on me. "Once I discover the man beneath the disguise, I will find those you love and kill them slowly."

Enlil frowns. "A merciless woman?" He rakes his gaze down her body. "A beautiful woman." He steps toward her.

She retreats and shouts, "*Il'gis,* I command you to appear!"

The floor in front of her opens and a tall, lean man with one long, dark braid that reaches to his naked arse appears. The ground closes beneath him and he looks from Enlil to me, then hesitates. The vampire demon and I have met. If he recognizes me, there will be a bloodbath.

His gaze sharpens, but he turns his attention to Hazel and says, "Why am I here, witch?"

"Protect me," she orders.

Enlil takes two quick steps toward her. Il'gis hisses and shifts into bat form, but not quickly enough to avoid the back of Enlil's hand. The bat is thrown across the room and crashes into the wall in his human form. Hazel screams and throws her hands up as the god scoops her up, then disappears.

I whirl to face Il'gis, who now stands, eyes locked on me. "So, we meet again, Fae."

There are few things I fear. Even an ancient Fae like me understands that Il'gis is a being to be respected. The man I'd knocked out when I'd thrown Hazel onto him pushes to a sitting position. His wide eyes lock onto Il'gis. The Shadow inches toward him. The man shoots a sideways glance at the Shadow and fear fills his eyes.

The demon looks from him to the charred man, then to me and says, "I see you still like destruction."

"Not really my fault," I say. "I thought I was coming home with a woman for a good time."

"A Zidruhin high priestess?" Il'gis says. "I doubt that."

I recognize the intention in his eyes and shout, *"Flames."*

Fire leaps from the hearth toward the demon. He moves with vampiric speed and is standing in front of me, as the flames combust in the spot where he just stood. He seizes my shoulders and flashes white teeth, his incisors elongated. I throw my forearms up, breaking his hold. He kicks my belly. I slam into the wall and drop onto the carpet. Il'gis leaps onto me, straddling my hips, and lunges for my neck. I yank my knees up in an effort to ram his back, as his teeth graze my flesh.

A gun roars in unison with a shout. Il'gis is yanked off me. I leap to my feet, breathing hard. Il'gis is spread eagle against the wall, writhing and whimpering, his arms and legs shackled to the wall with what I'm guessing are silver manacles. Barry stands ten feet away, eyes pinned on the Shadow, which slithers across the body of the man who shot himself through the temple.

"About bloody time you showed up," I say.

His eyes shift to me. "What do you expect when you don't take the taxi waiting for you? You're lucky I was able to track you. That witch—" He breaks off and scans the room. "Where is she? Shit, did she get away?"

"Hardly," I say. "Enlil liked her."

Barry stares. "I can't wait to hear this story."

SIXTEEN

Leilah

MY EYES SNAP OPEN. HEAVY BLANKETS COVER ME TO my chin. I bolt upright. I lie in a bed in a small bedroom. The quilted bedspread, hooked throw rug beside the bed, and doily on a small nightstand remind me of a farmhouse. The tall wolf shifter sits in an armchair on the other side of the nightstand. His jean-clad legs are stretched in front of him, ankles crossed. His clasped fingers rest on his chest and his head has fallen back against the headrest. He's asleep.

His eyes open and he turns his head. I stare into tanzanite blue eyes. My heart skips a beat. Okay, so he wasn't asleep. Affection ripples through me. He protected me against the wolves and brought me here.

"Where am I?" I throw back the covers and swing my feet over the edge of the mattress. "Last I remember—"

Memory flashes of the guy hanging motionless from the noose. My heart lurches and I can't halt a sob. The wolf jumps from his chair and reaches me in two strides. He pulls me up and into his arms. I bury my face in his warm chest, as he whispers indistinguishable sounds and holds me close. I don't want him to hold me, but I don't want him to let go, either. I don't want to remember. I wish Stony were here. She would know what to do. I hope she's safe.

I cry harder. The wolf swings me into his arms, sits on the bed, and settles me onto his lap. He holds me like this, gently rocking and making soft noises until, at last,

I have no tears left.

"I don't understand. He shouldn't have died." I look up at the wolf and am overwhelmed by the need to kiss him. He stares down at me. "Why couldn't I save him?" I ask through a dry throat. "Wait. You could have saved him."

He frowns. "What?"

I jump to my feet. "You could have saved him. Instead, you were—" I can't believe it. "You were trying to protect me." I thrust my hand forward, palm out and shout, "Asshole!"

He is shoved backward across the mattress. I stare. That much power should have thrown him across the room. Fury explodes inside my chest. I center my magic.

He sits upright. "Don't force me to shift."

I stare. Is he daring me?

"Shift, motherfucker," I snap. "I double dog dare you."

He's upon me before I can blink, tosses me back onto the bed, and lands on top of me.

"You should have saved that guy." I twist in an effort to shove him off, but the guy is heavy as hell.

He seizes my hands and shoves them above my head. His face is inches from mine. "I won't apologize for protecting you." The words are spoken low, but with a steel that startles me.

"I wasn't the one being hung," I snap.

"No," he murmurs. "You were the one being stalked by Shadows."

Gooseflesh races across my arms. "Stalked?"

"That's what they do," he says.

A realization strikes. "You fought in the Shadow War."

He pushes off me and sits on the bed. "We all fought in the Shadow War."

I sit up. "Not true. Most of us just tried to survive."

"Is that what you did?"

My cheeks warm with embarrassment. "I was four when the war ended. I wasn't old enough to do anything."

"I bet you still practiced magic."

"Grams told me not to, but you know how toddlers are. They're dumb."

He shakes his head. "Not dumb. Children do what comes naturally, and magic comes naturally to you."

I tense. "How do you know?"

"It's obvious by the way you handled magic out there. Not a smart move, by the way. Shadows are drawn to magic. Didn't your grandmother teach you that?"

"Don't be an ass," I say. "I didn't have a choice. I couldn't let that mob kill Chelsea and that guy."

But I had let the mob kill that guy. I am useless.

"You should have saved him," I whisper.

"I'm sorry about your friend."

"He wasn't my friend."

"Okay, I'm sorry about that guy. Not everyone can be saved."

I pin him with a glare. "He could have been saved. I didn't need protection."

What would he do if he knew a Shadow had entered me? Was it inside me still? Am I a bad person now? I don't feel any different. Do I? Out there, my fury had consumed me. Is that how infection begins, we tell ourselves we have a right to feel extreme anger?

The wolf is staring at me.

"Where are we?" I ask.

"A farmhouse."

"A farmhouse, that's it?"

"It was the first house we came to."

I frown. "We? Who else is here?"

"Academy students and a kid named Jonas, who says he knows you."

"Jonas is here? I've been worried sick about him." The wolf starts to answer but I say, "The mob who tried to hang them isn't here?" My heart pounds.

His expression softens. "They scattered."

"They better fucking scatter," I mutter.

He studies me. "You sure none of those Shadows touched you?"

"You were there. Did you see any of them touch me?"

His eyes darken. "I wasn't able to watch you the entire time. After you interfered with the wolves earlier, I'd hoped you would have the sense to stay out of the fray."

I ignore the admonition and say, "Is Chelsea here?"

"Chelsea?" he repeats.

"The girl they tried to hang."

"I didn't see her amongst the students downstairs," he replies.

"What happened to Ariel—the bitch who instigated the hangings?"

He grunted. "She ran."

"Ran?"

"She had half a dozen people chasing her."

"Good," I say in a dark voice that unsettles me. "I hope they tore her limb from limb."

"Like she wanted done to the girl you saved?" he asks.

I scowl. "She's not a nice person."

A corner of his mouth lifts. "I believe you." The warmth in his eyes causes heat to rise to my cheeks.

"How long have we been here?" I ask.

"You slept for about eight hours."

"Eight hours?" I blurt. "I never sleep eight hours." I drop back onto the bed and stare at the ceiling. "How much longer are we going to be here?"

"There's no telling," he replies.

I turn my head slightly so that I can see him. "Who are you? No way you're a student."

"No," he says.

"So, who are you?"

"Caleb," he says.

"Where are you from?"

"Colorado."

I frown. "There's no Academy in Colorado. I thought only students were taken in the Reaping. You know, High Potentials, due to their strong abilities."

"Do you think all High Potentials attend academies?"

I grunt. "You got me there. If not for being forced to stay at The Academy…well, I wouldn't be there."

"But you probably would have been taken in the Reaping."

"I guess." I look at my lap. "Who will tell that guy's family that he's dead?"

"Someone at that New York Academy."

"Raith," I murmur.

"Raith," he repeats.

There's something in his voice that—

Jonas bursts into the room, eyes wide. "They're coming."

I jump from the bed. "Who's coming?"

He looks from the wolf to me, then says, "Ariel and her gang. They'll probably be here in an hour."

"Don't worry. I'll deal with them." I start toward the door.

The wolf grabs my arm. "Not with magic."

I pull free. "They won't hesitate to use magic."

"Do you want to get out of here?" he asks.

"Out of the Reaping—or this house?"

"Both."

I narrow my eyes. "Of course."

"Then we find an alternative to magic."

"Easy for you to say. You can shift. I'm hamstrung."

"Didn't they teach you anything at that Academy?" he asks.

"Sure, they did," Jonas says.

I frown. "Look, Jonas, if you're talking about the meditation and love shit, in case you haven't noticed, we're under attack."

"We have three other witches here and two wizards. Not to mention me," he says.

I pause. "You're Longthorpe?"

He shrugs, clearly embarrassed by the question. Longthorpe women are strong witches. Warlocks generally have less power than the witches and many don't really practice magic. I figure their male egos prevent them from trying that hard. If they can't do something better than a woman, they walk away. I bet Jonas won't be able to walk away.

"What do you think we should do?" I ask him.

"We can place a shield around the house."

"We need protection against aggressive energy," I say. "It's not as easy as throwing protective light around a house."

"It's also not that hard." He looks at Caleb.

"He's right," Caleb says.

"Holding them off indefinitely isn't an answer," I say.

"Don't be so sure," Caleb says. "We only need to do things the right way once to get out of here."

"I pin him with a hard stare. "You've been in a Reaping before."

"Yep."

I blink. I expected him to deny it. I want to know more, but later. I turn my attention to Jonas. "How did you figure out Ariel's coming?"

"Dot is a siren."

"She's that good?"

He nods. "Oh yeah, she's highly psychic. I didn't know she was in the Reaping until I saw Caleb carrying you and followed him to this house."

"Fuck," I mutter, and cast the wolf a glance. I start toward the door. "Let's get that armor up."

SEVENTEEN

Ethan

I ENTER RAITH'S OFFICE. HE'S NOT AT HIS DESK. I turn to head to his assistant's office but stop when she enters the office.

She halts, glances at his desk, and frowns.

"I guess you don't know where he is either," I say.

Rebecca crosses to his desk and picks up the cellphone lying there. She holds the cellphone up for me to see and shakes her head. "Doesn't do any good when he doesn't take it with him, does it?"

"No." I chuckle.

Raith enters.

"It's about time," Rebecca says.

He continues around the desk to his chair and sits down. "I assume you need something."

"A Detective Holly Mills is here to see Leilah Crowe," Rebecca says.

"What?" Raith blurts.

My heartbeat accelerates.

"What does the detective want with Ms. Crowe?" Raith demands.

"She won't tell me."

Raith's mouth thins. "Please show her into my office."

Rebecca nods, then hurries from the room.

"Any idea what this is about?" I ask in a low voice.

He grunts. "Anything is possible where *she's* concerned."

A moment later, Rebecca returns with a tall, thirty-something brunette.

"This is Director Raith Vanderkoff," Rebecca tells the woman and angles her head toward Raith.

"Detective Mills," the woman says before Rebecca can finish introductions. She extends a hand to Raith.

Raith shakes her hand, then says, "Thank you, Rebecca. Why don't you take off for the night?"

She hesitates, then says, "Thank you," and leaves.

Raith shifts his attention to the detective and says, "This is Ethan Bordeau, one of our instructors."

I clasp the hand she extends. Her grip is firm. "Detective." I release her.

"Please, have a seat." Raith motions for her to take the seat to her right.

She sits and I take the chair to her left.

Raith says, "I understand you would like to see Leilah Crowe. She's not on campus, today. Is there anything I can do to help?"

"Do you know when she'll return?" the detective asks.

"A number of the students have gone on a field trip out of state. They'll be back in a week."

"Do you know if Ms. Crowe has been to her grandmother's home recently?" she asks.

"If memory serves, it's been at least a couple of weeks since she left campus. Has something happened?" Raith asks.

"Someone broke into her grandmother's house last night."

I lift my brows. "Vandals?"

"That's what it looks like," she replies. "The neighbors thought a rowdy party was in progress and called the police."

"I gather they weren't having a party," Raith says.

"Not the sort of party the neighbors thought."

Raith frowns. "What sort of party?"

"I would say some sort of occult party."

"A ritual?" I ask.

"I'm not an expert on occult rituals, but that's what it looks like to me. We found incense and what I'm guessing is some sort of sigil."

I keep my expression neutral and lean forward in my chair. "They don't sound like typical vandals looking for a place to escape the cold."

The woman turns her dark, intense eyes onto me. "My thoughts exactly. Do you by chance know if Ms. Crowe is involved in any kind of occult or Wiccan religion?" She shifts her gaze to Raith.

"We don't ask our students' religion," he replies. "But Ms. Crowe left with the other students two days ago. So, I do know that she didn't participate in whatever ritual took place last night."

"I see. Do you know if she allows any friends to stay at her grandmother's house?"

Confusion shows on Raith's face. The last time Raith was confused was the last time we had Ciarah in our lives. He simply doesn't get confused.

"Were these vandals doing something illegal?" he asks.

"If they were trespassers, then yes, they were doing something illegal. If they are friends of Ms. Crowe's, then, as far as we can see, other than the noise, no laws were broken—as long as they don't start sacrificing live animals."

"We can have Ms. Crowe contact you when she returns," Raith says.

"Is there a number where I can contact her?" the detective asks.

"I'm sorry, no. The students are on a retreat. No phones, no iPads."

Thankfully, this much is true. No devices were allowed in the War Games.

A corner of her mouth turns upward in a small smile. "No cellphones? I didn't know kids today were capable of being separated from their cell phones."

He laughs. "That's the problem. Which is why, for this retreat, students aren't allowed to bring their devices. If you like, Ethan can show you to her room where she left her cell phone."

She flashes a smile designed to make people think everything is fine, and says, "That won't be necessary. Please have her contact me when she returns." The detective pulls a card from her pocket and sets it on Raith's desk. "Please give this to her, just in case she lost the one I gave her last month."

Raith blinks and I know, this time, he is surprised. "Was there trouble at her grandmother's house last month?" he asks.

"No. She came to see me." Her eyes soften. "She wanted information on her grandmother's death."

Raith slumps back in his chair. "She has taken her grandmother's death hard."

"Really?" A hard gleam replaces the softness. "I understood that her grandmother kicked her out when she was fifteen."

Raith sighs. "Yes. Which left Ms. Crowe with unresolved issues."

"That can happen." The detective stands and we follow suit. "Please have her call me."

"Of course," Raith replies.

She looks at me. "Mr. Bordeaux."

I angle my head in acknowledgement and she leaves.

Raith's expression turns distant, and I know he's listening to her departure.

When his eyes clear, he looks at me. "Rouse Blade. I haven't seen him today. I imagine he's still sleeping off last night. Take Penelope and get to the potionary. Find out who the hell was there."

I turn, then halt when he adds, "And make sure whoever Detective Mills assigned to watch the potionary doesn't catch you."

An hour later, I turn the Toyota Camry I'm driving—my Martin Aston is too easily recognizable—down the street where the potionary is located. Penelope is sitting in the passenger seat to my right and Blade occupies the seat behind her. As Raith predicted, I did have to rouse Blade from his bed. Thankfully, he seems none the worse for wear, though Olympia wasn't pleased to learn that his mission didn't garner any information. I suspect Blade stayed in bed not because of his confrontation with the Zidruhin witch, but because of his worry for Leilah and, like me, he's glad to have something to take his mind off her.

I squint against the late afternoon sunlight that glints off the rearview mirror.

"There." Penelope says in her soft Portuguese accent. She's staring up ahead and to the left where a brown Crown Vic sits across the street from the potionary.

Penelope Fairbrandt is a petite blonde with a pixie hair cut that makes her look a bit like Peter Pan's mischievous Tinker-bell. The likeness is not that far off. Her mother is a witch and her father a Fae. The combination is common. In Penelope's case, her mother is a past member of the Kispu Order. Penelope inherited that power which, combined with her Fae nature, makes her particularly sensitive to magic, not to mention a powerful witch.

Two men sit in the front seat of the Crown Vic. The police aren't even trying to hide.

"How cliché," Blade murmurs.

I drive past the house and their car.

"Doesn't look like anyone is inside the potionary," he says.

I take a right at the corner, drive another block, then park and face Penelope. "Invisibility or illusion?"

"Illusion," Blade says.

Penelope twists and looks at him past the headrest.

He grins. "Illusion spells are so much more interesting than invisibility."

Penelope shifts her attention onto me. "Illusion is much easier to cast than invisibility."

She's right. Invisibility requires disappearing. Illusion is about blending in like a chameleon.

"Illusion it is," I say. "Cast the spell once we're out of the car." I open my door and cool air washes over me. "Let's make this quick before someone decides to take a walk."

I cast a quick glance around, detect no activity in any of the houses, and nod to Penelope.

We huddle on the grassy curb beside the car and she pulls her right hand from her jacket pocket, points her index finger heavenward, then makes a circle in the air as she murmurs, "Eyes of darkness, eyes of light, keep hidden those within my sight." She drops her hand to her side. "Ready?" She looks from Blade to me.

We're still visible to one another, but neither of us question whether or not the spell worked. Penelope is a strong witch. If she's confident the spell works, then we're good to go. I nod and we head toward the potionary.

"We're going to have to go in through the back door," Blade says. "Can't have the police seeing a door open by itself." The amusement in his voice tells me he wouldn't mind doing just that.

Five minutes later, we jump the backyard fence and enter the house from the back door, which isn't locked.

"Let's stick together," I say.

"Shall we take a look upstairs first?" Blade meets my gaze. "Just to be sure?" he adds, and I know he wants to get a look a Leilah's room and check on the absence of her chemistry book.

"Yeah," I reply.

We check the master bedroom and bathroom and a den with no issues. We reach Leilah's room and I enter. Penelope halts in the doorway with Blade behind her.

"Whoa," she murmurs.

I turn. "Whoa, what?"

She scans the room and takes a tentative step inside. "There's been strong magic here."

"This was Miriam Crowe's house," I say. "There is bound to be much strong residual magic."

"Yeah," she says slowly. "But this is recent."

"The vandals?" Blade asks.

"I don't know. Whoever was here, is a powerful witch." Her gaze shifts to the desk to the left of the door. She takes two steps, holds her palm an inch over the desk where the chemistry book used to sit, then frowns. "There's something strange."

"Strange?" I exchange a glance with Blade.

She withdraws her hand. "This spot is devoid of any magic."

"What? Like…a black hole?" I ask.

"That's an apt analogy." She looks from Blade to me. "We've encountered lots of residual magic in the world. Really, you can't throw a stone without hitting even a little fairy magic." Penelope's gaze returns to the desk. "It wouldn't be strange if there was no magic in the room. But for the room to hum with residual magic everywhere except one spot is…well, like I said, odd."

Even odder when one knows that a charmed book used to occupy that spot.

"Any idea why the spot is devoid of magic?" Blade asks.

She blows out a breath. "No."

"Let's go to the basement, then." He meets my gaze. "We can give more thought to this oddity later."

I lead the way to the basement. The sun has set and the room is full of shadows. I command a small flame to illuminate the hole in the middle of the cement floor. I've seen the hole half a dozen times, but the sigil drawn around the edge sends a chill through me.

"Well, well," Blade murmurs. "Someone did go to a lot of trouble, didn't they?"

"Wow." Penelope squats to my right and traces a finger along the sigil. "So intricate. The artist is a master. I cant distinguish where one letter melds into another." She frowns and looks up at me. "These aren't English letters."

Blade squats beside her. "I believe she's right. I can't discern any letters. Do you recognize the language, Penelope?" He rises.

She stands and rounds the hole to the opposite side and studies the sigil for a long moment, then looks up at us. "I have no idea."

"Let's find out, shall we?" Blade asks.

Penelope reaches inside her shirt and pulls out a gold chain with a gold pendant encircled with semi-precious stones. She grasps the chain three inches above the pendant and murmurs, "Time and space reveal in this place those who created this."

A shimmer begins at the wall behind Penelope, ripples across the room, passes through us, and halts at the far wall. Four translucent, cloaked figures descend the stairs. By the time they step onto the cement floor, they are fully formed. We step back as they approach. They reach the hole and throw back their hoods.

"Zedkeil? Bloody hell," Blade curses in unison with my, "What the hell?"

Penelope glances our way but says nothing.

Zedkeil kneels and traces a finger around the hole and a sigil begins to take form in the concrete. Our attention remains glued on the angel as each stroke connects to another.

When he finishes and rises, I look at Blade and say, "The letters must be of the angelic language."

"Yes," he whispers.

The angelic language is a hidden language the angels share with no one. There can be only one reason angels would deign to enter the same space where Shadow magic had been cast. They came to free their god from Hell.

How can angels possibly think that angelic magic could open any kind of door to Hell? But even as I wonder, the angels lift their arms heavenward and tilt their heads backward as they chant, "Son of Hades we command you to show yourself."

Son of Hades? Damien? I whip my head in Blade's direction. He's staring, open-mouthed, clearly as shocked as I.

Nothing happens.

Big surprise. Even if Damien has come out of hiding, why would he obey the command of angels?

The angels look at each other, then chant in a louder voice, "Son of Hades we command you now show yourself."

Still nothing.

Anger flashes in Zedkeil's eyes and the room lights up as if lightning has struck. "Damien, son of Hades, appear before us now!" he shouts.

A clap as loud as thunder rumbles. I wince, then freeze when a tall, faceless male figure appears over the hole. Damien? Have the angels actually managed to command Damien?

"Impossible," Blade whispers.

"Who are you to command me?" the figure thunders.

Zedkeil's eyes flash again. "We are the servants of the Most High, the Ancient One, the Creator of all that exists."

"So that god claims." His laughter shakes the floor.

I stumble back two paces. Penelope cries out and Blade yanks her against him and widens his stance to steady them both.

"What do angels of the Most High want with the son of Hades?" Damien demands.

"It's him." Blade looks at me. "So close. Had we known, we could have killed him."

"We know you gave aid to the witch Miriam Crowe in her quest to enter hell. We command you to aid us, as well," Zedkeil says.

"Angels? In hell? You wish to join the ranks of the demons? Have you angered your god?" Damien asks. "Or have you just seen the light and understand his true nature?"

Something in his voice gives me pause.

"We command you to give us aid as you did Miriam Crowe," Zedkeil snarls.

"It is not I who helped the witch, but my Shadows. Do you wish their help?" An obsidian ribbon floats away from the apparition.

"Command them to open the Hell Gate," Zedkeil orders.

"They are yours to command," Damien replies with amusement.

My heart beats faster when Zedkeil says, "We know nothing of Shadows. I command you to open the doorway into Hell."

Another laugh. "Foolish angel. Do you think that if I could open the door to Hell, I would've done so long ago—then crushed you puny angels with legions of demons?"

"We know the witch found a way into Hell," Zedkeil says.

"Then follow her there," Damien shouts in a voice devoid of warmth.

A dozen shadows separate from him and attack the angels. Swords appear in their hands. Blinding light flashes from the metal, and Blade, Penelope and I throw our arms up to shield our eyes. The angles' holy swords cut through the Shadows and they vanish. One of the angels screams an earthly scream as a Shadow passes through his chest and emerges out his back with a trail of silver-white light close behind. The angel falls to his knees, breathing heavily. The angel closest to Damien swings his sword in an arc clearly intended to sever Damien's head. The demigod leaps back as the blade whizzes past with a whoosh of air. From my vantage point, it looks as if the tip of the blade nicks his arm. Damien vanishes.

My heart thunders. He feared the holy blade. At last, after all these eons, we have found a weakness in the demigod.

The other two angels rush to the side of their fallen companion and lift him to his feet. A pounding on the front door interrupts. The cops must have arrived.

Zedkeil steps up to his companion and they vanish.

EIGHTEEN

Leilah

FIVE MINUTES LATER, I SETTLE CROSS-LEGGED ON the living room floor with Jonas, three other witches, who are thirteen, fourteen, and fifteen, and the siren. The configuration is simple: armor that hugs the outside of the house like a second skin. White light outside the armor that radiates at least ten feet out and a mirror on top of that.

I close my eyes and envision turtle-shell like armor encasing the exterior walls of the house. An unexpected sense of strength washes over me. It's the other students, I realize. I've never experienced this sense of unity. The kids are well-disciplined. The sense of unity is gentle, yet persistent.

We quickly construct the armor. I've never been a witch who believes putting up protection is a lengthy ritual. White light follows in a near blinding wave that covers the house in seconds. Already, the armor is a sight to behold. Next follows the mirror, closed to anyone who can enter through doorways that mirrors open, and intended only to reflect magic directed at us.

I love mirrors as a final layer of armor. Usually, the intent that bounces back to the sender is simple negative or hateful thoughts from a grudge-filled mortal, and the sender as no idea why their luck takes a turn for the worse. In this case, Ariel could be knocked onto her ass. I might have to watch from a window. I wonder if we should add terra-cotta colored light to ground us to the earth.

Suddenly, I'm standing in a meadow surrounded by trees. I blink against sunlight, then smile. I know this place. I came here often as a child. I consider lying down in the ankle high grass that dances in a breeze to stare at the sky.

Rustling grass draws my attention left and I cry out in delight. Stony is trotting toward me. I rush forward and reach her in seconds. I drop to my knees and hug her. She snorts in obvious happiness and nuzzles me with her wet nose.

"It's about time you showed up," I say.

"Too cold in the Reaping," she replies in piggy snorts.

"I would've kept you in my pocket," I chastise, still holding her close. "I was worried. You have to come back with me. I can use your help."

"I will help here."

"Here?" I draw back and look at her.

She stares back with those beady black piggy eyes and, as usual, her thoughts are inscrutable.

"Stony," I begin, then stop. What's that noise? I strain my ears. "Do you hear that? Sounds like tramping feet."

Stony snorts.

"Yeah, someone's coming." I stand, turn in a slow circle, and scrutinize the surrounding woods. Why did I come here? "Just a minute ago, I was at a farmhouse in the Reaping. Strange, huh?"

"You think everything is strange."

"*Hey.*" I narrow my eyes. "Not everything is strange."

The stamping grows louder.

"Though, this is strange," I continue. "I've always come to this place alone."

Stony shakes her head.

I roll my eyes, "You know, I'm glad you're here. I just can't figure out who else is here."

She nods.

"Yeah," I agree. "Let's have a look."

We head toward the sound, which comes from the far end of the meadow. The meadow is much larger than I remember. I had never done anything other than sit or lie on the ground near the middle of this meadow.

A woman emerges from the still distant trees.

Ariel.

I halt. "What is *she* doing here?"

The urge to race to Ariel and punch her as hard as I can nearly overwhelms me and I realize I've fisted my hands. More people emerge. I recognize Anthony, who helped chase Jonas, and another dozen people I don't recognize. They halt behind Ariel and stare at us.

I frown. "They're supposed to be attacking the house."

Stony grunts loudly.

I jerk my gaze onto her. "This is a lucid dream?" I never thought of coming here as a lucid dream. "How did you follow me here?" I ask Stony, but immediately know the answer. "When I began the creative visualization for the armor around the farmhouse. Well, fuck a duck. I get why you were able to tap into my psyche. But how did they do it?" I ask, but mean *how is Ariel able to intrude upon my special place?*

Stony snorts a laugh. "Do you think lucid dreaming is any more private than buying stuff on eBay?"

I blink. "You're joking?"

She shakes her head and her floppy ears flap.

"You do too joke," I say, my attention on Ariel.

I can't decide whether to grab the bitch or run. The fury inside me is eating its way through my intestines. She has to pay. Half a dozen Shadows emerge from the trees. What the hell? Shadows in my lucid dream—in my special place? This is Ariel's fault. She brought them here. Oh, I'm going to make her pay. I force a slow breath. I'll deal with her in the real world, where she doesn't have Shadows to do her dirty work for her.

"Let's get out of here," I tell Stony.

"Why?" she asks.

"Because a gang of students are headed this way—one of which is a killer. Do you want to become bacon?"

She plops her butt down on the ground and lifts her snout in the air with a loud grunt.

"I am not afraid," I shoot back. "At least, not of them. Look." I point at the half-dozen Shadows hovering behind the group.

"So what?" Stony says. "We're in a lucid dream."

I finally understand. Rules are different here.

We were taught at The Academy that our soldiers—Raith, Ethan, and Blade—turned the tide of the Shadow War in our favor by battling The Shadows in a lucid dream, using harmony, peace, and love. Oh, and *some* magic. Not the full magic we normally use. Our instructors didn't specify spells, but said the soldiers used earth magic: magic related to nature that somehow didn't make them susceptible to infection by The Shadows. The one thing the instructors emphasized was that the person wielding the magic in the lucid dream had to be at complete peace with themselves.

"How am I supposed to be at harmony with myself?" I mutter. "Fuck, half the time, I argue with myself."

Stony snorts.

"Hush," I say. "This is crazy. How am I lucid dreaming while in the Reaping? "God, I hate when I wake up from a dream only to find out I'm still dreaming. It's just too weird."

The group starts toward us, the Shadows flanking them. To my surprise, my anger has subsided.

"Lucid dreaming," I say. "Be at complete harmony with

myself." I'm most in harmony when practicing magic. Magic isn't about fighting. Magic is about embracing the forces around us.

I shift my attention to the Shadows and touch the spot where the Shadow entered me. A tremor of panic ripples through me. I hadn't let myself think much about the Shadow inside me. I don't feel different—at least, not unless I get really angry.

All I have to do is not get angry. I focus on Ariel. If she challenged me in the real world, I would walk away because she isn't worth my time. But a murderer is worth my time. Sadness weighs down on me.

Focus on getting out of this lucid dream, I tell myself, *then out of the Reaping.*

The students fan out to reveal Jonas, hands tied in front of him. A rope around his neck is attached to a stick someone is holding, as if he's an animal.

Fury sweeps through me and I take a step forward.

"Lucid dream," Stony says.

Lucid dream....

I conjure a regular bow and a foam arrow, aim, and send the arrow hurtling toward the guy holding Jonas' rope. The arrow moves like lightning and goes straight through the guy's chest. He falls to the ground in a deep sleep.

Someone seizes Jonas' arm as I send another arrow flying toward them, this time aimed at Ariel. She throws up a circular wall of black that makes it look like they're standing in a black hole. A sense of disorientation makes my surroundings twist around me and I list to the left before catching myself.

The arrow misses Ariel and disappears into the darkness behind her. A wall of energy hits me and I'm thrown backward. I land on my ass yet feel as if the wind has been knocked out of me. Stony looks over her shoulder at me as I push to my feet, breathing hard.

Ariel shoots a narrow-eyed look at me. What did I do to make her hate me so much? I thought she disliked me because I'm Miriam Crowe's granddaughter. Grams betrayed us by dabbling in Shadow magic, so I must be the same. Right? But the burning light in Ariel's eyes is personal. She's jealous.

"Brace yourself, Stony," I say, then widen my stance, my right foot slightly in front of the left and chant,

"Earth and wind, heed my request.

"Put this bitch in her place."

I never believed spells had to rhyme.

A loud rumble follows and the ground shakes. I rock, but the students stumble and grab for each other. Screams fill the air. What the hell? I lock gazes with Jonas in the instant before the ground opens up and he—and the rest of the group—drop from sight. I stare, unable to move. I-I killed them all. I hadn't meant to. I'd just wanted to…. Wanted to what? Teach Ariel a lesson?

I stumble forward several drunken paces before my mind registers Stony at the edge of the crevasse. Shouts and screams within the crevasse yank me from my stupor and I launch into a run. At the edge of the hole, I look down to find everyone, Jonas included, balanced on ledges on the jagged wall. I can't prevent a small cry of relief. I ignore the Shadows hovering ten feet from me while I center my core. I start and lose my concentration at sight of a shadowy form crawling up at turtle speed from deep within the crevasse.

Gooseflesh rises on my arms. "What the hell?"

One of the guys balanced on one of the ledges on the opposite side of the crevasse leaps up onto the ground on the other side of the hole. I take a step back in surprise before catching myself.

Vampire.

He flashes a smile, incisors long and white. Vampires don't extend their incisors unless provoked or ready to feed. I center my energy on the anger and fear that is always far too close at hand, then freeze when the Shadows drift closer. The vampire laughs softly.

"Back off," I command in a quiet voice, and make a back-handed wave at the vampire.

He's forced backward but manages to keep his feet and halts ten feet back. He starts around the crevasse toward me. Stony runs around me faster than a person would think a pig could, then stops between me and the vampire. He halts, clearly surprised and uncertain what threat a pig might pose.

"*Phillip,*" one of the female students calls. "Help me!"

He ignores the plea and again starts toward me. Stony shifts into her true form. At nearly seven feet tall with talons like the raptors in Jurassic Park, she's a formidable sight. The vampire stops and hisses. Stony bellows.

Students are shouting and pointing at the shadowy figure creeping up the crevasse. My heart pounds. I can't make the same mistake I made with the guy who got hung. The Shadows seem oblivious to Stony and hover within reach of me. I center my magic and, with a force of will that feels as if I am regurgitating a spleen, I chant in a gentle sing song,

"Mother Earth, gently please.

"Lift my friends from the crevasse onto solid ground."

Jonas rises on a mound of rich, dark earth just large enough for him to remain steady and is deposited onto the ground beside me.

"Mother fu—" I shake off the curse. I'd made the mistake of asking Mother Earth to save my *friends*. I am so stupid.

I quickly chant,

"Mother Earth, gently, please,

"Lift the others from the crevasse onto solid ground."

Jonas backs away so that I stand between him and Stony, who is half snorting in what I think is laughter at the vampire's expense. A great weight presses down upon me as if an anvil is balanced on my shoulders. I try to take a deep breath, but pain slices through my lungs. I breathe in short breaths like a woman giving birth, and the ground rumbles as the others are lifted up en masse.

The vampire growls, Stony stands her ground. Thank God for Stony. My legs shake under the weight of the spell. One of the female students screams and loses her balance. I gasp. Pain rips through me.

Jonas jumps to the edge of the crevasse and shouts, "Eagle."

An eagle the size of an elephant appears and swoops into the crevasse. Jonas' attention remains on the crevasse while I watch in horror as a Shadow slithers around my neck, then down my shirt an instant before the group of students rise out of the crevasse followed by a large eagle with a girl in its talons. Did the Shadow enter my chest?

The students are placed gently on the ground and I fall to my knees. The eagle sets the girl on the ground then, with a loud screech, flies away. I draw in gulps of breath and can't halt the tears. A second Shadow has invaded my body. I taste bile. I'm going to go insane. I'll hurt people. What am I going to do?

Ariel and Anthony whirl to face me.

"Get her," Ariel snarls.

I can't muster enough strength to care if they throw me into the crevasse. Does she know I'm infected? She might be right to throw me into the crevasse. Jonas looks from me to her. The other Shadow floats closer to Jonas. The things don't have eyes, but I *know* it's got the kid in its sights. Jonas is considering using magic to stop Ariel and Anthony.

Stony bellows and swipes at the vampire, who isn't quick enough to miss the backhanded blow. He's thrown back and Stony whirls as I push to my feet.

"Don't do it, Jonas," I order in a hoarse voice.

Stony bellows again and rushes Ariel and Anthony. Ariel and Anthony back away as the rest of the group scatters.

"You're infected with Shadows," I tell Ariel and Anthony. I don't remind her that she instigated a hanging—and leave out the part about me being infected. "We have to work together to get out of here. Remember what they taught us at The Academy. Peace, harmony, and love." Anger bubble in my chest. How can I possibly work with Ariel? "Listen, Ariel," I say. "Hate me all you want, but think of the other students. We can get them out of here."

She sneers and pain seers through me as my soul is ripped from my body.

NINETEEN

Blade

I SIT ON THE COUCH IN RAITH'S OFFICE. ETHAN SITS on the opposite couch and, like me, he's ignoring the conversation between Raith and the Kispu witch, Delta Winterling. Neither of us are fond of the Atlantean gods and we care even less about their problems. The Atlantean goddess paid us another visit this morning, demanding we immediately call a Kispu witch to help them. Olympia will do almost anything to avoid contact with the Kispu, so she assigned Raith the task of sending the witch to the gods.

My eyes are heavy with exhaustion and I contemplate my bed. Despite my fatigue, my head spins with unanswered questions, not the least of which is how can we convince Zedkeil to call forth Damien again so that we can attempt to kill him? I still can't believe the angel called forth Damien. I close my eyes and, as has happened the last two days, Leilah's face rises in memory. I am completely powerless to help her.

I snap my eyes open and straighten. "Wait a minute."

Ethan frowns. "What?"

"Wait." I nod toward the witch. Kispu witches are half witch half empaths who read a person's energy and sometimes their thoughts.

"I can't say when Eldione will arrive," Raith tells Delta. "But it should be soon. The gods are worried."

Delta gives a low laugh. "They should be, considering the way they treated us the last time we helped them." She adds in a mutter, "Ungrateful bitch," then stands. "I'm going to get a cup of your cafeteria coffee. It's pretty good. Send the goddess to me when she arrives."

Eldione won't like having to search for Delta. Raith knows that, but nods. The witch leaves and I shove to my feet. "I think there's a way we can help—"

Approaching bootfalls cause me to close my mouth. A Watchman enters. He glances from me and Ethan to Raith. "We've had a demon try to enter the grounds on the northwest wall."

"What?" Ethan says in unison with my "Happens every time."

Though frequency of occurrence doesn't make the attempt any less unnerving. Which is why four parents took their children out of school and won't allow them to return until the Reaping is over. More parents might have pulled their children, but most are out-of-state students.

"It wasn't successful, I assume?" Raith says.

The Watchman shakes his head. "No. We've reinforced the wards. Anyone—or anything—that shouldn't be here and tries to enter"—he shrugs—"are in for a big surprise."

"Good. Keep patrols tight," Raith says.

The Watchman leaves and I cross the room and close the door. "I think there's a way we can help Leilah," I say.

"What are you talking about?" Ethan asks.

I look from him to Raith. "The blood pact."

Ethan stands. "Why didn't we think of it before?"

"If you mean try to connect with her psychically, you're insane," Raith says.

"Why?" I shrug. "We all know that a blood pact connects the signers of the contract."

"There is no way to contact someone in a Reaping," Raith says.

"How do you know?" I ask. "Have you ever tried?"

He waves me off. "It's a ridiculous idea."

"I disagree. I think—"

At a shout outside Raith's office, I glance to Ethan. We hurry to the window overlooking the main concourse. At least four dozen students are headed our way. Teachers David Cornwall, Linda Walker, and two martial arts instructors have joined the approaching students. Some students are walking arm in arm, some are crying. Leilah walks at the head of the group, gripping Ariel's right arm. Ariel tries to twist free but Leilah yanks her and half drags her several paces before Ariel gains her feet. Jonas walk to Leilah's right with her pig to his right and—

"Bloody hell," I mutter. "That's—"

"Caleb," Ethan finishes.

Caleb strides in wolf form on Leilah's left.

"It seems Matthias was right," I say.

We look at each other, then race from the room, down the stairs, and out onto the front steps as the students halt in front of the building.

"Can you believe it?" Fran Shelton says. "Only two days, and they're back."

She's right. We've never had students return from a Reaping in two days.

Caleb and the pig plop their arses on the ground. Caleb looks up at us and pricks his ears. Chelsea stands sullenly beside William at the rear of the group. Chelsea has to be escorted away from the other students, but we mustn't make a scene. William's eyes are downcast. A student who returns from the Reaping and avoids eye contact is never a good sign.

"Here." Leilah shoves Arial toward us.

The girl whirls on Leilah and snarls, "Touch me again and I'll turn you into a toad."

Leilah ignores her and locks gazes with Raith, "She led a hanging that ended in one student's death and she tried to hang Chelsea."

Raith scans the crowd. "Is this true?"

A chorus of voices reply as several try to talk at once.

Raith gives a shrill whistle and they stop talking. "Where's Chelsea Nightlow?" he asks.

A tall boy nods at someone in front of him, who's blocked by other students. Chelsea pushes past them to the front of the group.

"Ms. Littleton tried to hang you?" Raith asks.

Chelsea nods. "Yeah, her and another student that isn't from here."

"David," Raith says, "take Ms. Nightlow to the infirmary and have Ms. Littleton escorted to her dorm room by two Watchmen. Someone will be there presently to speak with each of them."

David Cromwell says to Ariel, "Ms. Littleton."

She narrows her eyes on Raith. "You have no right to do this."

"Don't force me to use magic," Cromwell says in a calm voice that belies his power. The short, portly man is not the pushover he appears.

"I want to speak with my father," Ariel snaps.

"Don't worry," Raith says. "We will both be speaking with your parents."

She doesn't move and Cromwell steps toward her. Ariel shoots him a dagger filled look, then starts walking. David waves Chelsea to follow, and the three head toward the infirmary.

Raith addresses the three teachers, "Please take the students to the auditorium and begin debriefing. Blade and Ethan will get the other instructors."

I want to tell Raith to go to the devil, that I plan to debrief Leilah, but he's right. We have to attend to the students. The two martial arts instructors start walking and the students follow.

Leilah starts to follow, but Raith says, "Ms. Crowe, you'll stay here, please."

Her mouth thins, but she doesn't argue.

Jonas looks from us to her and says, "Can I stay, too?"

So, their friendship grew while they were in the Reaping.

"Go along," Ethan says. "You can see Leilah tomorrow."

He looks at Leilah, who nods, then he follows the rest of the students with Linda taking up the rear.

Raith locks eyes with Caleb and says, "Hello, Caleb."

Leilah frowns. "You know him?"

"Quite well," I reply.

She narrows her eyes at the wolf. "I should have known."

Ethan sends Raith a warning look, then heads toward the retreating students.

I hesitate, but I can't show favoritism, so start after the students. Our first order of business is a roll call to make sure everyone returned. I'm glad Leilah's familiar is with her. The creature won't let Raith abuse her. Neither will Caleb, I suppose. I glance over my shoulder to find they are halfway up the stairs. I turn away and realize Olympia isn't here. How could she miss the commotion of the students' return? I catch sight of Delta Winterling standing on the steps to the admin building, a strange smile on her face.

TWENTY

Leilah

Stony and the wolf flank me as I follow Raith up the Administration building's steps. The vampire is the last person I want to talk to about an Academy student's murder. Once again, I see the guy's body making a slow turn as he hangs from the tree. I stumble but catch myself. Stony looks at me, but I keep my attention on Raith's heels as we cross the foyer and start up the stairs to his office.

Were we really in the Reaping only two days? How did students became so quickly infected by Shadows that they hanged a fellow student? I'd heard stories of people infected during the war committing atrocities. Despite the millions that died, I had no idea how bad it really was. I blink against a sting of tears.

The wolf still walks beside me. I'd like to know how he knows *The Three*. I should have known they had a connection. He is just too skilled a shifter. The wolf protected me in the Reaping. He saved my life.

I resist an urge to look at him. Why did he single me out? Why did *The Three* single me out? Had they sent him into the

Reaping? No, that wasn't possible. Was it? I recall the night of the War Games. As we broke into the crime boss's house, a wolf had howled. A chill prickles my arms. A wolf howled right before I was taken in the Reaping? That's weird. This time I can't help but look at the wolf. He looks up at me, eyes intent. I step onto the second floor hallway. A woman emerges from his office. I remember her. Raith's assistant, Rebecca, is in love with him. Raith gives her a curt nod as we pass her and enter his office.

He's such an ass.

Suddenly, I'm exhausted, I wonder if I can keep my eyes open. I need to go to my dorm room. No, I need to go to the home that's mine now that Grams is dead. She might not have wanted me to have the house but, legally, it's mine. I have the right—

Gram's spell book. Oh God, what if they found the book? No, I've been gone only two days. Not enough time for anything to have gone wrong.

Two days? How is that possible?

I'll fill Raith in on what happened in the Reaping, then Stony and I are getting out of here. Seton is around and he knows I'm back. Maybe he can help me decipher Grams' spell book.

Raith points at the chair in front of his desk as he circles to his vacant chair. I drop into the chair. Stony plops down onto her stomach to the left of my chair and the wolf sets his butt on the floor to my right. The walls feel as if they're closing in on me.

Raith lowers himself into his chair and, to my surprise, looks at the wolf and says, "Don't tell me you were in the Reaping."

"He sure was," I say. "And I'd like to know why you sent him there to watch me."

Raith leans back in his chair. "If I had the power to send

someone into the Reaping, I would be the most powerful being on earth, maybe even the most powerful."

I study him. "You didn't send him?"

He shakes his head.

I look at the wolf. "You'd better shift into human form before I sick Stony on you."

Stony pushes up onto her forelegs. The wolf looks at her, sneezes, then shifts into human form, clothes, and all.

I narrow my eyes. "You can shift with clothes on?"

"When you've lived as long as Caleb, you learn a few tricks along the way," Raith says.

"You're old like *them*?" I ask.

"By them, if you mean Raith, Blade, and Ethan, then yes," he replies in his deep drawl.

Now I understand—partly, at any rate. The very old Margiddians all know each other.

"I—I heard a wolf howl in the War Games," I say.

His brows lift. "And that means...."

"It's just too coincidental, don't you think? You said you'd been in another Reaping."

He nods. "About a hundred years ago."

"I've never heard of anyone being taken twice."

"Neither have I," Raith says.

We both pin Caleb with a stare.

He shrugs. "It's not as if I had a choice."

I know he's right, but I can't escape the feeling there's more to the story. More to him.

"Was the Reaping you were in like this one? Are they all the same?" I ask.

"The one I was taken in was essentially the same as the one you and I were in. There were lots of Shadows, people got crazy, and people died."

"What was the deal with that stadium of people?" I ask.

"Stadium of people?" Raith says.

"There were—what"—I look at Caleb—"thousands of people in the stands?"

He gives a single nod. "Sounds about right."

"What stands?" Raith asks again.

The memory of fear tightens my stomach. "In the field where Ariel led the two hangings."

To my surprise, sorrow clouds his eyes. "What happened?"

I force myself to describe Chelsea and the guy with the ropes around their necks, the strange audience in the coliseum, and the weird wolves. Raith casts somber glances at Caleb as I describe the satisfaction Ariel took in bending the group of students to her will.

"Did you recognize the four students who were handling Chelsea and Robert's ropes?" Raith asked when I finished.

"Sorry." I shrug. "I didn't. Maybe they're from another school?"

"Maybe," he replies. "Did you recognize any other students there?"

"One girl who ran. I don't know her name."

"That's a start," he says. "We'll have you look at some pictures. I want to know who was there and what they were doing."

"The girl I recognized didn't do anything," I say. "When Ariel told the four students to get me, two of them ran. The girl was one of them."

"Okay. Tomorrow, we will take written statements and look at pictures." He regards me. "Did the Shadows touch you at any time?"

"Me?" I blurt. "No. In fact, I was surprised by the way they stopped when I told them to." I'm blabbing.

Raith straightens. "What?"

Oh God, I said the wrong thing. I look at Caleb. "You know, when the wolves were attacking you and Jonas was running? I-I shouted at them to stop and they did."

"They did what?" Raith demands.

"Stopped, halted, you know, stopped chasing Jonas."

"Ah," Raith says. "They didn't actually follow commands. Shadows instill fear by staying in sight, hovering, and chasing their victims."

"Oh," I say, and resist looking at Caleb—or Stoney, who I know is staring at me.

"I first saw Ariel when she led the gang that chased Jonas," I continue. I have to change the subject. "Her and another guy had a band of kids with them. Anthony is the guy's name. Strangely, he wasn't present for the hanging. I don't really know anything about Shadows and how they...control a person."

"They don't control a person," Raith says. "They play upon a person's fears, anxieties, and lust."

"Lust? How does anyone have time for lust in that hell-hole?" I think of the wolf and how beautifully naked he was, but that hadn't put me in the mood for fucking.

Raith shakes his head. "Lust of anything—sex, power, money, you name it. Everyone lusts after something."

"I guess Ariel lusts after power," I say. "I think others were infected too, but not everyone turned into a monster. That must mean there's some choice involved."

"Well, it implies that the results show what's in a person's heart," he says.

Raith Vanderkoff is talking about heart? I wasn't sure he believed people had hearts.

"What does that mean for Ariel?" I ask. "That chick is a psycho. I guarantee you no one will want to attend class with her—and I'm at the head of that line."

"You won't have to attend classes with her."

I hesitate, wondering why Raith gave in so easily, but decide to see what he does. I'm too tired to fight. "Can I go?" I ask.

Raith hesitates. I've never seen Raith hesitate about anything and that worries me.

"There's something I have to tell you," he says, and I'm surprised by the compassion in his voice. "It's about Seton Alexander."

I draw a sharp breath. "Has something happened to him? He was taken in the Reaping?" Aside from Stony, Seton is the only other friend I have. Tears rise to the surface. "He can't—"

"No, no," Raith cuts in. "He wasn't taken in the Reaping and he's unharmed. In fact, he can't be harmed. There's no way to say this but straight out. Seton is the Greek demigod Tychon."

I stare. Of all the things Raith could have said, the ridiculous idea that Seton is the demigod Tychon wasn't even in the universe of possibility.

I jump to my feet and Stony stands. "What kind of bullshit is this?" I snap.

To my shock, compassion appears in Raith's eyes. "We had a visit from the goddess Eldione. She recognized him and he disappeared before we could react." Raith motions with his head toward the fireplace where a small fire burns. "He was sitting right there on the couch opposite Olympia and I."

I glance at the sofa and back. "You're lying."

He keeps his gaze locked with mine. "Why would I? Seton is a graduate of The Academy. I promise you, we do not consider this a positive development."

I shake my head. "I don't believe you."

But I see the truth in his eyes.

~

CALEB WANTS TO WALK ME TO MY DORM ROOM. Thankfully, Raith tells him I was safe on campus, especially with Stony at my side. I'm a little surprised Raith didn't insist I get locked in my room again, but I'm not one to look a gift horse in the mouth.

The campus is a ghost town. Stony and I pass only two students, each accompanied by a teacher. I'm grateful. I'm not in the mood for small talk.

We reach the room and I close and lock the door. Stony snorts in delight and trots to the bed. She jumps onto the mattress and plops down on the blanket she slept on before we were taken.

I cast out my senses in an effort to determine if anyone has been in my room. I detect no disturbance. We've been gone for two days. Two days. I still can't believe it. Just as I can't believe that Seton is an Atlantean demigod. I want to hate Raith, but what are the chances he's lying—or wrong?

Gods do visit Margiddians—and humans—all the time. They even have relationships with us. Seton simply decided he liked me well enough to look after me. What other motive could he have for befriending me? He never tried to get me into bed. He was my friend. He taught me magic, stuck up for me.

With a sigh, I cross to the bed and sink to my knees between the bed and the desk. I listen for sounds of life outside my room, detect nothing, then murmur, "Book."

The book hidden beneath the floorboard materializes in my hand. I remain still for a moment while listening for sounds of approaching feet, but all remains quiet. Maybe my tiny spell didn't attract attention. I rise and sit on the bed. Stony snorts.

"I know," I reply. "But it's early for bed. I don't want to wake at two in the morning." I'm exhausted but don't think I can sleep.

I'll need some time to get through the spells in Grams' spell book. I remove my cell phone from the charger, unlock the device with my thumbprint, and go to the last picture I took: the first page of the spell book deciphered by my magic.

I remember the first two lines by heart.

The power in The Shadows is unmistakable.

There is no doubt they are the key I have been searching for these last ten years.

My chest tightens. I still can't believe Grams began using Shadow magic three years before she kicked me out. I have no doubt that is at least part of the reason she kicked me out. How could she betray us like that...betray me? I can't blame Blade for leading the investigation into her death. She broke our most sacred law: do not practice Shadow magic.

"Listen to this," I say to Stony, and read the next line in the book, *"I know God will forgive me—though everyone else will condemn me, and some would kill me if they knew the truth. I pray He is still able to help me."*

"Some Margiddians *would* kill her," Stony snorts.

"Yeah, but I'm talking about the part where she says she hopes God can still help her. What do you make of that?"

"Weird."

"The Shadows are not as difficult to control as I'd expected. That frightens me," I read, then add, "That frightens me."

Memory rises of me commanding the Reaping Shadows to halt. Despite what Raith said, I know they obeyed. I resist the urge to touch the place on my chest were the Shadows entered my body and read.

In the end, though, does fear matter? Once I control them, nothing else will matter.

Denique in occursum mihi Fatum meum.

"At last, I meet my destiny," I murmur.

Yeah, and that's what got her killed.

I open the spell book to the first page. The words on the page look like an ancient language, but I'm still convinced they're a code created by some spell Grams cast. I have no talent for decryption. I suspect the code would take even an expert some time to decipher. My options are simple: Show the book to *The Three or* use magic to decipher the book as I did the first page. Yeah, like I'm going to share this book with *anyone*.

The magic I'd used to reveal the book's first page had been gentle. No one had noticed that I'd used magic. If I decipher one page at a time several times, however, someone might notice the continuous use of magic. I think I can risk a page or two.

I used my wand to cast the spell. I should do the same, as the spell worked well and without any negative effects. I get my wand from my backpack in the closet, then grab my phone and drop down onto the bed. I open the book to the second page, then tap the camera icon on my phone and position the phone over the book.

I take a deep breath, then chant the same spell I used on the first page,

"Words on this one page only.

"For the barest of three heartbeats.

"Decipher me your riddles."

As happened the first time, a breeze blows across the pages. The words shimmer then come into focus in English. I snap the picture before the words return to their original form.

I wait, but all remains quiet outside my room. I start to get up to put the wand away, then hesitate. Should I do a second page? I look at the next page, as if I expect some clue as to whether or not I should take the risk. Magic abounds in The Academy. Likely, the students often dabble in magic outside the classroom.

I position the camera over the third page, repeat the spell, and snap the picture. Without waiting, I stow my wand in the backpack and stuff the spell book under Stony's blanket. She snorts a small recrimination but doesn't open her eyes.

I position my pillow against the wall, sit on the bed, and lean against the pillow. A thought strikes. What day is today? I think back. The War Games took place on Tuesday. We'd been gone two days, so today is Thursday. Tomorrow is Friday, and Friday evenings I'm obligated by that damned blood pact to spend two hours studying magic with Raith in his office.

Raith was oddly kind today. Thank God for small favors. Raith being kind to me *ever* is more than a small favor. A strange sorrow pricks at the center of my chest. I stiffen. Did that prick occur where the Shadows entered my body? Did they come with me when I returned to the real world? I'd never heard anyone talk about Shadows returning with anyone from a Reaping. When we got back, Ariel hadn't been the crazed bitch she'd been in the Reaping—though she was still cruel.

I'm becoming paranoid. No one likes being hated. I know from personal experience. So why does Raith's dislike bother me? Because I didn't do anything to deserve his hate. His dislike is personal. I scoot down and rest my head on the pillow. I close my eyes. What woman did him wrong?

TWENTY-ONE

Caleb

LETTING CIARAH OUT OF MY SIGHT IS THE SECOND hardest thing I've ever done. Watching her die my arms was the hardest. I comfort myself with the knowledge that her familiar is watching over her. It's obvious the animal would protect her with its dying breath.

Leilah closes the door as she and the pig leave, and Raith says, "Where the fuck have you been the last forty years?"

"What do you care?" I ask.

His eyes blaze, but I don't break our stare.

"We could have used your help during the war," he says.

"I doubt that," I reply.

"Ethan has worried like hell."

I believe that, but say, "Ethan is a big boy."

Raith leans back in his chair. "You think you can just walk back into Ciarah's life?"

I shrug. "That's always how it's been."

"Not this time. She's a student at The Academy. She lives here—you don't."

"I imagine there's a place here for an old wolf like me."

He bares his teeth. "Not if I say otherwise."

I stand. "I'm not in the mood to argue."

"How did you end up in the Reaping with her?" he demands.

Footfalls approach in the hallway and, an instant later, the door opens. Ethan and Blade enter. Ethan crossed the room and pulls me into a hug. He steps back and looks at my face "You had us worried."

Blade slaps me on the back. "Matthias said you would return soon. I'm glad he was right."

"Matthias is here?" I ask.

"Not right now," Ethan says. "We saw him for the first time in thirty years two nights ago."

I frown. "Thirty years?"

Blade grimaces. "He decided to become a bishop."

I snort. "That sounds about right."

A shadow stretches across the hallway in front of the door, then a tall vampire enters the room. His gaze flicks to me.

Ethan says, "Carter, this is an old friend, Caleb Dakota. He was in the Reaping. Caleb, a new old friend, Gabriel Carter."

I angle my head in acknowledgement. He does the same, then says to Raith, "We found the body of Robert Janson in the woods."

"Have the Watchmen prepare the body for return to his parents," Raith says. "Thanks for your help."

Carter nods. "I'm going to check with Cromwell and see if he needs a hand with the debriefings."

"We can use the help," Raith says without his usual condescension.

I guess it takes a vampire to command respect from another vampire.

Carter turns and leaves.

Ethan says to Raith, "We called Ariel's and Chelsea's parents. They're on their way."

"You'd' better hope Robert's mother doesn't figure out that

Ariel is responsible for his death," Blade says. "Kathryn is a well-connected siren."

Raith's lips thin. "Then Kathryn better hope nothing happens to Ariel. Olympia will deal with the woman if that happens."

"Speaking of Olympia," Blade says. "Has anyone seen her today?"

Ethan and Raith both say no.

"Odd," Blade says. "I haven't seen her since I gave her my report on the Zidruhin this morning. No sign of her assistant, either?"

"I had Rebecca leave messages for both Olympia and Franklin," Raith says. "But haven't heard back from either of them."

"What about Domini?" Ethan looks from Blade to Raith.

"I'd completely forgotten about him," Blade says.

"Haven't seen him," Raith replies.

Blade arches a brow. "You don't think...?"

Raith grimaces. "Anything is possible, though I'd be surprised if Olympia was fucking around right now. For the moment, however"—his eyes cut to me—"I'm interested in learning how Caleb ended up in the Reaping with Leilah."

"Oh, I figured that out," Blade says.

We all look at Blade.

"Come on," the Fae says. "The answer really is too easy."

"The War Games," Ethan murmurs.

Blade nods and locks gazes with me. "The wolf we heard in the virtual world was you."

"Is that true?" Raith demands.

I nod.

Raith frowns. "How long have you known she was back?"

"I figured it out a couple days before your War Games. I got on the first flight from Colorado to New York."

"Colorado?" Blade whistles. "Whatever were you doing in Colorado?"

"Not much," I reply.

The Fae regards me with a small smile. "I suspect that isn't quite true." He doesn't wait for a reply but asks Raith, "How is Leilah?"

"She's okay, considering she saw a student die."

"You shouldn't have sent her back to her room alone," Ethan says. "She needs protection."

She's with that damned night howler pig," Raith says.

Ethan releases a breath. "She's so young. This is probably the first time she's seen someone die."

"She sells fake IDs," Raith shoots back. "She's anything but innocent."

"Selling fake IDs? What the hell's been going on here?" I glance toward the door, wondering if I should find Leilah now. Is she safe?

"Raith is right," Ethan says. I turn my attention to him, and he adds, "Leilah is safe."

"Didn't you think she was safe when she came here? I blurt. "You were wrong, very wrong. How do you know she's safe now?"

The three of them exchange a glance.

"I'm not in the mood for games," I growl.

"We know because we made a blood pact with her," Ethan says.

"What?" I blurt.

Jealousy surges through me before I recall her words *"If a vampire, Fae, and dragon ever ask you to make a blood pact with them, don't."*

"If you forced her," I snarl.

"For God's sake, sit down," Blade orders.

I whip my head in his direction. "I warn you, Fae."

"Stop your posturing," he says in a patient voice. "Does Leilah strike you as the sort of woman who could be forced into anything?"

"She's young," I shoot back.

He grunts a laugh. "She stood up to Raith the first day they met. Half kicked his arse."

"I wouldn't say that," Raith mutters.

"We made a deal with her," Ethan says.

"What kind of deal?" I say warily.

"Sit your arse down and maybe we'll tell you," Blade says.

I cast another glance at the door, then reluctantly sit. They fill me on the blood pact. I'm not thrilled with what appears to be trickery, but I have to admit, with Leilah sneaking out of The Academy and an attempt on her life, I might have gone along with the blood pact had I been here. The time I spent with her in the Reaping taught me that she's a proud, headstrong woman who doesn't always listen to sense. She's also brave.

"I feel certain if she were in danger, we would sense it," Blade says.

I regard him, then Raith, who has been silent through the telling of the story.

"How about you, Raith?" I ask. "Would you sense it if she were in danger?"

"I signed the blood pact," he replies.

"Would you tell us, if you thought something was wrong?"

"Yes," he says without hesitation. "My feelings toward Leilah won't stop me from ensuring her safety."

I believe him. He was kind when he spoke with her about the Reaping, as well as when he delivered the news about her friend.

"Once she learns that we found her would-be killer, she'll want to nullify the pact," Blade says.

"No way," Raith says.

Ethan and Blade look at him in surprise.

"You weren't keen on the idea to begin with," Blade says. "I would think you'd be happy to void the contract."

"I owe her six months of tutoring," he replies.

Blade whoops and slaps his leg. "I should have known."

I shoot Ethan a questioning look and he says, "Leilah was... persnickety when the time came to sign the blood pact. She goaded Raith and he demanded the lessons in magic so that she would learn some discipline."

"I can't blame him there," I say.

Raith's gaze sharpens. "She tested your patience in the Reaping."

"There was a time or two I wanted to paddle her ass," I say.

"The fun stuff," Blade says with a laugh.

"She has courage," I say. "Misplaced courage, but courage. She thought she had to save me from the Reaping wolves."

Blade's amusement vanishes. "That was foolish of her."

"She put up a good fight against the Shadows that were present at the hanging," I say.

"She didn't mention that." Raith scowls. "What happened?"

"She conjured these swirling black balls and—"

"Swirling black balls?" they say in unison.

I look at each of them. "Yeah, why?"

Ethan leans forward in his chair. "Matthias said she used swirling black balls to fight the Thol'guk that attacked her at the potionary."

"Thol'guk?" I repeat.

Blade grunts a laugh. "Hard to believe, isn't it? That was one of the times Leilah sneaked out of The Academy—the first time, actually, during her first week here. Turns out Matthias was there—along with a Thol'guk."

"Who sent the demon?" I ask.

"We haven't figured that out yet," Blade says.

"Christ," I mutter. "You all have a little soap opera going in here."

"Nothing so dramatic as that," Blade says with amusement.

"Shit always happens when Ciarah reappears in our lives," Raith says.

"You seem to have forgotten who she is." Ethan's tone is gentle. "She's saved us more than once."

A soft light enters Blade's eyes. "Remember when that dhampir tracked us all the way from Romania and caught Caleb and Raith in our cabin on the Warsaw Vienna Railway? She was a tricky one, that dhampir. I had no idea she hid a short sword beneath her greatcoat. I would still like to know what spell she used to incapacitate you two. You're bloody lucky Ciarah returned to the cabin when she did." Blade shakes his head. "I wish I could have seen her kill that bitch. Ciarah is magnificent when she's fighting." His eyes darken. "And when she's making love."

"We all know that Ciarah can take care of herself," Raith says with asperity.

"And us," Ethan says.

"She's caused her share of trouble for *us*," Raith snaps.

Blade lifts a brow. "One of these days, she's going to remember our past lives, and you will have to ask her why she put that knife through your heart."

TWENTY-TWO

Leilah

Something in the way I walk feels...off. I look down and frown at my short, red, flared skirt. I never wear skirts. The shoes, however, are pretty damn cool. Three-inch heels, teardrop shape, tapered heel with t-straps in red suede. The kind of shoes one would expect to see on a woman twisting her hips on the dancefloor to the beat of Latin music.

"Nova," a woman with an accent—Spanish, I realize—calls to me.

As I turn, I breathe in the scents of baking bread, sugar, cinnamon, chocolate, and other indefinable sweets. I'm in a bakery, one of my all-time favorite stores. A woman, maybe forty-five years of age, stands in a doorway at the back of the store where an oven as tall as me commands the rear wall. She's beautiful in a regal sort of way, with dark hair swept up onto her head and a hint of gray at her widow's peak. Dark brown eyes in a face of beautiful brown skin. The merest hint of crows feet crinkle the corners of her eyes and faint smile lines extend from each side of her mouth. There's something familiar about her that I can't place.

"Nova," she says, "bring the two lower trays from the case, please."

I frown. She lifts her brows and looks to my left. I follow her gaze to a display case filled with beautiful sweets, everything from eclairs to cream filled pastries, cookies, cakes, and more.

"Nova."

I look back at her.

"Bring the two bottom trays, please. I have a batch of marzipan cookies that are ready."

"Uh, sure." I take a faltering step forward. The voice coming out of my mouth vibrates in my chest in a way that my voice doesn't.

The woman frowns. "Is something wrong?"

I shake my head, then hurry around behind the case, and pull out the two bottom trays, which are about a quarter full. I start toward the kitchen. I glimpse myself in a small decorative mirror on the right wall, stop, and take a step backward to get a better look. The young woman staring back at me has long, wavy, raven hair, dark eyes and olive skin that almost glows. She's at least four inches shorter than me and stacked like Sophia Loren.

"Nova," the woman calls.

I hurry to the back where she's pulled a tray of rolls from the oven. The scent of fresh baked bread envelopes me like a warm blanket. I set the trays on the counter to the left of three dozen colorful marzipan cookies. The woman sets the hot baking sheets on a stainless steel counter that faces the oven.

"Ah, thank you, *carino*. Now please—"

A bell tinkles in the front of the store.

"Go help that customer, will you?" the woman says.

I hurry into the front of the store and halt at sight of the tall, handsome vampire staring into a display case. He turns his head and I look into eyes so unlike those of the vampire I know at The Academy that I think for an instant that I've mistaken him for Raith. He's hard, that hasn't changed, but there's a soft light in his eyes, a hunger—for me. My heartbeat quickens. He turns toward me. His attention shifts over my shoulder to the woman behind me.

I hurry forward. "Can I help you?" I say, as I step behind the counter.

"Can you get away for a few minutes?" he asks.

His voice is the same deep voice I know, but the anger is absent. I had no idea this Raith existed.

He lifts his brows. "Well? Can you get away?"

I open my mouth, but what do I say? I don't know if I can get away? What are you doing here? Why don't you hate me? Why do you hate me?

The bell on the front door tinkles again and Raith turns as another man enters. He's tall, though not as tall as Raith, and he has a hard look about him that I instantly dislike.

"Vanderkoff," the man says.

"Cordero," Raith's reply is cold.

Cordero? Sounds like a crime boss—which I realize, he is. Dread prickles my spine. He's here to see me. I know him. I know him well, in fact. Revulsion roils in my stomach. Why would I have anything to do with this man? His gazes remains fixed on Raith and I tense. Are the two men going to throw down right here? I realize there is an Italian stiletto knife strapped to my leg, hidden by my skirt. I step around the counter and allow my hand to drop toward my hem.

The woman enters the room. She halts, eyes locked on Cordero. She glances at Raith, and says, "Mr. Vanderkoff," then her attention returns to Cordero. "Can we help you, Mr. Cordero? We have a dozen of the chocolate tarts you're so fond of."

He flashes white teeth. "No one can refuse your pastries, Mrs. Elias."

She gives a curt nod and walks to the counter. She pulls a pink cake box off the shelf against the wall, then slides open the display case and puts half a dozen of the small round chocolate cakes in the box. With crisp efficiency, she closes the lid and tapes the cover.

She meets Cordero's gaze square and I know she's telling him to leave me alone. "That will be three-seventy-five, please," she says.

Three-seventy-five? Those half dozen cakes should be twelve dollars.

But they're not, comes the whisper of a reply.

Because this is some time in the past. I glance around the bakery for clues to what *era* this is but, aside from the prices on the baked goods, the bakery could be any bakery in a diverse city neighborhood.

Cordero pays and, again, flashes that smile at Mrs. Elias. His proprietary gaze lingers on me, which causes my cheeks to warm, then he angles his head in Raith's direction. Raith doesn't so much as flinch a muscle until the bell tinkles again as the door clicks shut behind the man.

Mrs. Elias shakes her head, then looks from the door to me. "I have told you, Nova, to stay away from that man." She blinks at Raith, as if having forgotten he is there "I am sorry, Mr. Vanderkoff."

Raith shakes his head. "There's no need to apologize. I can deal with Cordero for you."

Her face softens. "That is kind of you, but do not bother yourself. I'm sure he'll give up—once Nova makes is clear she is not interested in his attentions. Now, if you'll excuse me, I have bread in the oven. Nova, please help Mr. Vanderkoff." She heads toward the kitchen.

Raith waits until she leaves, then asks, "Why do you encourage him?"

Irritation flares. "I didn't encourage him. I didn't say a

fucking word to him."

He frowns. "Nova, what's gotten into you? If your mother hears you talking like that, she'll—"

"Mother?" I cut in. That woman is my mother? I look through the door into the kitchen, but she's out of my view.

"Is something wrong? It's Cordero, isn't it?" he demands.

I jerk my attention back to Raith. He's staring out the front door. I've seen Raith angry, but that anger was always directed at me. This anger is in defense of me. He starts toward the door. He's going after Cordero. Cordero, I suddenly *know*, plans to kill Raith. Cordero isn't just any crime boss. He hunts big game. Vampires, werewolves, and maybe even witches. More than once, I've wanted to kick Raith's ass. I'd even wished him gone. But not dead. No, not dead.

"Hey," I call to Raith.

He pauses at the door and looks over his shoulder.

"How about that moment alone?" I ask.

Surprise flickers in his eyes, then doubt. I hurry around the counter. He turns as I approach.

"Come on." I grasp his hand.

I startle at the warmth of his hand as he grasps mine. The gentleness in his grasp freezes me. I stare at our clasped hands.

"Nova."

I snap my head up. He stares down at me, eyes so filled with concern that I wonder what happened to change him so much.

"Nova."

I shake off the strong sense of déjà vu that washes over me. I hate déjà vu. "Come on."

I open the door and pull Raith outside onto the Chicago sidewalk. I look around and remember there's an alley to the right. The bakery delivery door opens into the alley, but I don't want Mrs. Elias—Mama—to know I'm taking Raith into the alley. She likes Raith. In fact, she would love to see me marry someone like him. Handsome, rich, and she's certain he's kind.

Sometimes he is. Like today. Still, Mama wouldn't approve of me being alone in an alley with any man, even a man she likes.

A kid on a bike rides past. I glance behind us to be sure Cordero isn't following. Sometime, he has one of his goons follow me. He thinks I don't know, but Cordero underestimates women. Even witches. He underestimates Raith, too, but that's because he's never encountered a vampire like Raith. There aren't many vampires like Raith. Then again, Cordero does know one very important thing about Raith. If anything can get Raith killed, it's his weakness for me.

Guilt washes over me. I'm not interested in Cordero. He's a criminal. Yet, I've played Raith against Cordero because I knew Raith would get jealous—and Raith jealous is a magnificent sight. Which makes mine a very dangerous game. I've got to convince Raith I'm done with Cordero. With a final glance behind us to be sure no one is watching, I pull Raith into the alleyway.

He halts and seizes me by the shoulders. "Cordero is dangerous. I told you to stay away from him."

"He said the same thing about you," I say before realizing my words. "He's right."

"You'll force me to kill him."

I know this is true, but anger flares. "Don't use me as an excuse. You've wanted to kill them for years."

"He hunts our kind. How can you let him touch you?"

I break free of Raith's grasp. "Who said he's touched me?"

"Men like that don't settle for a chaste kiss."

He's right, still, I say, "It seems you and he have more in common than you would like to admit."

"Are you comparing me to him—a murderer?"

"If you kill him, won't that make you a murderer?" I retort.

"Not a murderer," he shoots back. "A hero."

"Heroes don't murder people." And there's no guarantee Raith will be the victor.

"Pick a side, Nova."

I look up at him. "I'm on your side, baby. You know that."

A guy and a girl walk past the alley and stare until they're out of sight.

"Stop seeing him," Raith says.

Easier said than done. Raith is right. Men like Cordero don't settle for a chaste kiss and they don't handle rejection well.

"You don't have to be afraid of him," Raith says. "You know we'll take care of you."

The "we" he's referring to are him, Ethan, Blade, Caleb, and Matthias. Confusion washes over me.

"You don't have to worry that your family will ever know there are five of us," Raith says.

Five? "Have you boys decided which one of you would legally be my husband?"

"Me," he replies.

I blink. "Cordero will burn down the bakery," I say more to myself than Raith.

"We can protect you."

I start to tell him that he's a fool if he believes that.

Does Mama know that Raith, Cordero...and I aren't... human? No, she doesn't. Humans can't wield magic. Which means, somewhere in my lineage is a Margiddian, who married a human, then lived as a human.

"We can kill Cordero," Raith says.

They would try, but at least one of them would die. I played them—Raith in particular—against Cordero. I thought seeing Raith jealous was funny. I thought I was clever enough to control Cordero. I never considered the repercussions. I never considered that someone might die.

"*I* will kill him." Raith's incisors elongate.

His anger is pushing him dangerously close to looking for Cordero. Cordero is a coward and cowards hedge their bets. He won't face Raith alone.

Raith is right. Cordero has to die.

I grasp Raith's hand. "Forget about Cordero."

Raith shakes his head, but I pull him deeper into the alley, past the closed bakery door to an alcove between the bakery and the building next to it. I push Raith into the alcove until his back presses the wall.

I look up at him. His eyes have darkened. Not with anger, but with desire. The juncture between my legs tightens. I rise on tiptoes and press my mouth against his. He yanks me close and kisses me like a man who's starved. His mouth, warm, firm, and insistent, causes my head to spin. I want him. But more than that, I need him…I love him. Unexpected sorrow twists my heart and I force back tears.

His tongue flicks against my lips and I open for him. He thrusts his tongue inside my mouth and I'm suddenly aware of the hard bulge pressing against my abdomen. My heart pounds. Would he let me touch him? Would he let me wrap my legs around his hips and lower myself onto his erection? I moan and he growls in response. Yes, he would let me do anything I want.

I imagine wrapping my legs around his hips as he drives into me with all he's got. My throat goes dry. The image has a strange quality, as if I have already made love to him. I want so badly to make it real and undulate my mons against his cock. His fingers tighten on my arms. Why can't Raith be like this at The Academy? I could so easily give myself over to him. But I can't fuck him now. It's too cruel, too sadistic. I reach down and rake my nails over the front of his jeans where the bulge strains.

"Nova," he rasps against my lips.

He slides his mouth along my cheek to my ear. A shiver races down my arms. I reach beneath my skirt and inch the knife from its holster. I allow my head to drop back as Raith slides a wet kiss down my neck. I must be quick. Raith is in a haze of lust, but one tiny wrong move and he'll stop me before I have the knife out.

I grab a fistful of his hair and pull—hard. I smother his grunt with a kiss. I grip the knife, place my thumb on the switch. Then, in a hard upward swing, I open the knife and plunge the blade under his left ribs.

Raith stiffens. His eyes lock with mine. Confusion gives way to pain. The recognition of betrayal follows in the instant before he collapses. I release the knife and try to catch him, but his weight takes me down. We almost tumble out of the alcove, but I throw my weight forward, so that we slide down the left corner. My arm is pinned beneath his back, and my breasts press against his side as if we're still locked in an embrace.

My heart thunders and I remain frozen, unable to tear my gaze from his eyes, staring past me, unseeing. Tears break through my resolve. I want badly to pull the knife from his chest and beg his forgiveness. But vampires don't forgive. Worse, to free him now would sign his death warrant.

I grasp his shoulder and gently pull him forward an inch so that I can free my arm. My gaze catches on the knife protruding from his chest and a sob escapes me. I'm so glad Raith isn't aware of his surroundings. Unlike the movies, real vampires can't be killed with a knife or stake to the heart. But it can incapacitate them. If Cordero were to find him…. I shudder. I press a kiss to Raith's lips, then stand.

After I find Cordero and kill him, Raith will be safe.

TWENTY-THREE

Ethan

QUICK BOOTFALLS ON THE MARBLE FLOOR OUTSIDE Raith's office halts our conversation. Raith, Blade, and I exchange a glance in the instant before Headmaster Edd Domini enters the room.

Speak of the devil.

His glance takes us all in, then he focuses on Raith. "I just arrived from the City. The students have returned from the Reaping?"

"Yes," Raith replies.

Relief washes over Domini's features. "That's miraculous. To my knowledge, a Reaping has never ended within two days. All the students returned safely, I hope?"

Something in his voice gives me pause. He's almost... nonchalant, as if he's trying to act natural.

Raith's face clouds over. "All but one."

Fear flickers in Domini's eyes. "What happened?"

"Robert Janson was hanged."

"Hanged?" The color drains from Domini's face. "He was a promising siren. What a tragedy."

The words sound sincere, but something still seems off. I

have the strange feeling he expected another student to have died. Or does he fear a different student died?

A click of snowy sleet taps the windows.

"Who is responsible for the hanging?" Domini asks.

Raith shifts in his chair. "Ariel Littleton led the hanging."

"That slip of a girl?" Domini blows out a breath. "You just never know, do you?"

"Leilah Crowe saved Chelsea Nightlow from hanging." Blade's eyes are locked on the man.

Does he sense something off about Domini, as well?

"My God." Domini shakes his head. "A Reaping is never pretty. How is Ms. Crowe doing?"

"She's doing well," Raith says. "You were in the City?"

Domini nods. "Olympia sent me on an errand. She must be pleased the students have returned."

"I wouldn't know," Raith says. "We haven't seen her."

He frowns. "She isn't here? Have you no way to contact her?"

"I left a message with her assistant."

"Do you need me to help with debriefing?" Domini asks.

"You may report to Cromwell. He can assign you a student."

Domini angles his head, starts to turn, but halts, his eyes on Caleb. "Forgive me, but have we met?"

Caleb gives a single shake of his head. "No."

Domini hesitates, clearly surprised at Caleb's curt manner and, I suspect, hopes one of us will make introductions. When we don't, he leaves.

Blade crosses to the open door and closes it. "Is it just me or is there something off with that guy?" he asks.

"It's not just you," I say.

"Leilah Crowe?" Caleb cuts in. "She isn't related to Miriam Crowe?"

"Her granddaughter," I say.

"You're not serious?" He shakes his head. "That's a hell of a family to be born into."

"You have no idea," Blade says. He looks at Raith. "I assume you haven't filled Caleb in on the situation with Miriam?"

"What situation?" Caleb looks from me to Raith. "I thought the witch was dead."

Blade's expression goes grim. "We all thought that."

We tell him everything, including the current theory of Miriam being in Hell, along with the god of the angels."

Caleb stares at us for a long moment, then says, "Wow."

"You always had a way with words," Blade says.

"Does Leilah know any of this?" he asks.

Caleb is good at seeing Ciarah strictly for who she. He never refers to her as Ciarah, or by any other name than the one she has in the current lifetime.

Raith shakes his head. "We haven't told her anything yet. You saw how she reacted when I told her about Seton. I wasn't sure she was ready for the news about her grandmother yet."

Wow, Raith being considerate of Leilah's feelings. Maybe he's starting to mellow.

"Zadkeil let slip that their god is in Hell and they think Miriam was trying to join him," Raith continues.

Caleb frowns. "To reach their god?"

Blade shrugs. "That's Matthias's theory. He thinks she wants to free Yahweh. For all we know, she might want to team up with Hades and Damien to annihilate Margidda using Shadows."

Caleb humphs. "Wouldn't loosing The Shadows make her a prime target for annihilation?"

"Does anyone really know what will happen if The Shadows overrun Margidda?" I ask. "We learned during the war that there were many Margiddians who welcomed the power The Shadows gave them."

"I've never understood that," Caleb says.

"You've never been one to care for politics," Blade says.

Caleb grunts. "I've never been one to understand why someone would hand over their power to someone else. Especially someone who means to kill them."

"Everyone thinks they're smarter than everyone else," Blade says. "Which brings us to Seton Alexander."

"Fuck," Raith mutters.

"We have to tell him." Blade's gaze centers on Caleb. "Before Miriam kicked Leilah out—"

"Her grandmother kicked her out of her home?" Caleb cuts in. Blade nods and Caleb mutters, "Humans."

"Before Miriam kicked her out," Blade continues, "Leilah had a close friend, Seton Alexander. He's a graduate of The Academy. Turns out, he's Tychon."

"The demigod? Why weren't you guarding her better?" he snarls.

"Easy there, wolf," Blade says. "We could ask you the same." Caleb frowns, and Blade adds, "Then there's Chelsea Nightlow."

Caleb's expression darkens. "The girl Leilah saved from being hanged?"

"You were there," Blade says to me. "Want to tell him?"

I don't. I don't want to think about Leilah's limp body when I took flight for Raith's office. "Chelsea tried to kill Leilah."

"Twice, in fact," Blade adds.

I shoot him a narrow-eyed look, then wince when Caleb snaps, "What the hell have you three been doing?

"You've been gone for forty years," Raith says in a cold voice.

Caleb glares. "My being gone has nothing to do with you not taking care of her."

"Technically, it was my fault," I say.

"What?" says.

"The attempt on her life took place in my class. In the end, Raith saved her life."

"You forced me," Raith says with the belligerence of a child.

Caleb stands. "He forced you? You mean you didn't want to save her."

Raith didn't flinch. "You, of all people, should know how dangerous she is."

Caleb glances from Blade to me, then back to Raith, and stares. "Dangerous? She died in my arms. You're pissed I haven't been around? Where were you when Cordero shot her?"

"As Blade said earlier, I had a knife through my heart—one Ciarah put there."

Caleb growls. "I don't blame her. You dogged her like the damned IRS. You weren't supposed to be at the bakery that day."

"I don't care where I was supposed to be. She stuck a knife in my chest and left me for dead."

"Stop your whining," Caleb cut in. "Vampires can't be killed with a knife through the heart. You don't have a fucking heart."

Raith flashes a grim smile. "Only because Ciarah cut it out that day."

TWENTY-FOUR

Leilah

MY SURROUNDINGS SHIFT AND MY EYES READJUST AS I stare for three more heartbeats at Raith, then he's gone and I'm looking at Stony, who's sitting beside me on the bed watching me. I glance at the window. It's late afternoon, not quite dark.

I look back at Stony. "How long was I out?"

"Ten minutes," she replies in a snort.

"What a weird dream." But it wasn't a dream.

What prompted the vision? Then I remember. Before I fell asleep, I was wondering who had hurt Raith to make him hate me. I don't usually have visions. Well, not often. My thinking about Raith wasn't enough to prompt a vision. Was it? No, I realize.

"Fuck a duck," I murmur. "Damned blood pact."

"Blood pacts are dangerous," Stony says.

"No shit." I knew that thing would come back to bite me in the ass. "Now I understand why Raith is so angry," I say.

Stony drops onto her belly and waits. I take a deep breath and recount the vision.

"I guess I can't be as angry with him as I've been," I

conclude. "I would hate women, too, if the woman I loved put a knife in my heart. I wonder if he would believe me if I told him that Nova intended to save his life. Though now I can't recall how she intended to do that." I look at Stony. "He might feel better knowing she didn't completely betray him."

Stony shakes her head and sneezes.

I sigh. "Yeah, I guess not. He would call me a liar and hate me even more."

She snorts a mutter that I recognize as Chinese, then says, "Stop lying to yourself."

"What are you talking about?" I ask.

She stares.

"Hey!" I cry. "You aren't suggesting—"

Stony snorts a laugh, then farts. She does that sometimes when she's really amused.

"Christ, Stony." I wave a hand in front of my face, despite the fact there's no odor.

"Now you know why they chose you," she says in her piggy language.

"That's not possible," I whisper, but the chills that roll down my head and arms says she's right. "No." I shake my head. "I'm not Nova."

Stony's forehead stretches in an approximation of lifting her brows.

I sit up. "I've got to get out of here."

Stony pushes up onto her forelegs.

I shake my head. "You don't have to go. You can rest. I'm going to go back to Grams' place. I can work on the spell book there much easier than here."

"Blood pact," she says.

"Fuck." The pact stipulates that I have to get their permission to leave Academy grounds. I cut my gaze to Stony. "Wait a minute. The pact says I must *ask* for their permission. Oh my god, we didn't stipulate that they had to *give* their permission."

Stony laughs again.

"It might work," I shoot back in defense.

I jump up and pull paper and pen from the desk drawer. I spot one of the hard cinnamon candies I left there. I love cinnamon. I unwrap the candy, pop it into my mouth, and write,

Raith, Ethan and Blade,

I request permission to leave The Academy.

Leilah

A light knock on the door causes me to freeze. I look at Stony, then the door. I stuff the note into the front desk drawer, then cross to the door.

"Who is it?" I ask.

"Blade."

I mouth to Stony, *What does he want?*

She shakes her head.

I stare at the door. How can I face him?

TWENTY-FIVE

Blade

ETHAN WANTS TO SEE LEILAH AS BADLY AS I DO, BUT I left him and Caleb to argue with Raith over whether or not Caleb should be allowed to stay on Academy grounds. If Raith thinks he can order Caleb to leave Leilah, then he's forgotten who the wolf is. Caleb is angry enough with Raith to push the issue—or let Ethan push the issue. Caleb knows that his insistence he stay on Academy grounds is pissing off Raith.

I plan to pay Chelsea Nightlow a visit, but first, I have to see Leilah. I hurry from the building along the pathway toward her dorm. I'm still in shock that Caleb has spent the last fifteen years as a sheriff in a small Colorado town. He's perfect for the job, of course, but he might have dropped us a line to let us know he was alive. That's a wolf for you.

I catch sight of Watchmen in the trees. Aside from them, not a soul is walking the grounds. The students who returned from the Reaping are being cared for by staff and friends. The friends are sticking close in an effort to reassure themselves that their returned friends are really safely home.

Five minutes later, I reach Leilah's dorm and take the stairs two at a time. What will I say to her? How will I explain my need to see her? She witnessed a student get hanged. She can't be in good shape emotionally, yet Raith—and Caleb—let her go off alone. Not quite alone. She's got her familiar.

I reach her room and knock. A rustling in the room is followed by her calling out,

"Who is it?"

"Blade."

Silence follows and I fear she won't open the door. I flatten a palm against the metal. The light pad of feet on the wooden floor approaches the door. An instant later, the lock disengages and I pull my hand away as the door swings open. Leilah has changed from the leather pants and shirt and now wears white socks, sweatpants, and a long sleeve white shirt with no bra.

"Can I come in?" I ask.

She shrugs and starts back into the room. I push the door closed, then take two quick steps and pull her into a hug. She stiffens, and I expect her to resist. To my surprise, she melts against me and begins to cry softly. I lift her into my arms and cross to the bed. I'm surprised to find that her familiar is absent, and lay Leilah on the bed. I strip off my jacket, toss it onto the desk, and crawl in beside her. She curls into my arms and I hold her close, stroking her hair and making shushing noises.

Raith was wrong to send her to her room alone. I was a fool for not coming directly to her. Her experience in the Reaping has traumatized her—as is the case with all the students. Just the few snippets I gleaned when the students were talking in hushed voices on the walk to the auditorium told of the different—and even somewhat conflicting—experiences. That's what the Reaping does, taps into a person's fears.

What trigged the bloody Reaping? I badly want to take Olympia to task for creating the Virtual War Games but can't. No one can, at least not yet, and she knows it. I know in my bones her virtual world is responsible for trigging the Reaping.

She knows that, too. I take a slow, deep breath. Now is not the time to get angry. Leilah needs comfort, not conflict.

At last, her tears cease and the slight rise and fall of her chest tells me she's fallen asleep. Too much time has passed since I held her in my arms while she slept, and I want to cry with relief that she's finally back with me...with us. She has returned and we've all been drawn to her as we always are. She survived the Reaping. Now we can protect her.

Fear tightens my chest when I recall Caleb's recounting of his and Leilah's experiences in the Reaping. She protected Jonas, saved a dozen students from falling into a crevasse, and saved Ariel, the vicious bitch, and Chelsea—though the girl doesn't deserve Leilah's protection. Why did Chelsea try to kill her—twice? Did Leilah know her before The Academy? Doubtful. Not that Leilah would tell us, but I get the impression that she has no friend or acquaintance at The Academy. I knew Leilah would encounter some opposition here—she's Miriam Crowe's granddaughter, after all—but I can't imagine any of the students wanting to kill her.

Fury roils in my chest. Chelsea might be young, but she knew exactly what she was doing. No one gets away with trying to kill *any* of our students.

I take a deep breath to slow my heart and hold Leilah just a little tighter. We'll discover Chelsea's reasons for wanting to kill her. A terrifying thought hits. Does Chelsea know Leilah from a past life? I remember during the Salem witch trials, a witch who swore she knew Ciarah before even we met her in Persia. The witch had denounced her as a dark witch, and others who heard turned the gossip into an even darker accusation; a witch who practiced Shadow magic.

Part of me wants to race to the room where Chelsea is being held to demand answers, but I'm not quite ready to leave Leilah. Caleb and Matthias have returned, which means there will be less time alone with her. I grimace. She now knows that

Caleb is another man in her life. What will she do when Matthias reveals himself?

I think back to her last lifetime as Nova. That girl loved the attention of five sought-after men. Nova had been childish; in some ways, maybe even a little cruel—the perfect match for a vampire—but she wouldn't have allowed anyone to hurt us. I still haven't figured out why she stabbed Raith and left him in the alley, but I know she believed she had good reason.

Leilah stirs. If she wakes, I fear she will ask me to leave. Twilight has fallen and the room lays in shadow. I love this time of night when the night creatures are stirring.

Leilah is so different from previous incarnations. She's always been strong and sexy as hell. She usually knew who she was and often used the knowledge to her advantage. I didn't mind. In this lifetime, she's almost more...human than witch. Oh, she's a powerful witch. I'm still stunned at the story of how she lifted *all* the students out of the crevasse—and in a lucid dream. Ethan and Raith studied for five years to prepare for the lucid dreaming battle with The Shadows. But her power isn't what caught my attention, but her attitude and manner. She's more...down to earth than I've ever known her to be. I want to laugh. I doubt Raith would agree.

Leilah breathes deeply and I realize she's waking. My heart sinks. She slides an arm around my neck. I freeze when she nuzzles my ear. He warm mouth closes over my lobe and she gently bites my lobe. My cock jumps to attention. I want her so badly it hurts. I know what this is about, however. The Reaping has changed her, and she needs comfort, to reaffirm life.

"Leilah," I whisper.

She pulls the tie from my hair, then slides her fingers into my hair and tugs. This is a move that seems to follow her from lifetime to lifetime and I love it.

I resist the compulsion to yank her against me, and instead whisper, "Sweetness."

She whispers, "If you didn't want me, you shouldn't have gotten into bed with me."

I give a strangled laugh. "I never said I didn't want you."

"Do you hate me?"

"Hate you?" I pull back. Fae sight is excellent in the dark. She stares, eyes intent. I smooth back her hair. "Love, I'm in bed with you. Where you're concerned, hate is not a word that exists in my vocabulary."

"I would understand," she says.

Something her voice sounds a distant warning bell inside my head. "Why would I hate you?" I ask carefully.

She gives a low laugh, then throws a leg over my abdomen, pressing in the most wonderful way against my cock. Has Ethan made love to her, already? The dragon isn't one to kiss and tell. But he is one to kiss, given the opportunity. Why not comfort her, if that's what she needs? I roll on top of Leilah. Her soft curves mold to my hard planes.

I stare down at her. "I would think by now that my feelings would be clear."

She startles me by tracing a finger along my cheek, then my mouth. I press my lips against her fingers and close my eyes for an instant, as she slides her hand around my neck and pulls my mouth down to hers. I have never been able to resist Ciarah. The moment her mouth touches mine, desire rockets through me. She tastes sweet and a little like cinnamon. I love her and, whether she knows it yet or not, she loves me.

Still....

I break the kiss. "Are you sure?"

Her answer is to wrap her legs around my hips and undulate her mons against my cock. Need further hardens my erection in pleasurable torture. I hiss through my teeth. I think I am hungrier for her than ever before. I rock against her and the compulsion to climax nearly overwhelms me.

I kiss her, then thrust my tongue inside her mouth. She

slips her arms beneath my arms and wraps them around my back. My cock is making its need known in the most demanding way. Will she.... She slides her palms down my back and cups my arse.

I break the kiss and trace wet kisses along her jaw, her neck, then to the stiff nipple poking against the white fabric of her t-shirt. I take the nipple in my mouth and suck. She draws a sharp breath. Oh yes, she likes that. Her fingers dig into my arse through my jeans and she arches against my cock. I move my mouth to her other nipple and, this time, only ring the stiff bud with my wet tongue. She arches into my mouth.

We've got to get out of these clothes. I raise onto my knees, pulling her with me. I reach for the hem of her t-shirt, but she impatiently pushes my hand aside and yanks her shirt up and over her head.

I cup her perfect breasts. The luscious weight feels so right in my hands. Leilah pushes my hands aside, then pulls my hoodie over my head and tosses it onto the floor. My t-shirt follows. She shimmies out of her sweatpants and panties and pushes them onto the floor. I can't tear my eyes away from her. She's beautiful. I want so badly to toss her onto her bed and drive into her until she calls my name.

Leilah grasps a loop of my jeans and tugs. "These have to go."

I jump from the bed, toe off my boots, then shuck my jeans and boxer briefs.

She grasps my hand. I don't resist when she tugs me to the bed and onto her. My cock makes contact with the curls between her legs and the need to show her how much I love her pulses through my veins. I close my eyes and nuzzle her hair. She releases a soft breath that washes over my shoulder and sends a shiver across my flesh.

Leilah rocks against my erection. Pleasure draws my bollocks up. I kiss her and she sucks my tongue into her mouth. I taste every inch of her, then thrust my tongue in and out of her mouth as I intend to do to her channel. She moans. The woman will drive me mad.

Turnabout is fair play.

I pool my concentration—no easy feat with her rubbing against me, as she is—and command soft energy into my fingertips. I break the kiss and watch her face as I lightly graze my fingertips along her cheek. A tiny swirl of multi-colored energy sparks across her skin. Her brows draw together. I trace a finger along her neck, then…her taut, pink nipple. She gasps. The sound sends a message straight to my cock.

Leilah arches into my fingertips. I smile. Her fingers press into the flesh of my arse. Perfect. The tiny whirlpool of energy sparks. She wriggles restlessly beneath me.

"Blade."

The need in her voice tugs at my soul as much as my body. Ciarah is finally home.

I kiss her, slow, tender and with the intention of never letting her go. She releases a small sigh and traces her fingers along my spine. I shiver. Ciarah is the only woman who ever made me shiver.

I reach between us and fit my cock to her opening. I grit my teeth and force calm as I slowly ease into her tight channel. Wet heat surrounds the crown and squeezes until I'm hilt deep. Leilah releases a contented sigh. Then I pull back and drive deep. She gasps and her fingers tighten in my flesh. I pull back then thrust again, harder, faster.

Leilah draws her knees up so that she can lift her hips to meet my thrusts. She pulls my head down and sucks my ear lobe. Her hot breath on my neck sends a shudder through me. Pleasure coils around my cock and I groan. She angles her body so that the side of my cock slides along her sex. She sucks on my ear harder. I fear I won't last much longer.

I pull my ear from her mouth, press my mouth to her ear, and whisper, "Are you ready, love?"

"Blade," she whispers, and I know that I'm driving her wild.

I increase my speed. I won't stop until she is satisfied.

"Oh god," she groans.

I press a kiss to her ear, then slide my tongue along her jaw, then down her neck to the sensitive place where neck meets shoulder. I suck the flesh. She shivers. When she cries out, her channel tightens around my cock and I let my head drop into the pillow as my climax rolls over me. I thrust until her hold relaxes and I have milked the last of the pleasure from her.

When I roll to her side and pull her against me, she buries her face in the crook of my neck and I wonder how I can ever leave her again.

TWENTY-SIX

Leilah

MY HEART SKIPS A BEAT AS THE DOOR CLOSES BEHIND Blade. When he stepped into my room, I hadn't intended to fuck him. When I woke up with him beside me, I did. I've wanted Blade since I met him a nearly a month ago. But fucking isn't what we'd done. He made me feel so…vulnerable. I swallow. I hadn't known fucking—making love—could be like this. A part of me wonders if Blade actually touched my soul and I'm struck with the strange feeling that he *knows* me. Loves me.

Had he loved Nova? Had he *known* her? But I know the answer. Yes, and yes. Had it been like this with all of them? Had Nova known all of them intimately? The answer again, yes. My mouth goes dry. How was that possible? Why would four men love one woman like that? Wait. Not four, but five. Who is the fifth? God help me. How could a woman deal with so much intensity?

I have to get out of here. I jump from bed and grab a long sleeve shirt and jeans from the closet, then begin to dress. Another question echoes off the inside of my skull. Did Blade sense the Shadows that entered my body in the Reaping? Had they followed me here? My chest tightens, but I don't know if my reaction is normal fear or if it's *them*.

"Stony?"

Where the hell is that pig?

I pause in buttoning my jeans. Shit. When Stony disappeared, I should have realized what was about to happen. She always knows when I'm going to get busy with a man. Guilt washes over me. 'Getting busy' isn't what happened between Blade and me. I grab clean socks, then stuff first the left foot into one, then the right. I get my tennis shoes from the closet and sit back on the bed.

"Stony," I call as I put on the first shoe. "I'm going to Grams' You can stay—"

A mouse emerges from the closet and scurries across the floor toward me.

"About time," I say, as I put on the other shoe.

She reaches me and I scoop her up and set her on the bed, then stand. "If my loophole for the blood pact doesn't work, I might be knocked back on my ass. You sure you want to go?"

She squeaks.

I narrow my eyes. "I'll make sure I don't land on the pocket you're in." I roll my eyes and put on my coat.

I return to the bed and put an open palm on the mattress. She climbs on and I deposit her inside the front jacket pocket. She squeaks, but I ignore the recrimination and pull the note from the drawer. Guilt stabs and I look at the door. What will Blade think about my *loophole?* Will he consider my actions a betrayal? Raith will. I shake off the thought. Nothing has changed. Not only do I need to put distance between myself and these men, I need to work on Grams' book. The danger is too great to decipher the book here.

I set the note on the desk, my attention on my signature. A sliver of Nova's wickedness surfaces and I wonder what Raith would do if I signed Nova? Raith? What about the others? Who am I kidding? I'll never tell them I know anything about Nova. Stony's right. Raith wouldn't believe me, and he would probably hate me even more for what he would believe was a pretense.

I retrieve Grams' spell book from its hiding pace and slip it into the empty inside coat pocket. I slip my cellphone into my back jeans' pocket, then grab my debit card from the desk drawer. I stuff it into the pocket with the spell book, then close the zipper.

I gently pat the pocket where Stony is, no doubt, snuggled into the corner and fast asleep. I'm glad to have her with me. She must be as exhausted as I am. When we get to the potionary, we're taking a long nap in my room.

Fear uncoils in my stomach. Fear? What am I afraid of? But I know. I'm afraid of Grams' influence. She may be dead, but she isn't gone.

I ease open the door. All is quiet. I peek out into the hallway. As expected, no one's around. I slip from the room and hurry along the hallway, then down the stairs. I reach the front door without a problem. The campus is still a ghost town. So far, I'm experiencing no ill effect from the blood pact. Then again, I'm still on Academy grounds. Oh, this is going to be interesting.

I reach the trees, then minutes later, the wall. I'm damn glad to be wearing my jacket. The temperature has to be near freezing. I scan the grounds for Watchmen, but even they're absent. I reach the wall and stare up at the top. I kind of want to laugh. If I'm wrong about the loophole, the magic of the blood pact will knock me back on my ass. If I'm right, well... then I found the best loophole ever.

"Hold onto your ass," I tell Stony.

A squeak emanates from my shirt pocket.

I leap, grab the top of the wall, then pull myself up, and swing my legs over to the other side of the wall. No problems yet, only the gentle push of the ward intended to keep out baddies. Of course, technically, I'm not off Academy grounds yet. I consider the possibilities, one of which could be the magic of a blood pact so strong it yanks me back up and over the wall. That could be uncomfortable. I drop onto the ground.

I freeze in a half crouch and wait several heartbeats, then slowly straighten and face the wall. How about that? I found a bona fide loophole in that damned blood pact. How long can I be gone before *The Three* figure out I'm gone? I'm betting until morning. That'll work. I'll take a nap, work on the spell book, and be back before dawn.

I walk a quarter mile, then order an Uber. Half hour wait. Damn. I reset the address for the intersection a mile down the road and start walking. A fifteen-minute walk with nothing to do but think. I've got too much to think about. As if Raith and Nova aren't enough, I've gone and fu—made love with Blade. No, I'd rather think about Raith. I grunt a laugh. I never thought I'd see the day when I would think that.

I pick up the pace. So, I knew *The Three* in another life. No, not three...five. Five? What the hell? They had wanted to live with me as husbands? My mind whirls. How would that even work? God, I can't go there. But my mind does go there and I see Raith as I saw him in the vision, eyes dark with desire and so tender that I want to wrap him in my arms and warm that cold vampire blood. The fire in Blade's eyes when he—

My thoughts screech to a halt. Fuck. Blade knew about the sigil that night I ran into him after Ethan waylaid me at the Witching Hour Cabaret Club to inform me The Academy was drafting me. I blow out a breath of frustration. Did Ethan know who I was when he slapped his dragon sigil on me that night? Yeah, they all know me—the fucking wolf included.

I rub my temples. I don't know if I can handle this. Truth is, I don't know how I can face Raith again. Nova stabbed him to save his life, but she wouldn't have had to do that if she hadn't been fucking Cordero.

Raith loved Nova. He hadn't tried to stop her—me—when I stabbed him, but remained motionless as if the hurt held him by invisible chains that even he, a powerful vampire, couldn't break free of. No wonder he hates me. Fuck, I hate myself.

Forty-five minutes later, the Uber driver lets us off at the potionary. I hurry onto the porch. The comforting low pulse of the wards press against me as I enter the house. I lock the door behind me, then take Stony out of my pocket and set her on the floor. She shifts into pig form and shakes like a dog.

"I'm starting to get a little hungry," I say. Her eyes light up and I laugh. "Yes, I'll order Chinese." Actually, Chinese sounds good.

I turn right in the foyer, walk through the arched doorway into the living room and halt. There's no sign of the damage the Thol'guk wreaked when he attacked me and the stranger. Which one of *The Three* cleaned up that mess? Not Raith, that's for sure. Ethan or maybe Blade when they came to make sure Stony was being fed that first week. Do they possess that kind of magic? I'm thinking no.

I phone in the order and, an hour later, Stony and I are on the couch in the living room. I locate a comedy on my phone's Netflix app and we watch while eating. Stony finishes off her veggie lo mien, sweet and sour tofu, and egg drop soup, then flops onto the carpet and promptly falls asleep. I, on the other hand, can't stop thinking about Raith.

I can't return to The Academy. I don't care that the Wall has named me as a High Potential, I can't face Raith every day. Hell, I can't face any of them. As for Blade…. Embarrassment warms my cheeks. Fuck, sex has never embarrassed me. Then again, what happened between us was more than sex. I unexpectedly recall Caleb in the Reaping when he'd thrown me on the bed and come down on top of me. That had been…very nice. Not to forget my first day at The Academy when that stupid spell backfired and my ass almost caught on fire—literally. I'd stripped off my jeans and was searching for cooling herbs when Ethan caught me in the classroom dressed in a t-shirt and a thong.

What had he said to me? *"You need a little…" he leaned closer and added in a whisper, "taming."*

The same shiver of desire that had rocked me last time slid along my arms. The dragon is pure heat. The memory flares with a vividness that steals my breath.

I arch my back and push against him. His cock is rock hard—and huge. He grasps my hips and I draw a sharp breath when the fingers gently squeeze. I need him.

His hands slide over my skin and leave blessed coolness in their wake. A new heat builds that sends a different electrical current straight to my core. I close my eyes and will his fingers lower. He slips a finger under the lace of my thong and I draw a sharp breath at the warmth of his touch.

The classroom door creaks open.

I jar from the memory, the juncture between my legs pounding with every beat of my heart. I breathe in and out slowly until my heart slows. The damned desire persists. I rub my temples. These guys are all too intense for my comfort. Hell, even as a wolf, Caleb exuded power.

Warmth ripples through me. The wolf probably saved my life more than once in the Reaping. He stuck to me like glue. Why? Because he knew me in another life? That's no small thing. Still, why did I meet them in this life? Given how I left things in that life, they can't possibly think any more highly of me than Raith does. A damned good reason not to return to The Academy.

I knew these men in another life. My most recent life? What's even more frightening is that they know I am that woman Nova. How do they know I'm her?

I shake my head. This whole thing is just…too strange. Too much. I should be loving the attention from these gorgeous men. That, I'm pretty sure, was Nova's mistake. I can never make that mistake again. I have to stay away from them.

Truth is, even without *them*, can I face those students who were with me in the Reaping? The mental picture rises of the guy turning slowly, head lolling to one side, the noose around his neck. My throat tightens. Why hadn't I saved him? I'd gotten cocky. And he'd died. There is some of Nova in me.

Nova?

Where have I heard that name before? Then I remember. Oh god, the Wall named me as a High Potential, but not just me. Nova and others. I close my eyes and envision the Wall that first day at The Academy. He names appear in memory, Ciarah, Brin, Emma and Nova.

I snap open my eyes. Nova was a past life. That has to mean the other three are past lives. How did the Wall know of these four incarnations? I suddenly wish Grams was here. She would know what all this means. I hysterical giggle escapes my mouth. Grams and I now have more in common than I ever thought we would. She practiced Shadow magic, I have Shadows inside me. Maybe Ariel was right—after all, even a psychopath like her can be wrong all the time—maybe I am like Grams.

I jam my eyes shut. Here we go, the bottom line. These five men frighten me, but they're just the excuse I'm using not to admit the truth. I'm a coward. That's the *real* truth. I don't want to face anyone who will discover that Shadows are inside me.

I *am* a fucking coward.

TWENTY-SEVEN

Caleb

An hour later, I leave Ethan in Raith's office to discuss business that doesn't interest me. Raith gave grudging permission for me to stay on Academy grounds. As if he could force me to leave. I emerge from the building into the night. I love brisk winter nights like these. I take the half dozen steps to the walkway, then reach the trees a moment later. I shift into wolf form and locate Leilah's scent among the myriad of other human scents. I follow it to a dormitory called Penncarrow. I halt within the trees and scan the windows of the building for any sign of her. I sigh. She could be anywhere. I could enter the building and follow her scent to her room. Would she allow me inside? Yes.

I shift into human form and emerge from the trees, wearing jeans, a long sleeve shirt, and a swede jacket and boots. I enter the building and shift back into wolf form. I easily pick up her scent and climb four flights of stairs and track her to room 410. I sniff at the crack beneath the door. The Fae has been here and he and Leilah—

We all know we share Leilah, but for her to have turned to Blade mere hours after we returned from the Reaping hurts. I sniff the crack beneath the door again. They were here, but they're gone now. I back up several steps. They didn't leave together. I return to the front door, then raise up on my hind legs and push the door open. I bound outside and follow her trail through the trees to the south wall.

I stare up at the eight-foot-high wall. So, she broke out of this prison. How did she leave without getting permission to leave? I laugh mentally. I'm betting she got permission from Blade, who didn't tell Raith. I'm half tempted to return to Raith's office and tell him how well his blood pact is working, but I'm not going to out Leilah—though I'm not thrilled with her taking off on her own. There's only one way to make sure she's okay.

I back up thirty feet, lunge forward into a run and, seconds later, sail over the wall. I land on the other side in snow trodden only by Leilah's booted feet. I don't need a wolf's keen sense of smell to follow her trail south. I follow her boot prints along the side road to the main road where large houses sit on acres of land. Ten minutes later, I discover that she got into a car at a deserted intersection. I catch a strange scent. The driver? Maybe, but the scent is—

Demon.

My hackles raise. Demons near The Academy? I recall Blade telling me about the Thol'guk at Miriam Crowe's home. This scent isn't the large green demon. I lower my head and slowly scan my surroundings for anything those sneaky creatures might shift into but detect nothing. I sniff the air, but still catch only the hint of its scent. I jerk my head in the direction of Leilah's scent. Is a demon tracking her?

An approaching car draws my attention behind me. I can't see the car beyond the curve in the road, but it'll be here soon. Even on a cloudy night like tonight, the car's headlights are sure to illuminate me. I race across the street and into the trees as the car's headlights appear around the curve and a large, black SUV with tinted windows speeds past.

After half a dozen paces, I halt. Another scent captures my attention. *Vampire*. And he's been here recently. I scan the trees. Nothing. Is he one of the students? Leilah is likely not the only student who plays hooky.

I continue south for half a mile before reaching an intersection. I wait for two passing cars, then pick up Leilah's scent. I duck back into the forest and follow the road until the trees quickly thin, where I race across open field. A wolf sighting in Westchester County, New York, would cause a stir after the absence of wolves these last centuries. Another car approaches. I drop onto my haunches on the snowy ground behind a fallen tree and wait until the small sedan passes, then follow the trail for two miles before I catch a whiff of the demon again.

I halt among the trees and a growl rumbles from my chest. I concentrate my sense of sight and smell but, still, can't get a lock on him. Demons are among the most difficult creatures to track.

I follow Leilah's scent and get lucky when her driver doesn't jump onto one of the parkways but stays on backroads until, twenty minutes later, I enter the shadows of a sparse residential area. It's still early evening. Traffic is light, but I'll have to be careful. A wolf sighting will put the entire county on my trail. As a human, my sense of smell isn't good enough for me to track Leilah. Where is she headed?

I weave between houses while following her trail another mile to where she exited the car and crossed the street to a three-story house. The nearest streetlight is forty feet away. Leilah doesn't have the front porch light on. No light shines on the porch of the neighboring house. Good.

Crouched in the yard across the street, I peer through dense shrubbery at Leilah's house. A small sign to the right of the front door reads Crowe Potionary. Crowe Potionary? Her grand-mother's house? This is where Miriam Crowe died—or drilled her way into Hell—using Shadow magic. What does Leilah want here? Knowing her, she's running her own little investigation.

A hint of light seeps over the backyard fence between her house and the neighbor to the right. I catch the smell of some-thing…. The pig. I sneeze. Leilah's familiar might be as formidable a protector as I am.

Three cars approach. I drop to my belly and watch until they pass. A figure crosses in front of the front curtained window of the house. Hunger ignites in me. Leilah. I need to be near her, to see for myself that she is still well. Memory flashes of her falling into my arms and the blood that stained the front of the red dress she wore the day Cordero shot her forty years ago. I block the image. She's here, alive and well, and as strong and beautiful as ever.

Pride fills me. I know she had to be afraid when the wolves in the Reaping stalked her, but she stood her ground. She tried to protect the boy…and me. The little fool.

If I shift into human form and knock on her door, will she turn me away? I sigh. Yes. She would likely never forgive me for following her. I catch a whiff of the demon. My hackles rise. Where the hell is the creature and what does it want with Leilah? I rise. Another car whizzes by. I sniff the air and catch another scent.

This scent isn't the demon.

TWENTY-EIGHT

Leilah

A LOUD KNOCKING STARTLES ME. I TURN IN A SLOW circle in the living room of Gram's house. What was I doing? Had I come in here from the kitchen?

"Stony," I call.

Where is that pig? I haven't seen her since…. I can't recall. I shake my head. She's got to be off napping in some corner of her house.

The knocking on the door resumes, insistent this time. What the hell? I hurry to the foyer and yank open the door. Seton Alexander stands on the porch. Am I dreaming? The last time I saw Seton was the night he'd shown up below my window after I'd awoken to find Grams standing over my bed chanting. She'd kicked me out the next day.

At six feet two with shoulder length, dark hair—and he still wears the same leather jacket—his bad boy look appears much more dangerous than I remember. But the soft light in his eyes tells me he's still *my* Seton. I throw myself into his arms. He hugs me tight and our seven-years separation melts away. I'm that fifteen-year-old girl who tagged along every chance I got.

He watched out for me and even helped me practice magic, now and then.

I draw back and look into his eyes. "What are you doing here?"

He pushes aside a lock of my dark hair and smiles. "Did you think I wouldn't come?"

Of course, he would come. He's my best friend, the only best friend I'd ever had. Except for Stony.

"Why did you leave?" he asks. "I looked for you."

Guilt washes over me. After Grams kicked me out, I searched for, but didn't find him. Seton often disappeared for a month or two. He never told me where he went, but I assumed he found a girl to hit the road with on his motorcycle and after a couple months he grew bored of her and returned.

I shrug. "You weren't around."

"Bad timing." He kisses my forehead. "Sorry. But that doesn't explain why you ran away."

"Ran away? Is that what she told you?"

He lifts a brow. "If you mean your grandmother, yes."

I can't believe it. She couldn't even own up to throwing me out. Had I known her at all? I pull free of Seton's arms and plop down on the old porch swing to the left of the door.

"She kicked me out."

He sits beside me and takes my hand in his. "I had a feeling."

I turn to face him and draw my left leg up under my right. "You always knew when something was wrong."

A shadow passes over his face. "Not well enough to figure out where you were."

I shrug. "I made a point of keeping a low profile." Not that I always succeeded.

He studies me. "That doesn't sound good."

"Forget it," I say. "What have you been up to?"

He leans back against the swing. "Not much. After I gradu-ated from The Academy, I spent some time on the road."

I wonder if he was looking for me, but say, "That's right. You graduated from The Academy. What in the world made you decide to go to school?"

He groans. "It wasn't my idea, if that's what you're thinking."

I laugh. "That damned Wall named you, too, huh?"

"No, I was named an honorary student."

"What? Honorary student? I thought all Academy students had to be named by the wall." That had been my misfortune. Though there had been several other names named with me. I have yet to understand why.

"It used to be that an honorary student might be named every few years," he says. "But now a student is chosen about once a year. I think it's politics. You know, *the powers that be* notice someone with strong powers who hasn't been named by the wall and"—he shrugs—"they induct us into the school. I always wondered if your grandmother brought me to the atten-tion of The Academy."

"Grams?" I frown. "Why would she do that?"

His brows lift. "I'm a pretty powerful warlock, if you recall."

"Maybe," I say with a laugh. I still find it odd that she might do that, but don't say so.

He stands. "You up for grabbing a bite to eat?"

I hesitate, struck by a sense of déjà vu that makes my surroundings spin for an instant.

"You okay?" he asks.

I stand and, thankfully, the feeling has passed. "I'm great. Where do you want to go?"

"I know this great Korean place. You still have a leather jacket?"

. . .

SETON AND I RIDE HIS BIKE. I TIGHTEN MY ARMS wrapped around his waist as he takes a curve on the rural road. It feels as if we've been riding for less than a minute, but I know it's been at least twenty minutes. I'm wearing the leather jacket I had when I lived with Grams, though I can't quite place how that's possible. I lost that jacket a year after I left New York. Seton feels so familiar, yet there's something missing I can't quite identify. I shake off the feeling. All that matters is that my friend is here with me.

We round the curve and I catch sight of two guys and a woman walking on the side of the road up ahead. Another déjà vu washes over me and I claw at the images that feel so close but remain out of reach. I hate déjà vu. I never see the images clearly, but the sense of familiarity often drives me to distraction. It's like an itch I can't quite reach.

We near the people and I tense. I know these people. Of all the roads in all of Westchester County, why did they have to take this one? Seton and I had a run-in with these shifters down in New York City about a month before Grams kicked me out. That was seven years ago. Maybe they won't recognize me. Even as the thought forms, I realize what a fool I am. They aren't likely ever to forget me.

I lean close to Seton's ear and shout over the roar of the motorcycle, "Turn around."

He ignores me—just as he'd done last time. We near them and they don't bother to look back or get off the road but walk side-by-side as if they own the road. Just like most fools who walk on the roads out here.

Seton veers far left and maneuvers around them. I look into the righthand mirror. The girl's head turns enough that I know she's looking in our direction. She points and shouts something.

The three of them launch into a run and, in seconds, they've shifted and are racing after us. I swear, I can hear Seton laugh. That's like him. He's cocky as hell and loves stirring up trouble. I watch in the mirror as the wolves draw closer. I glance over Seton's shoulder at the speedometer. He's slowed to thirty-five.

Fuck.

Shifter wolves are fast as hell. A strong wolf can rival a cheetah at sixty miles an hour or more. We take a left-turning curve and I hug close to Seton as we lean into the curve. I watch in the mirror as the wolves veer off the road to our left on an intercept course. We round the curve and the wolves race across open ground to our left. Anger whips through me. After seven years, they're still angry because we didn't let them steal our wallets.

"Mother fuckers," I mutter. I lean against Seton's back and say in his ear, "They intend to cut us off."

He nods and, to my surprise, picks up speed. They run faster as we approach the intercept point. On the open road, a motorcycle can outrun a shifter any day. On two-lane, curvy rural roads, they have a real chance of catching us. Fuck this shit.

"Slow down," I tell Seton.

He glances over his shoulder and I nod. He shrugs and slows down. I envision a mirror likeness of Seton and I on his motorcycle and chant,

"Mirror, mirror on the road,

"Who's the fastest of them all?"

As our mirror image separates from us, I whisper, "Cloak of invisibility shield us from their eyes."

The wolves keep running as if to intercept the mirror image of us.

I grin. "Dumbasses."

My smile drops away when the wolves turn toward us. Seton picks up speed and whispers something I can't discern.

The trees melt away and the roar of the motorcycle recedes until we're standing on a dark street in—

We're in New York City on that same street where the wolves tried to rob us.

"Seton," I cry.

He steps past me, just as he did that night, and I catch sight of the shifters standing ten feet away. What are we doing here? How did we get here? Where is the country road and his motorcycle?

"We can take them," Seton says in a low voice. "Remember what I taught you."

What? I stare, uncomprehending.

"Remember," he whispers. "Anger."

Then I remember. Seton taught me that anger is one of the strongest forces in magic. *"Draw on anger, and you can't lose. Anger brought about one of the biggest catastrophes in history,"* he'd said with a laugh. "Be that sorceress."

Elexea, Damien's Demon Bride, had been so enraged when the Atlantean king sent an assassin to kill her that she unleashed magic powerful enough to sink Atlantis. She killed herself in the process, but she took the assassin with her.

The same anger I'd felt then wells up and I shout, "Suck this, mother fuckers."

Wind breaks through the ground and curls into a tornado with a deafening rush of air that nearly drowns out the shifters' screams. They whirl and lunge away from the tornado, but it yanks them up into its swirling center. My hair snaps with stinging force around my face.

"Woo hoo!" Seton scoops me up and swings me around. "I knew you could do it," he shouts. The rest of his words are lost in the roar of wind.

A police siren blares in the distance. I whip my head in the direction of the street. The cops are on their way. Release of so much magic is sure to have alerted the Margiddian Watchmen, as well. They'll want to be sure we're not practicing magic that will draw Shadows to us. I'm not Grams.

"I don't practice Shadow magic," I say, and realize I'm lying on the sofa in Gram's living room, staring up at the ceiling.

TWENTY-NINE

Ethan

DESPITE RAITH'S ANGER TOWARD LEILAH, I GET THE feeling that he wants to confirm she's okay. If not for the fact that he's headed to the infirmary where they were keeping Chelsea when she escaped, I would almost guess that he gave Blade and I assignments so that he could check on her himself. But that's just my jealousy. Chelsea's mother has arrived. I don't envy Raith that meeting.

Once I finish my interview with Ariel, my next duty is to assign two Watchmen to the potionary. We want to be ready if the angels make another attempt to conjure Damien. I'm still stunned—we're all stunned—that the angels were able to conjure him. I wouldn't have believed they had the power. I can't recall a single instance where anyone conjured Damien. He's a powerful demigod. More powerful than some gods.

I round the cafeteria when I catch sight of a student headed my way on the walkway. Jonas. His eyes lock with mine and I read relief. I increase my pace and reach him a moment later.

"Is something wrong, Jonas?"

"I—" His gaze drops. "I'm probably just being stupid."

I lay a hand on his shoulder. "Not a chance. What's on your mind? Have you spoken with your parents?"

He looks up at me. "Oh, yeah. They want me to come home, but I told them I'm okay."

"Maybe a short visit wouldn't hurt?" I suggest.

"I'm not a baby," he shoots back.

"Maybe going home for a day or two isn't about you," I say.

His brow furrows, then he says, "Oh, you mean it might make my parents feel better?"

"Maybe," I say.

"I guess I could go for two days. You won't let them take me out of The Academy, will you?"

"Is that what they want to do?"

He shrugs. "My mom worries about everything. She didn't want to let me come to The Academy in the first place. She might try to say that I'm too upset to come back."

"Everyone who's taken in a Reaping goes through counseling," I say. "How about we tell your mom that she and your dad can talk to the counselor—with your permission."

He considers. "As long as the counselor sees that I'm okay. I am okay, so it's not a lie," he quickly adds.

"Talk to your folks and let them know you're fine with coming home for two days, You will talk to the counselor again before you go. Does that work?"

He nods.

"Now, what did you want to talk to me about?" I ask.

"I...I want to know if Leilah's okay."

I smile. "She's resting—which is what you should be doing."

"I didn't have it as bad as she did."

"What do you mean?" I ask carefully.

"I know it was only a lucid dream, but it was so real."

"Lucid dreams *are* real," I say. "They're an alternate reality."

"Are you sure?" he asks, and I get the distinct feeling he doesn't want the lucid dream to be real.

"It's kind of like the Reaping," I say. "That's an alternate reality, too."

"Like the virtual War Games," he says. "Only, the rules are different there than here."

"That's right," I say.

"We couldn't be hurt in the virtual War Games, but we could be hurt in the Reaping. And the lucid dream, I guess," he says, more to himself than me.

"But you didn't get hurt," I say. "Neither did Leilah."

He hesitates and a chill stirs in my belly. Something is wrong with Leilah. "What happened, Jonas?" I ask.

"I-you're sure she's fine?" he asks in a half whisper.

"I am," I say, despite the fear clawing at my insides. "Why do you think she isn't?"

"I don't know that she isn't okay. I just..."

I force calm and wait.

"Ariel got into trouble for what she did in the Reaping," he says.

What in God's name did Leilah do? "Did Leilah do something wrong?" I ask in a neutral voice.

He shakes his head vigorously. "No. She saved everyone—including Ariel, which she didn't deserve. She hurt a lot of people. She tried to hurt me, but Leilah didn't let her. I wasn't there for the hanging." His brow creases. "I was a coward. I was hiding."

"Hiding doesn't make you a coward," I reply. "Discretion is often the better part of valor."

He regards me. "Really?"

"Really," I say. "Now tell me what has you worried?"

He swallows. "The Shadows that went inside her."

THIRTY

Blade

———

Leaving Leilah's bed has never been easy. Tonight, was nearly impossible. Once I finish my business with Chelsea, I'll return and make love to Leilah all night long. Despite the fact I just left her, my cock begins to harden, again.

I reach the infirmary where Chelsea is being held. Anger flares in the center of my belly. Fifteen and she tried twice to kill another student. I enter the building and close off my mind. Chelsea is a gifted mage and empath. She might know I'm on my way to see her. If not, she will sense my feelings once I'm in the room with her.

Cromwell emerges from the nurse's office. "I'm immensely relieved you're here. I called the girl's parents. They're on their way—and furious."

I grunt. "I would be surprised if they weren't. House Nightlow is an influential house. Lady Nightlow won't ever believe her daughter is guilty of attempted murder." I recall running into Chelsea on campus a couple weeks ago and thinking that she hadn't displayed any of her mother's fanaticism. She has now.

"Her mother is going to make trouble," Cromwell mutters.

"No truer words have ever been spoken. Olympia will deal with her." I frown. "Speaking of Olympia, have you seen her?"

"No," he replies. "One would think she would want to welcome the students back."

"Yes," I murmur. "One would."

Cromwell unlocks the exam room door and I enter an empty room. I race across the room to the window, which stands open. Cold air pours in.

"Cromwell!" I shout.

He bursts into the room. His eyes lock onto the window and widen.

"When did you last see her?" I demand.

He hurries to the window. "About two hours ago, when we locked her in the room."

I curse. This is my fault. I should have come directly here, instead of going to Leilah.

"The window was sealed with magic." He runs a finger around the window seal.

"The girl is a strong mage," I mutter.

"Penelope cast the spell," he says. "Chelsea is no match for her."

"I think you're wrong on that score," I say.

"I'm not mistaken." He pulls a small wand from his back pocket and waves the tip over the window as he murmurs *"Revelare."*

A whisp of smoke-like energy appears and slides along the seams of the window, then fades.

Cromwell looks at me. "A *libertas* elemental. Is Chelsea's mother a powerful enough mage to command elementals on Academy grounds all the way from Pennsylvania?"

"Maybe," I say.

His mouth thins. "We've strengthened the wards around The Academy. At the very least, we would have been alerted if someone tried to enter the grounds. I think someone here at The Academy cast the spell. I should have sensed the magic."

"The girl created magic strong enough to thwart Ethan, Leilah Crowe, and other students when she made the attempt on Leilah's life," I say. "Chelsea is stronger than we realized."

"I'll get a search team together," he says.

"She's long gone."

"Maybe. But no matter how strong her mother is, she couldn't have reached The Academy yet. That means someone else helped her. If they're still here, I'll find them."

"Let's expedite things," I say.

An hour later, Penelope Benedict has used her considerable ability to trace Chelsea's trail over the south wall.

"How the bloody hell did she elude the Watchmen?" I demand of Cromwell, but know her escape isn't his fault. It's not even the Watchmen's fault. Students rarely sneak out of The Academy—they understand the penalties—so we don't add extra patrols to keep them in. Keeping attackers out is the real goal. "Double the Watchmen guard," I order Cromwell.

The three of us hurry toward the Admin building, where our cars are parked.

"I've got to follow the girl," I say.

"She's probably headed home," Penelope says in her light Portuguese accent.

"Maybe, but if anything happens to her, Lady Nightlow will cause problems," I say.

"I'll go with you," Penelope says.

"Excellent. We'll go straightaway. Cromwell, please report our findings to Raith and let him know I'm looking for Chelsea."

At the administration building, Cromwell continues inside while Penelope and I head to my car, parked in the parking garage attached to the admin building.

Half an hour later, my blood runs cold when I realize where Chelsea is headed.

The potionary.

"Hold on," I tell Penelope, and step on the gas as we round the curve in the road.

THIRTY-ONE

Leilah

I TURN MY HEAD SO I CAN SEE STONY SNORING SOFTLY on the carpeted floor nearby. The movie is still playing on my phone. I return my gaze to the ceiling, then close my eyes and release a deep breath. Thank god Stony's asleep. This was a bona fide dream. Still, I'd rather not tell Stony about it. I open my eyes. Given that Raith told me Seton is the Greek demigod Tychon, I'm not surprising I dreamt about him.

I want to believe Raith lied about Seton being Tychon, but I know he didn't lie. Raith is a lot of things, but a liar isn't one of them. I told myself the gods often involve themselves in the lives of humans and that Seton simply decided he liked me, but I can't help wondering why me? A memory surfaces and I draw in a sharp breath, then look quickly to be sure I haven't woken Stony. She doesn't stir.

In my dream, Seton told me that the Wall hadn't named him as a High Potential, but that Grams nominated him. I search my memory but find no reference to such a thing ever happening and come up empty. What a strange thing for him to tell me.

I sit up. I'm being stupid. Dreams are weird. That's all. I

stand and scoop up the phone. I really don't want to think about Seton right now. If he did show up on my doorstep, I honestly don't know what I would do. I need time to process... whatever this is.

I jab the screen of my phone and turn off the movie. I shove the phone into my back pocket and grab Grams' spell book from my coat pocket, then head upstairs. At my room, I stop. The door stands open as it had been the last time I was here. I hadn't expected anything to change, but I suddenly wonder if I can work here. It's just so strange to see the room look the same as when I lived here.

"Stop being such a coward," I mutter, and enter the room.

I glance from the bed to the desk, then decide on the desk. With a deep breath, I sit in the chair and lay the spell book on the desk, open to the first page. I pull my phone from my back pocket, open the camera, then lean back and begin reading the picture of page two in the spell book.

I considered telling the other witches who fought with us during that last Shadow battle what we learned during that battle, but they would believe me even less now than they would have then.

I draw a sharp breath. *The last Shadow battle?* Is she referring to *the* battle *The Three* fought? No, it couldn't be. I never heard that. She never told me she'd been there. Would she have told me?

"Dammit, Grams. One of these days I'm going to figure out how to raise you from the dead. Then you'll answer my questions."

I continue reading.

I wouldn't have thought the bond we witches shared during that last battle could be broken, especially our bond, Olympia.

Olympia was there, too?

I glance at the book laying open on the desk. It's the size of an average spell book, smaller than a mass market paperback. Each page is roughly large enough for an average spell. I've only looked at two pages, but so far not even a tiny spell. Is this a journal? I pick up the book and flip through the pages until the writing stops a quarter of the way through the book. Shit, even as a journal there's not much here. I set the book back on the desk and read the next line.

The most important thing is that I've found a way into Hell.

"What the fuck?" I blurt.

I reread the line.

The most important thing is that I've found a way into Hell.

Grams found a way into Hell? How is that even possible? The Hell Gates have been sealed for thousands of years. Maybe she'd been right, she was crazy. Even if she could find a way into Hell, why go? Did she want to break the seal on the Hell Gates? Was Grams a follower of the Zidruhin? The Zidruhin worship Damien and swear that one day they'll help him open the Hell Gates so that he can combine his Shadow magic with the powers of his father, Hades. I realize my hands are shaking and set the phone on my desk. I consider not reading more, but my eyes move to the next line almost of their own volition.

We can't go on living in fear. Death is better than fear. He must be freed.

Who is "he"? Whoever the fuck "he" is, isn't worth risking Damien being able to team up with Hades. Margidda wouldn't survive. What the hell was wrong with Grams?

Fear constricts around my heart like a vice. Am I in over my head? Maybe I should show the book to *The Three*.

Raith's face flashes in memory as he was when Nova left him in that alcove, a knife protruding from his chest. Forget Raith. I could give the book to Ethan or Blade—then disappear. Will they let me disappear?

I can't stop myself from reading the last line on the page.

Who would have thought Shadow Hell was the key?

THIRTY-TWO

Caleb

VAMPIRE.

A demon *and* a vampire lurking around Leilah's house?

I scan the shadows to the left and right of the house. Raith is the only vampire I've ever been able to tolerate for any length of time. Based on what I saw in his office earlier today, Leilah only tolerates him. I'm betting she's not a lover of vampires, either. So why is a vampire hanging around her house? Whatever the reason, my blood sings with the need to rip his throat out.

Leilah lives at The Academy and just returned from the Reaping. No one could know she would decide to come here tonight. Unless they followed her from the Academy—which the demon had.

This demon isn't the Thol'guk that attacked Leilah. The green demon has a distinct smell. This demon is an upper demon with the power to take other forms. But he could be a dozen different types of demons with powers that varied from shape shifting to spell casting almost as sophisticated as a witch's magic.

If word got out that Miriam was looking for a way into Hell, demons would want that knowledge. Demons on the earthly plane have been stuck here since the Hell Gates were locked. A ticket home is a damned good reason for a demon to be hanging around Miriam Crowe's home. Would a vampire have an interest in finding a way into Hell? Or maybe communicating with someone in Hell?

Why didn't Raith post Watchmen around the house? He, Blade or Ethan should have realized that demons—and maybe vampires—would be prowling the vicinity.

I might be able to kill the demon and vampire, but maybe not before one of them breaks into the house. Leilah isn't helpless and her familiar is fearsome, but how can I risk a demon or vampire getting near her? Hell, I have yet to catch sight of either of them. I could sniff them out, but they might spot me before I spot them. Should I get Leilah out of the house? She might be angry I followed her, but she would be safe. She, the pig, and I would make a damn good team.

Why hasn't the demon or vampire made a move? If they'd entered the house, the pig would have raised a ruckus. Then I understand. There must be wards around the house. Pride fills me.

That's my girl.

I've got to draw them away. *Then* kill them. How do I get a demon to chase me? Hell, how do I get a vampire to chase me? I've chased demons and run from demons. But never purposely tried to get one to chase me. Maybe that's the wrong tack. Since Leilah has wards around the house—

Shadows shift in the side yard between Leilah's house and the neighbor's. A human form. Probably the vampire. That's all I need. I jet across the street to the yard in front of the porch, out of sight of whatever moved to the right of the house. The wards around the house pulse. Good. Hunkered low, I creep along the porch to the side of the house, then peer into the darkness.

I discern a slight shift in the darkness at the rear of the house where a tall wooden fence separates the back yard. The tiny bit of light from the back yard makes him even easier to see. Hugging the wall, I slip around the side and creep forward. The scent of the vampire is strong. My heart picks up speed. I easily distinguish his form at the fence. Blood pounds through my ears. I creep, inch by inch, head low, the need to clamp my teeth into his flesh gnaws as I draw nearer. Wolves are one of the few creatures that can kill a vampire. Killing them—truly killing them—isn't easy. I have to get my jaws around his jugular and rip him apart.

He's got his back to me. I start forward again. I approach within five feet of him and crouch. I lunge. He turns and I recognize the vampire who'd entered Raith's office earlier today.

THIRTY-THREE

Ethan

I reach Ariel's dorm room and force thoughts of Leilah and Shadows from my mind. I nod to the two Watchmen standing outside her door, then knock. No answer.

I knock again and call, "Ariel, it's Ethan." Still no answer. I look at the Watchman to the left. "Any sounds inside?

"She's been pretty quiet," the Watchman, Kane, replies.

"Thanks," I say, then, "Ariel, I'm coming in," and enter.

Ariel turns from where she's staring out the window. "Is my father here?"

I leave the door open and take only two paces into the room. "I'm sorry, not yet. Domini should be here soon. We need to talk."

She crosses to her bed and drops onto the mattress. "I don't have to talk to you."

"You don't have any feelings about killing a fellow student?"

"I didn't kill anyone," she says.

"We've got a dozen witnesses who say you orchestrated the hanging of Robert Janson and the attempted hanging of Chelsea Nightlow."

She shrugs. "That was The Shadows' fault."

Bootfalls echo in the hallway outside her room and, an instant later, Headmaster Domini enters.

"Ethan." His gaze shifts to Ariel. "Ms. Littleton."

"I was just asking Ariel how she feels about leading the hanging of Robert Janson," I say.

"Say what you want, I can't help that Shadows got to me," she replies without emotion.

"No one is blaming you for being infected by Shadows," Domini said. "But you do have some responsibility for how you responded."

"It wasn't my fault," she shoots back.

I glance at Domini, who asks, "Who's fault was it?"

"Leilah Crowe."

I blink in surprise.

"She was using Shadow magic—just like her grandmother," Ariel rushes on. "She was using Shadow magic before we were taken in the Reaping."

"What proof have you that she was practicing Shadow magic?" Domini asks.

"In the Reaping, we saw her. She was communicating with the Shadows. She ordered them to stop, and they obeyed. They were crawling on her arms and shoulders."

Fear seizes my heart and squeezes. Is Jonas right? Did Leilah get infected?

"According to reports of other students, Shadows were crawling all over you and the other students who participated in the hanging," I say carefully.

Ariel shrugs. "Like I said, that was her fault. She commanded them to chase us. Ask Anthony. He was there."

"I understand you and Anthony were chasing Jonas," I say. "Anthony threatened him and other students with a tree branch."

She rolls her eyes. "The tree branch was to fight off the wolves. Leilah Crowe was there—with one of the wolves. I bet she didn't tell you that. We were trying to save Jonas from her. She was feeding black balls of energy to the Shadows."

"What?" Domini blurts.

I snap my head in his direction.

"What do you mean 'feeding black balls of energy'?" he asks, his voice calm.

"She conjured these black balls of energy and tossed them at the Shadows," Ariel says. "Everyone could see that she was using Shadow magic. I mean, who conjures black balls of energy? Things got way worse after that."

Domini opens his mouth to reply, but I cut him off, "How could things get worse, Ariel? You instigated a hanging."

She scowls. "I didn't instigate the hanging. The students who were pulling the ropes are the murderers."

"Witnesses say you ordered the students holding the ropes to hang Chelsea and Robert."

She jumps to her feet and narrows her eyes on me. "Is your witness Leilah Crowe?"

"We have several witnesses," I say. "Ariel." I take four steps to where she stands, grasp her shoulders, and ease her onto the edge of her bed. I squat so that I'm eye level with her and say, "A student is dead. You aren't the only person responsible, but you did play a major role in his death." Fear flickers in her eyes, but I know that fear is for herself, and no one else. "You won't be staying at The Academy."

"You can't kick me out. My father won't let you."

"Do you really want to stay here when your fellow students know of your part in Robert's death?"

"Do they know of Leilah Crowe's part?" she hisses. "She made the ground open up and swallow us."

I nod. "Yes, she told us about that. As did other witnesses."

"Jonas, you mean," she retorts. "He's her puppet. He would say anything she told him to say."

"I understand you had him tied up and led him by a rope," I say.

"That was just so that he wouldn't run away. He's a danger to himself. Leilah had the ground swallow us. She tried to kill *all* of us. Is she being expelled?"

"That is a good question," a male voice says.

I rise as Ariel's father and mother enter the room with Kane close behind. Mrs. Littleton pushes past him and rushes to Ariel.

Ariel jumps to her feet and throws herself into her mother's arms. "I didn't do anything wrong, Mom. Honest, I didn't."

Mrs. Littleton strokes Ariel's hair. "I know. It's all right. We're here now."

I nod to Kane, who returns to his post in the hallway.

Mr. Littleton crosses to his wife and daughter. "How dare you interrogate her without us present?"

"We didn't interrogate her, Mr. Littleton." Domini steps closer and extends a hand. "I'm Headmaster Ed Domini."

The man ignores him and locks eyes with me. "We're taking Ariel home."

"Good," I say. "But please be aware that you will be hearing from the Grand Witch about the next steps."

"Next steps?" Kathryn Littleton says, and looks at her husband. "Philip."

He motions her and Ariel forward. "Come on. We're going home."

Arm wrapped around her daughter, Kathryn walks with Ariel from the room.

Philip Littleton says to me, "Where is Olympia? I want to speak with her."

"She is indisposed at the moment," Domini says before I can reply.

I resist the urge to tell him to shut up and say, "Philip, we have two dozen witnesses who attest to Ariel's actions." He opens his mouth to reply, but I cut him off, "She instigated two hangings. We're lucky the other girl was saved. But a boy died, and Ariel threatened and terrorize other students."

His mouth twists in anger. "Is the person who *saved* the girl Leilah Crowe—daughter of Miriam Crowe? You can't possibly take the word of the granddaughter of a witch who killed herself practicing Shadow magic over the daughter of upstanding Margiddians."

"We not only can, but we do," Domini says with more force than I've seen him exhibit. "Mr. Littleton, Leilah Crowe is by far not the only witness to your daughter's crimes."

"Crimes?" Philip blurts. "These are children who were taken in a Reaping." His gaze swings back onto me. "You remember what a Reaping is, don't you, Bordeaux?"

"Yes," I reply. "I remember. I also remember the Shadow War where some Margiddians preyed on other Margiddians. Being infected by Shadows is not an excuse for cruelty—or murder."

Philip's eyes blaze and I tense in readiness for the heat that suddenly radiates off him. He isn't as powerful a dragon as I am, but he's no slouch.

Domini steps between us and says in a voice so dangerous that the hairs on the back of my neck rise, "Do not test us."

Philip blinks, then his mouth thins. "I will expect to hear from Olympia."

"You may count on hearing from her," Domini replies. "I suggest you prepare your daughter for the stripping of her powers."

"Stripping of her powers?" His hands fall into fists, but he turns and stalks from the room.

Domini watches him go, then says to me, "I believe we need to talk at length with Ms. Crowe."

THIRTY-FOUR

Leilah

WHAT THE FUCK COULD SHADOW HELL POSSIBLY BE the key to? Could Grams believe Shadow magic has something to do with Shadow Hell? That might not be a stretch. In the eons since the Hell Gates have been locked, not even the most powerful witches have been able to communicate with anyone in Hell. On the other hand, there are those who swear they talk to souls in Shadow Hell.

I snort. If we can communicate with souls in Shadow Hell, that means Grams is ignoring my efforts to contact her. Unless she didn't end up in Shadow Hell. Yeah, a white witch who turned to Shadow magic, she's going straight to Hell—or Shadow Hell.

Could Grams have communicated with someone in Shadow Hell? She easily had the power to talk with the dead. There are some powerful badasses in Shadow Hell who could tell her how to use Shadow magic. My insides quiver with anger. She killed herself trying to master the darkest magic that exists. Now she's in Shadow Hell with whatever asshole she was trying to contact. I hope they're having a big party roasting each other over an open fire pit. She can burn forever, for all I care.

Grams was one of the most powerful witches around. What if she teams up with the assholes in Shadow Hell? So what? It's not possible for anyone to escape Shadow Hell or to make trouble for us in the earthly plane. Shadow Hell is a one way trip. *In.*

My eye catches the line *Hades and Morningstar will also be freed.* There's only one way the ruler of Hell and the Underworld—an extension of Hell—could be freed. If the Hell Gates are opened. Was Grams trying to open the Hell Gates? She wouldn't be the first witch to try.

Tears spring to my eyes.

"Stop being stupid," I order.

Detective Mills was right. People change. Or maybe Grams was never who I thought she was. I don't have to worry about who she was or her trying to open the Hell Gates. She's dead. Still, I can't help wondering what she meant by *We can't go on living in fear. Death is better than fear. He must be freed.* Who can't go on living in fear and who is the "he" that must be freed? Hades? The Morningstar? I yank my gaze back onto the line *Hades and the Morningstar will also be freed.* Also? That implies "along with" someone else. The "he"?

"Goddamn you, Grams." I tap the image for the next page in the book.

If anyone is capable of finding this book, it's you, Olympia. Yes, I know you are reading this book.

I blow out a breath. Of course. I should have known. Grams left the book for the Grand Witch to find. Unexpected hurt coils in my belly. I'm stupid. I never really thought she'd left the book in *my* room for me to find. Grams probably hadn't thought of me since kicking me out. After all, she had better things to do.

I read on.

When I'm gone, you will move heaven and earth to find out what I was up to and what happened to me. If all goes well, you won't find so much as a molecule of my remains. (Which will drive you to distraction and please me just a little.) You can stop looking. If you can't find any remains, that means I reached Shadow Hell.

I grunt. "Good for you, Grams. You killed yourself in order to go to Shadow Hell."

Wait. Had she used Shadow magic to try to get to Shadow Hell? Practicing Shadow magic ensured she would go to Shadow Hell when she died. Another thought strikes and I yank my eye back to the line that reads *If all goes well, you won't find so much as a molecule of my remains.* When a person dies, their body remains on the earthly plane and decays. Why hadn't Grams' body remained behind? Not just her body. Like she said, not so much as a molecule remained. Why?

Because she didn't die.

I collapse against the chair back. This is fucking Twilight Zone shit. No one can go to Shadow Hell alive. Then why were no remains found? Did she disappear? What if someone kidnapped her and—

Now I'm being stupid. She didn't disappear any more than she entered Shadow Hell without being dead. Though, if anyone could do find a way into Shadow Hell alive, it would be Grams. But what could she hope to accomplish? The next line reads:

I know, my old friend, that the god of the angels is locked in Hell.

What-the-fuck? I quickly reread the line and the one that follows.

I know, my old friend, the god of the angels is locked in Hell. Can you imagine the god's bad luck to be visiting his son the Morningstar when the Hell Gates were locked all those eons ago?

God—The god who claims to have created this world—has been locked in Hell all these years? No way. No fucking way. The world would be overrun with demons, if that god weren't around to keep them in check. But the thought niggles in a way I don't like.

If Grams left the book for Olympia.... Why leave this information for the Grand Witch? So she could follow in Grams' footsteps and blow herself to bits, too? Even if Grams is right—and there's no way she can be—and the god of the angels is in Hell, there's not a damn thing anyone can do to free Him.

Maybe. Over the years, some have tried. The Zidruhin, in particular, have made it their mission to try. But no one has come close to succeeding. No. This isn't about anyone following Grams into Shadow Hell. This is about the Grand Witch understanding what happened to her. We know Grams was practicing Shadow magic, but we don't know why—or, I guess, I should say, we assumed she wanted power, but we couldn't know for sure. I'm also betting the Grand Witch doesn't know that Yahweh is in Hell. Then again, what do I know? Maybe she does. Grams didn't seem to think so.

I grimace. I'm acting like this insanity is real. My head begins to throb. I'm out of my depth here. I should turn this book over to Olympia. But I won't.

Two hours later, Stony lays on my bed snoring and I've read most of Grams' book, which contains thoughts on how The Shadows would return sooner than we think—yeah, thanks to people like her who are practicing Shadow magic—and how the gods are experiencing nightmares again—I have no idea what that's about and I'm not sure I want to know. Still, I read on.

Olympia, you, and I know, to save Margidda, we must open the Hell Gates. Tell the world otherwise, but I was there with you when Raith and Ethan fought The Shadows in the dream world. We kept quiet and allowed Margidda to continue to believe that Damien needs Hades to control The Shadows. But Damien only needs his Demon Bride. She's close. I felt her. You felt her.

Perhaps I should have told someone. I know that's why you distanced yourself from me. Had we told anyone that opening the Hell Gates is Margidda's salvation, our powers would have been stripped from us. I don't blame you for distancing yourself from me. You knew I wouldn't be able to remain silent forever. At least this way, you needn't worry that I'll take you down with me.

You and I are the only ones who can open the Hell Gates. But without you, I can't break our spell. I know you're betting on that keeping you safe, and you are right.

I jerk my eyes back onto the words *our spell. Our spell?* Grams and the Grand Witch cast a spell? I jump to my feet. My chair topples over and thuds to the carpet. Stony stirs, but I ignore her, my heart thundering, eyes on the book. What the motherfucking hell is going on? Grams is—I choke on the thought. Grams is saying—

I can't even think the words. It's not possible. It's just not possible.

Stony snorts. I whirl to face her.

Her black eyes bore into me. "What's wrong?" she says in perfect English.

I can only shake my head. She looks from me to the book, then jumps from the bed and trots to the desk.

"No, Stony."

I take a step to the desk, but she bumps me with her sizeable rump and I fall on my ass. She rises up on her hind legs and braces her front hooves on the edge of the desk, then reads the page. I remain seated and hold my breath. A moment later, Stony snorts a true piggie snort that has no meaning, then twists her head and looks at me over her shoulder. Night howler pigs can live to be centuries old, but I have no idea how old Stony is. Until we returned to New York, I hadn't known what she was, nor had I seen her in her true form. Even if I had, I wouldn't have been able to guess her age. How could I know what a young or old night howler pig looks like? At this moment, however, despite the fact that pigs really don't have any facial expressions, something in her demeanor tells me that she is very ancient, and I am suddenly very thankful.

"I don't know what to do," I whisper.

"Believe," she replies.

I stare. "Believe that my grandmother was one of the original sorceresses that locked the Hell Gates? That's—that's insane."

"Why?" she snorts.

"Stony," I whisper, "the sorceresses have never returned to Earth. They're believed to be trapped in Shadow Hell or maybe ascended to another plane."

"You don't know that they have never returned. No one knows that. Your grandmother and the Grand Witch are powerful witches. They are good candidates." She returns her attention to the book and uses her nose to turn the page.

I hesitate. Should I read more? Aw, hell. I jump to my feet and stand behind Stony.

Your position as Grand Witch may survive the coming battle. Then again, you may fall. Strange, isn't it, that we're now on opposite sides?

The Shadows will rule Margidda and eventually the human world. Do you think you can survive if Margidda falls? I can't wait any longer. We must have a fighting chance. I must give Leilah a chance at a real life.

My heart thunders. She must give me a chance at a real life?

"Stony," I whisper.

Stony drops back onto all fours and sets her butt on the floor, as my eyes catch the final lines in the book,

If I don't return, you must follow me. You must try where I failed. You must save us.

I command the power of the darkest Shadows,

Open your door and let me safely enter.

I yank my eyes from the spell. "Did you see that?" I say in a hoarse voice.

"I can read," Stony says in Chinese.

"What does she mean that she has to give me a chance at a real life?"

"Shadows must be stopped," she replied.

"Grams kicked me out," I say.

"She can't take you with her."

I frown. "You're being stupid."

"You're stupid."

"None of this can be real," I say.

"Then where's her body?"

I narrow my eyes. "I hate you." I shoot a sideways glance at the spell. "I haven't gone into the basement."

Stony pushes off her butt and trots toward the door. I hesitate for two heartbeats, then follow.

THIRTY-FIVE

Ethan

I CAN'T BELIEVE THAT I WAS SO FOOLISH AS TO ALLOW Domini to accompany me to Leilah's dorm room. The thought occurred to me that she would likely be sleeping, even though it's only eight in the evening. But the truth is, I longed to see that she was well, that Jonas's concern about her and Shadows is unfounded.

I'm a stupid, selfish bastard.

Domini and I stand at Leilah's desk. He holds the note she addressed to me, Blade and Raith, requesting permission to leave The Academy.

Domini looks at me and frowns. "Why is Ms. Crowe asking you, Blade, and Raith for permission to leave The Academy?"

"We instructed all students that they were to stay in their rooms. She's clearly breaking the rules." In more ways than he can possibly know.

His frown deepens. "Asking Raith's permission, I could understand—though why she's asking permission through a note...."

I shake my head. "I don't know. Maybe she's hedging her bets."

"By asking permission in a note?" he asks.

Yeah, I silently fume. That was how the little fool got around asking our permission, per the agreement of the blood pact—and she must have gotten around us, otherwise, we would have *felt* her trying to violate the pact. I should have known she would find a loophole. Raith is going to lose his cool over this, and I can't blame him.

"Where is she going?" Domini says. "Her only living relative was Miriam Crowe."

"Home, I would guess."

"As in the potionary?"

"Yes."

"Then we had better track her down," Domini says.

"Track her down?" I don't want Domini anywhere near the potionary. I don't trust him as far as I can throw him. "We can send Watchmen," I say.

He shakes his head. "No need. I can go."

"Domini—"

"She has been through a great deal," he cuts in. "She deserves better than to be dragged back to The Academy by Watchmen."

I can't stop him from going. Raith can.

"Let's go see, Raith."

"You can fill him in. I'll head to the potionary."

Yeah, the only way to stop him is by force, and that would raise too many suspicions. If Leilah were any other student, I would be sending him on his way.

"Let's go," I say.

We head out and I pull my phone from my jacket pocket and text Raith.

.   .   .

Leilah left Academy grounds—I'll explain how later. Domini is insisting on going after her. We're on our way to the potionary. I'm taking the long way. I suggest you try to get there first.

Ethan

THIRTY-SIX

Leilah

I OPEN THE BASEMENT DOOR AND STARE DOWN INTO the darkness. I'm going to live in this house for the rest of my life. I can't be afraid of the basement. The washer and dryer are in the basement. The thought makes me laugh. Yeah, I have to conquer my fear so that I can do laundry. I look at Stony. There's no leaving her here. She'll just shift into a monkey or something and open the door, then follow me down the stairs.

"You have to get down the stairs on your own," I say. "You're too heavy for me to carry.

She gives an indignant sniff.

"You're the one who finished off the lo mien and fried rice." I flip on the light switch.

Stony shifts into a mouse and quickly climbs up my pant leg, then my sleeve to my shoulder. I start down the stairs. The fourth step doesn't creak like I remember. Now that I look closely, the stairs look new. Three quarters of the way down, I catch sight of the hole in the cement to the left. I continue to the bottom, then cross to the hole. Stony squeaks.

"Yeah," I say. "I thought the hole would be bigger, too."

I'd expected a hole the size of an abyss, but it's only about a foot deep and didn't break through the cement to the ground below the house, much less into the ground. Stupid, I guess. It's not as if the hole would really open into Hell—or Shadow Hell.

I groan. "Grams, you really did lose your marbles."

I recall her words in the book *I must give Leilah a chance at a real life.*

My heart squeezes. "Damn you, Grams."

Had guilt driven her to grasp at straws in an effort to find absolution for abandoning me? Now that's stupid. Grams was a tough old bird. Her body would go long before her mind. Right or wrong, she believed what she wrote in that book. If I'm honest, she was right far more often than she was wrong. She believed the god of the angels had to be freed...to help fight The Shadows? If He really is locked in Hell, could that be why The Shadows were so powerful during the last war? They were also very powerful during the fifth century war in Greece. His angels hadn't done a great deal to help us during the war. Was their power diminished with Him in Hell?

If He really is locked in Hell, why isn't that public knowledge? The answer is too easy. No way the angels would want that tidbit to make the evening news. If demons knew the god of the angels was trapped in Hell, they would call forth the four horsemen and we would be living Armageddon, baby. Yeah, I can see why the angels would keep that secret. How did Grams find out?

I track my gaze around the hole. We love to think of Hell as *down below*, but it's just another plane of existence that sometimes intersects with ours. That hasn't happened since the Hell Gates were locked, though. So why does it feel like we intersect with Hell all the time?

I recall Raith and the sadness and hurt in his eyes when Nova stabbed him. Raith has had one foot in Hell since that day just as I have since the day Grams locked her door against me.

I squat and Stony scampers down my arm to the concrete, then shifts back into a pig. I touch the edge of the hole. Grams wasn't trying to dig her way into Hell. The Shadow magic she used was so powerful it simply blasted a hole in the concrete.

"If Grams wanted to open the Hell Gates, why try to enter Shadow Hell?" I murmur.

Stony's brows scrunch in an approximation of a frown and she grunts, "Good question."

"Grams said that if she didn't return, Olympia was going to have to follow her. Did she mean follow her into Shadow Hell?"

Stony nods.

"No one returns from Shadow Hell," I say. "Unless…. Fuck," I whisper. "If she manages to open the Hell Gates, then everyone in Shadow Hell will be freed, including Grams. If she's not dead, then she can travel through Hell and return to the living."

I drop onto my ass. "Can we open the Hell Gates through Shadow Hell?"

Stony gives a loud squeal.

"I know it's nuts," I shoot back. "But is it possible?" I lock gazes with Stony. "Do you think the god of the angels really is locked in Hell?" Another thought hits. "She's been dead—gone —for about three months. If she was successful, wouldn't we know by now?"

Stony shakes her head. "Who knows."

I stand and walk around the hole. "You know the Grand Witch will never risk herself to save Grams."

Stony snorts loudly.

"Okay, she'll never risk herself to save any of us."

"You can't rescue her," Stony says in perfect English.

"Probably not," I reply. "I don't have any Shadows."

Or do I?

I resist the urge to touch my chest where the Shadows entered my body. I didn't tell Stony that part. I haven't told anyone that part. If the Shadows are inside me, then I can use them. Fuck a duck. I've hated Grams for using Shadow magic, now I'm considering doing the same. No, it's not the same. I'm not looking for Shadows to use. If they're inside me, then they're a part of me. But they're not inside of me. The Reaping is another plane of existence that intersects with our dimension *only* to snatch us up. Nothing from there can come here. Right? I've never heard anyone say anything from the Reaping can come here. What if Grams didn't reach Shadow Hell? What if she ended up somewhere else altogether? But where?

I stop circling the hole. A sense of dread ripples through my midsection.

"Time to go?" Stony snorts.

I release a breath. "Yeah."

She trots over to me, then shifts into a mouse. I scoop her up, then deposit her into my hoodie pocket. I turn, then freeze. Chelsea is standing at the bottom of the stairs, dressed in a leather jacket and jeans. A woman, at least ten years older than the teenager, steps from the last stair onto the concrete floor.

I frown. How did they get all the way down the stairs without me hearing them? Dammit. Grams replaced the stairs and they don't creak even the tiniest bit. I look from Chelsea to the older woman. It's strange enough that Chelsea is here, but the older women's presence explains my unease.

"What are you doing here, Chelsea?" I demand.

"Did you think you could hide?" she sneers. "I should have known you would return here. Like grandmother like grand-daughter." She looks at the other woman. "You wanted proof. She's right here where Miriam was when she died practicing her blasphemous magic."

"What the hell?" I blurt, then I understand. "The lightning bolt wasn't an accident."

"The only accident was that I missed." She steps toward me.

I will my speeding heart to slow and take step to the side, keeping the hole between us. "You tried to kill me in Ethan's class."

Her eyes narrow. "You were all but dead. How did he save you?"

She suspects Raith helped me. "Too bad I saved your life instead of the guy who got hung," I say.

Stony stirs inside my pocket. *Easy*, I telepath. The two women have no idea the danger they're in if they threaten me. Where my safety is concerned, Stony takes no prisoners.

"How did you know I was here?" I ask.

Chelsea reaches into the front of her shirt and pulls out a chain with a crystal pendant. "Easy."

"You sure as hell didn't use that to get past my grandmother's wards," I say, but I know Gram's wards have weakened significantly. Why hadn't I set up my own wards?

"Maybe Miriam wasn't as powerful a witch as everyone thinks she was," Chelsea says.

"You had your say," I snap. "Now get the fuck out."

Malice gleams in Chelsea's eyes. "It's time you follow your grandmother into Shadow Hell."

"Haven't you heard?" I say. "My grandmother isn't dead."

Chelsea blinks in surprise and the other woman whips her head in Chelsea's direction.

"That's right, you heard me," I say. "My grandmother isn't dead. And if you're not careful, she's liable to return home and be fucking pissed that you're in her house uninvited."

"That's a lie," Chelsea says, but I catch the slight tremble in her voice. "Everybody knows she died using Shadow magic. Just like you." She throws her arms forward and shouts, "*Flamma*."

Flame bursts from her palms. I dive to the floor as flames shoot so close past me that I smell burnt hair. I roll into a squat and pin her with a glare. I glance at the hole in the cement, then swing my gaze back onto Chelsea.

I grin.

Her eyes widen.

"*Lateo*," the older woman shouts, and disappears.

I know she's only invisible.

"Into the hole," I command, and swipe my hand as if shoving them into the hole. Chelsea stumbles as I chant: "*I command the power of the darkest Shadows. Open your door and let them*"—Blade lands in a crouch behind her at the foot of the stairs as I utter the last two words—"*safely enter,*" on a gasp.

A loud whooshing fills my ears. Two women scream.

Chelsea is yanked by an unseen hand over the hole and vanishes.

"Leilah! No!" Blade shouts, and leaps toward me.

The room spins. I glimpse a blonde woman stepping from the stairs into the basement. A gargoyle appears in front of me and throws his wings around me, blocking my view.

Then a banshee shriek deafens me.

THIRTY-SEVEN

Caleb

THE VAMPIRE CARTER HISSES AS I CRASH INTO HIM. We hit the ground and I roll aside onto all fours. He leaps to his feet and crouches in readiness to attack as I shift into human form.

He blinks. "Dakota?"

"What the hell are you doing here?" I demand.

"Following a demon we suspect made an attack on The Academy wall. What are *you* doing here?"

"I caught the scent of the demon and followed it here," I reply.

"Any idea where the creature is now?" he asks in a low voice.

I shake my head. "I know it's close."

"A wolf can't nail down the scent. I don't like that. "

Neither do I. "What does the demon attack have to do with Crowe Potionary?" I ask.

He shakes his head. "I wish I knew. It's weird."

So, he has no idea Leilah's in the house.

"I would like to find out," he says. "You want to shift back into wolf form and see if we can catch this bastard?"

I answer by shifting—and immediately catch the demon's scent. I bound past the vampire, leap over the backyard fence and land in lush grass that needs to be mowed. An instant later, the vampire lands behind me with only a whisper of movement in the grass. A light from a lamp in an upper room casts the barest of light in the yard. I scan the area but see no sign of the demon. Where the hell is the creature? I creep forward. The demon has been here. The damn thing has eluded me all the way from The Academy.

I catch the scent. The demon is close. I creep toward the rear of the yard. A shadow moves in the far left corner. What shape has the demon assumed? Another shift in the darkness. The creature is trying to hide in the shadows. What demon can so easily blend in shadow? I discern movement, the outline of a human body. Did I really see something or is that just my eyes playing tricks on me? I definitely smell the creature. Though I'm not certain what I'm smelling.

Carter creeps alongside me. We near the far corner. I get the impression the creature believes it's invisible in the murk of darkness. Yes! That is definitely movement. Carter leaps forward. I halt, startled by his sudden attack. He lands on the thing and an unearthly growl emanates from the demon. They roll across the lawn, vampire and a man-size silhouette. I gauge a way to bite the demon, but Carter is wrapped around the thing like an octopus.

The vampire growls and sinks his teeth into the demon's shoulder. The demon thrashes and I see an opening at its feet. I leap forward and close my jaw around a muscular leg. My teeth penetrate soft tissue, then clamp down on nothing so hard my head jars. I shake my head and snap at the demon's feet, but the shadow figure disappears. Carter collapses onto his back breathing so heavily, I'm afraid Leilah will hear.

I scan the yard but no longer smell or see the demon. I shift into human form and pin Carter with a glare as I demand in a low voice, "What the hell happened?"

He pushes to a sitting position and drops his head between his knees, still breathing heavily. "I don't know," he pants. "It just disappeared."

"The object wasn't to kill the creature," I hiss. "We needed to interrogate it."

He lifts his head. "When is the last time you interrogated a demon?"

Not that long ago, by my standards, a hundred years. But I say, "Why did you kill it?"

He stands. "I meant to incapacitate it."

"Good job," I mutter.

"What else would you have done but bite it, wolf?"

This is why wolves hate vampires. They're arrogant dicks.

"If you think you can catch a Shadow demon then, by all means, I'll leave you to it, next time," he says.

"Shadow demon?" I exclaim.

Surprise flickers on his face. "You didn't know?"

"I thought they were myths."

Rumors that circulated during and since the Shadow War spoke of abominations such as Shadow-infected Margiddians mating with demons. Though rare, Margiddians and demons do mate, and their offspring vary from almost-human to near demigods like Kelvozaun, who is imprisoned in Belyy Rassvet, the White Dawn Russian prison, one of the half dozen Margiddian prisons in the world. During the war, however, rumors of half demon, half-infected Margiddians brought to life the rumor of a demon that was more shadow than corporeal. These rare demons can't infect like Shadows, but are said to possess the ability to project fear. I hadn't experienced that, but perhaps the demon's effect varies by person? They are also believed to be able to possess a body like old-fashioned Christian demons are said to do.

"What happened to the demon?" I ask.

Carter shrugs. "No idea."

"Then it isn't dead," I say more to myself then him.

"Doubtful," he replies. "I didn't do any real damage to its body."

If what the demon has can be called a body.

"It could still be nearby." I scan the darkness, but my human eyesight can't compare to my wolf eyesight.

The pad of footsteps on the front porch causes me to snap my head in the direction of the gate I leapt over. The vampire freezes. The front doorknob turns and at least two people enter the house. Carter and I both head for the back door. I reach the house and take the half dozen stairs two at a time. I grasp the doorknob and find the door unlocked. I look over my shoulder at Carter and press a finger to my mouth in a "stay quiet" command. He nods, and we slip inside.

THIRTY-EIGHT

Raith

Like Blade, I borrowed a nondescript car, my assistant Rebecca's Hyundai, as my McLaren would stick out like a sore thumb in this middle-class neighborhood. I spot the unmarked police car parked across the street half a block before Crowe Potionary. The two police officers act as if two men sitting in a parked car at twilight is normal.

I turn right at the next corner and spot Blade's Camry parked at the curb. I take the next right and park Rebecca's Hyundai sedan one block up. Two minutes later, I jump the back yard fence in time to see Carter enter and close the potionary back door. What is he doing here? I race across the yard to the steps and burst into the kitchen. Carter halts at the basement doorway and looks over his shoulder at me.

"Leilah, no!" Blade shouts from the basement.

Carter snaps his head forward and races down the steps. I reach the stairs and leap to the concrete floor an instant after Carter reaches the bottom. Caleb, Penelope, and Blade are staring at an empty room.

I pin Blade with a stare. "What the fuck happened?"

He turns stunned eyes on me. "Leilah, Chelsea, and another woman I didn't recognized disappeared. Leilah—" His voice breaks. "Leilah was chanting a spell."

"A spell?" I repeat.

"She commanded Shadows," Penelope whispers.

"Show me," I order.

Penelope's eyes widen and she looks at Blade.

"Do as I say," I snap. "*Now.*"

She casts a quick glance right, toward the small basement window then, with trembling fingers, withdraws a gold chain with a gold pendant encircled with semi-precious stones from a shirt pocket.

She extends chain and pendant as far as they will extend and murmurs, "Time and space reveal in this place those who just disappeared from our sight."

A shimmering wave travels through us and across the room to the far wall. We stand aside as Chelsea and another woman I don't recognize step onto the concrete floor from the steps. Chelsea locks gazes with Leilah, who stands near the hole.

Leilah demands to know why she's there.

"Did you think you could hide?" Chelsea demands. "I should have known you would return here. Like grandmother like granddaughter." She looks at the other woman. "You wanted proof. She's right here where Miriam was when she died practicing her blasphemous magic."

"What the hell?" Surprise on Leilah's face gives away to under-standing and she says slowly, "The lightning bolt wasn't an accident."

"The only accident was that I missed." Chelsea approaches her, but Leilah retreats around the hole.

"You tried to kill me in Ethan's class." Sadness tinges Leilah's voice.

Chelsea's eyes narrow. "You were all but dead. How did he save you?"

"Too bad I saved your life instead of the guy who got hung," Leilah says in a tired voice. "How did you know I was here?"

Chelsea pulls a chain and crystal pendant from inside her shirt. "Easy."

"You sure as hell didn't use that to get past my grandmother's wards," Leilah says.

Satisfaction shines in Chelsea's eyes. "Maybe Miriam wasn't as powerful a witch as everyone thinks she was."

"You had your say. Now get the fuck out," Leilah orders.

"It's time you follow your grandmother into Shadow Hell," Chelsea snaps.

A cold light appears in Leilah's eyes. "Haven't you heard? My grandmother isn't dead."

I yank my gaze onto Ethan and Blade who are staring, mouths open. Which one of them told Leilah that her grandmother isn't dead?

"That's right, you heard me," Leilah says. "My grandmother isn't dead. And if you're not careful, she's liable to return home and be fucking pissed that you're in her house uninvited."

"That's a lie," Chelsea says. "Everybody knows she died using Shadow magic. Just like you will." She throws her arms forward and shouts, "Flamma."

Flame shoots from her palms. Leilah dives to the floor as the fire shoots past her. She rolls into a squat then grins.

"Lateo," the older woman shouts, and disappears.

"Into the hole," Leilah cries, and swipes her hand left. Chelsea stumbles as Leilah chants, "I command the power of the darkest Shadows. Open your door and let them safely enter."

"Shadow magic!" I shout, as the Blade in the vision jumps onto the floor from the stairs.

A loud whooshing fills the room. Women scream.

Chelsea is yanked by an invisible hand over the hole and vanishes.

"Leilah! No!" the Blade in the vision shouts, and leaps toward Leilah.

A gargoyle appears and throws his wings around Leilah.

Where the hell had he been hiding?

"Matthias," I growl.

A banshee shriek rocks the room and I whip my head in Blade and Ethan's direction as Caleb shifts into wolf form. Their eyes meet mine as the spell in the vision yanks us from the basement into gray.

Sneak Peek

Outlaw Witch

AN ILLUMINA ACADEMY REVERSE HAREM NOVEL BOOK THREE

ONE

Ethan

I DELAY MY AND DAMIEN'S ARRIVAL TO THE potionary by maybe eight minutes. Raith can drive like a maniac when necessary. I hope he reached Leilah first and can get rid of any possible incriminating evidence. There's no telling what that girl might be hiding. My headlights shine on the unmarked cop car parked just before the potionary. The two men in the car act as if they're deep in conversation as we pass.

"That's the potionary." I motion slightly with my head at the house on the right.

"Shouldn't we park?" Domini asks when I don't stop.

We haven't told him—or anyone else—about Detective Mills' report or the angels conjuring Damien in the potionary. Explaining why the police are staking out the potionary will spill that secret.

"The neighbors are nosy," I say. "I want to go in through the back."

"Ah," he intones. "We will sneak over the back fence through the neighbor's yard?"

"Right."

He chuckles. "I haven't snuck into a house since I was a boy. Let's go."

I turn right at the next block and barely control my surprise at sight of Blade's Camry parked at the curb. What is he doing here? I turn at the next street. Rebecca's Hyundai is parked up ahead. Raith must have borrowed her car.

"Is that Rebecca Hathaway's car?" Domini asks.

I give up worrying. There never was any way to keep Domini from learning that Blade and Raith are at the potionary. "Yes," I reply.

"What would she be doing here?"

"She isn't here." I park my car at the next block and cut the lights. "I imagine Raith borrowed it. His McLaren would be too conspicuous in this neighborhood."

"How did he beat us here?" The frown in Domini's voice is clear.

I grunt. "Raith is a maniac behind the wheel." That is true.

When we drop from the rear fence onto the grassy yard of the potionary minutes later, I glimpse the flicker of dim light to the right of the house, low to the ground.

The basement.

I resist the desire to race to the house. We jog to the porch and I find the door slightly ajar.

"Leilah, no!"

At Blade's shout, I burst into the kitchen, turn a hard right, and nearly fly through the open basement door. I glimpse Carter at the bottom of the stairs.. Caleb's in wolf form beside him. An unearthly scream pierces to my soul. I leap the last four steps. The light vanishes and I land in an empty basement. A single, faint beam of moonlight shines through the small ground level window. I take two quick steps and turn wildly, heedless of Domini who stands at the bottom of the stairs staring.

"Lights," I order.

"What?" Domini says.

"Lights—at the top of the stair—the switch. *Now*."

He races up the stairs and, an instant later, light flares. I blink the room into focus—the empty room.

Domini hurries back down the stairs. "What happened?" he demands. "That was Blade's voice. Don't deny it."

I whirl and take a threatening step toward him. "Beware, mage." Flames ignite in my palms.

His eyes widen and he retreats a pace. "I mean no disrespect. Please understand, that was Blade's voice, yes?"

"Do you see Blade here?"

"No, but"–he throws up his hands, palms out—"that was his voice, and he shouted Ms. Crowe's name."

I face the room in an effort to keep him from seeing the irrational need clawing through me to ram my fist into his face.

"Something is wrong," he says.

I inhale a breath and close my palms around the flames. They extinguish. Yes, something is wrong—*very* wrong.

I need to get rid of Domini and figure out what happened. Blade and Raith were here. Caleb—Carter. And Leilah. All gone.

A shadow moves on the wall to the left of the washer and dryer.

I whirl to face the apparition. "Come out before I kill you," I order.

The shadow separates from the wall and expands from a thin line into human form. I squint.

"Olympia," Damien says.

I take a faltering step back.

She locks eyes with me. "You have two choices. Tell me what is really going on. Or tell the Assembly."

www.ingramcontent.com/pod-product-compliance
Lightning Source LLC
Chambersburg PA
CBHW021314190726
48288CB00003B/837